MOONLIGHT KIN
TRISTAN

JORDAN SUMMERS

Moonlight Kin: Tristan

Copyright © 2014 Jordan Summers

Cover Art by: Wicked Smart Designs
Formatted by IRONHORSE Formatting

ISBN-13: 978-1-942237020

Armed with a lodestone and a magical sword, Lycanian enforcer Tristan Chevalier is on the trail of a Darkling, who's already killed a werewolf and a human female. He knows where it's going and who the Darkling is after, so he needs to reach her first. When he finds Isabel MacDougal, Tristan believes he's discovered the perfect bait to draw his enemy out.

Isabel "Izzy" MacDougal has always known monsters were real. She spent her childhood hiding her psychic abilities until they nearly drove her mad. When she runs into Tristan, Izzy believes the giant arctic werewolf is the one who's been hunting her and that her life is over. But for Tristan Chevalier and Izzy MacDougal life isn't over—the cat and mouse game is just beginning.

CHAPTER ONE

In New Orleans you'd better like your sushi deep-fried and your saxophone dipped in a coating of bluesy jazz, or you wouldn't survive long in the Big Easy.

Music rang out through the Jackson Square courtyard as street musicians turned up the volume and charm to compete for tourist dollars. Tonight the jazzy band at the end of the square attempted to lure their crowd away from a lone trumpet player and a violinist.

Along with the musicians, tarot and palm readers had already set up their tables, staggering them just enough to give the pretense of privacy.

Isabel "Izzy" MacDougal did a quick head count. There were ten tables in total. Her table would make eleven, but she only counted the ones in Jackson Square. Others would be set up along the side streets near Bourbon Street, hoping to catch the stray drunk ready to part with their hard-earned cash.

Izzy scanned the growing crowd as she unfolded her small card table and spread her purple shawl on top of it. She spotted her friend Everly Watts a few tables over and waved.

Everly waved back then returned to reading the woman

seated across from her. Izzy had met the short, dark-haired Goth when she first arrived in New Orleans a month ago.

Despite resembling an anemic vampire, Everly was down to earth and turned out to be a good friend. Most nights she could be found at The Dungeon with all the other Goths and vampire wannabes in town. The pancake makeup disguised her sensitive nature and fierce intelligence, but nothing hid her street smarts.

Izzy smiled as a few people slowed to browse her table. They didn't notice that enterprising locals were shadowing them, waiting for them to drop their guard.

Not even dusk yet and the French Quarter already bursting at the seams with sunburned tourists and crafty pickpockets.

Izzy finished setting up and took a seat. She kept her expression open. Hard to do when she was continuously bombarded by impressions from the growing crowd, but she managed. Unlike some of the others situated around the square, Izzy had a true gift of Sight.

She snorted. Some gift.

She and Everly had glommed onto each other when Izzy discovered that Everly suffered from the same "gift" that she'd grown up with. It wasn't easy being psychic, especially in a world populated by skeptics and monsters.

Instead of growing up in a loving household like Isabel, Everly had been kicked out of her home when her *gifts* arrived. According to the petite Goth, she'd been living on her own ever since. She survived by taking on menial jobs and never staying in one place for too long. Another thing that they had in common.

Izzy shuffled her tarot cards and smiled at a passing group of women. The women wore flowery nametags across their chests, advertising a local conference.

"Would you like to know what your future holds, ladies?" she asked.

One of the women giggled, but the ash blonde stopped to

chat. "Can you tell me if I'm going to meet someone soon?" she asked.

"Sure," Izzy said. "Take a seat."

The woman's hand clasped the back of the folding chair as she pulled it out to sit down.

"Lisa, you're not really going to waste your money on that crap, are you?" her friend asked.

Uncertainty filled the blonde's green eyes. Before she caved to peer pressure, Izzy flipped the first card over.

"He has dark hair," she said.

The woman scooted forward on her seat. "Really?"

"Yes," Izzy said. "And he's tall."

"Is his name Mike?" Lisa asked, peering into the cards in search of answers.

Izzy closed her eyes and concentrated. She saw the dark-haired man in her vision drop down to one knee in front of the blond woman.

"I see him proposing," Izzy said. "It's quite a ring."

Lisa squealed. "Oh my God! When?"

Izzy examined her vision. The leaves on the trees around the couple were orange and red, but no limbs were bare. "The fall." She opened her eyes. "He'll propose in the fall."

The woman whipped her head around to search for her friends. "Did you hear that? Mike is going to propose to me in the fall."

The skeptic among them simply shook her head in disgust. "Mike's a jerk," she muttered.

Izzy turned her attention away from the cards and stared at the woman. Her black aura came into view. The color startled her. On occasion when Izzy looked at people, shadow obscured their entire face. She had no idea what the darkness meant, but it always felt evil and frightened her.

This was different. The woman's dark aura didn't obscure her features. Izzy peered deeper, past the outer layer to see what caused the woman's pain.

A red-haired man appeared in her mind, then his image

quickly faded into a tombstone with the name Thomas carved into its rigid gray face.

"I'm sorry about Thomas," Izzy said. "He really loved you."

The woman's face went from red to white, as the blood drained from her cheeks. "How did you know about him?" she whispered.

Izzy shrugged. She couldn't begin to explain where her gift came from and certainly not to someone who wasn't ready to listen.

"Think she's still a fraud?" Lisa asked as she plucked several bills out of her wallet and laid them on the table.

"Let's go," the skeptic said. "I need a drink."

The crowd swallowed them. More people approached her. Izzy got ten more readings done before her head threatened to explode.

The pain happened every night. She could only read for so long before her gift exerted too much pressure and her body gave out. At least she'd made enough to pay rent. All in all a good night.

Izzy was packing her things, when the first inkling of unease struck. She casually scanned the crowd, but no one seemed overly interested in her. She finished gathering her fortune-telling tools and shoved them into her backpack. She quickly folded her table and chairs then took them over to Everly.

"Can you keep these for me until tomorrow?" Izzy asked.

Everly's back stiffened, and she frowned. "Sure," she said, scanning the faces around them. "I feel it, too."

"It's okay," Izzy said. Whatever was out there didn't know about Everly—at least not yet. She'd lead it away before it detected her friend. "I'm going to head out. Catch you later."

Everly nodded, but she didn't relax. She continued to covertly scan the crowd.

Izzy weaved her way through the throng, cutting along

Pere Antoine's alley before hanging a left toward St. Peter Street. She glanced up and down the sidewalk to be sure she wasn't being followed, then ducked into Yo Mama's Bar and Grill.

The bearded doorman greeted her with a friendly smile. Izzy grinned back then bounded up the stairs to where her friend Heather bartended.

A red light illuminated the small space. Two couches, a couple of long tables, dancing statues, and a small bar filled the room. Classic rock from an old jukebox blared out of speakers mounted in the ceiling. The place reminded her of a bordello, but it had *amazing* hamburgers.

Izzy's stomach growled. She wished she had time to order a burger, but she needed to use Heather's phone then get back to her apartment on Dumaine Street.

Heather had just popped the cap off a longneck, when she spotted Izzy. She smiled, then without saying a word, she grabbed her cell phone and tossed it to her. Izzy caught it easily, mouthed the word "thanks," and quickly called her sister, Mindy.

She didn't want to alarm her sister, but Izzy needed to let Mindy know that someone was following her and she might have to lay low for a while.

It would hurt to be out of touch with her sister, but Izzy didn't have much choice. The darkness she'd sensed in Breakbend, Oregon was here and getting closer. She'd felt its presence growing, and it terrified her.

Izzy finished up her call and handed the phone back to Heather. "Thanks," she said.

"Anytime," Heather said. "Catch you later?"

She shook her head. "Not tonight. I have a headache." Izzy rubbed her temples for emphasis.

"Catch you next time," Heather said then moved onto a waiting customer.

Izzy hurried down the stairs but stopped before she stepped out onto the sidewalk. The doorman watched her, but didn't say anything since this wasn't exactly new behavior from her.

"It's all clear," he said.

"Thanks." Izzy slipped out the door and headed toward Bourbon. She'd just passed Royal Street, when the sensation of being observed returned.

Izzy glanced over her shoulder but didn't see anyone. Didn't see anything out of the ordinary. Ordinary being a relative term in the French Quarter. Nothing to alarm her, but Izzy knew he was there.

She *felt* him.

She wound her way through the heavy crowd, hoping to lose her pursuer on raucous Bourbon Street. With the sun going down, the mood on the street changed. Izzy turned down Dumaine Street.

The crowd thinned, and she caught sight of Louis Armstrong Park in the distance. The trees swayed as the sun dipped below the horizon and darkness took over. A shiver tracked down her spine.

This was their time. The time when they were most active. The time when the real monsters came out and hunted.

Izzy hurried along the uneven sidewalks. She heard music coming from Bourbon Street. The jumble of sounds and the collision of smells should've comforted her, but Izzy knew she wasn't alone.

She tripped over a raised concrete slab and fell forward. She grabbed the wrought iron fence that ran along the front of one of the old gentrified homes to keep from falling.

The metal felt good in her hand. Cool. Hard. Real. Real as the heavy footsteps coming up fast behind her. Izzy pushed away from the fence and sprinted on.

Her blood pumped so hard she could barely hear herself think. Izzy turned to see who approached and collided with a wall. She cursed under her breath and looked at the offending object in her way. It wasn't a wall at all. Somehow she'd buried her nose in a man's hard chest.

Strong hands grasped her arms. Whether to keep her from falling or prevent her from leaving, she didn't know. Izzy craned her neck to see who she'd run into. Her gaze collided with a pair of mercury-colored eyes, and she shivered, despite his handsome face.

Her body went from hot to cold to hot again. Staring in his eyes was like staring into the face of the Arctic. His white-blond hair and stern expression mirrored the harsh, unforgiving environment.

Izzy opened her mouth to apologize, but before she uttered a single syllable, the image of a white wolf obscured his striking features. She felt the blood drain from her face. He was one of *them.*

"Let me go," she said, struggling to break his grasp.

He didn't release her. Instead, the man's grip tightened. "You're being hunted," he said.

She knew that. Izzy had known that for days. Weird that he announced it like he wasn't the one hunting her.

The man had to be the biggest monster she'd ever seen. Given his size, he'd be unnaturally large for a werewolf, and that was saying something, since they leaned toward massive.

"Let me go or I'm going to scream," Izzy said.

"This is the French Quarter," he said. "No one will notice or care." His sensual lips tilted into a smirk.

Izzy wanted to knock that smirk right off his face.

As if reading her mind, his smile vanished. "If you don't come with me, you're going to die."

Despite the ominous and rather clichéd warning, Izzy had no intention of going anywhere with him. She'd seen his true form. She would be safer locked in a cage with a half-starved polar bear. Everything about this man screamed danger.

A trashcan lid banged at the end of the street. They both turned to see what had caused the noise. Izzy took his momentary distraction as a chance to get away. She twisted out of his hold and took off running.

She didn't get far. He was on her before she'd made it ten feet. Given his tremendous height and long legs it wasn't really a surprise, but she'd had to try.

A small crowd of men and women wandered by. Izzy flagged them down. As they slowed to a stop, the giant beside her swung her around, and his mouth descended upon hers.

* * * * *

Tristan needed her to shut up and listen, but short of gagging her, he had no way of making her comply. He'd expected to find a flighty, air-headed female, but Isabel was also far smarter than he'd anticipated. Manipulating her wasn't going to be easy. When she flagged the small crowd down, Tristan used the only thing he had on hand to silence her. Himself.

He spun her around in his arms and pulled her close. His mouth came down upon hers before she understood what was happening. The second their lips met, something unexpected occurred, something entirely unwanted.

Tristan's body hardened, and heat exploded inside of him. Urges that he viciously suppressed surfaced in an instant. His hands tightened on her shirt, and his arms locked. He felt her nipples harden against his chest a moment before her body melted into his.

Instead of keeping the embrace superficial, Tristan deepened it. He nipped Isabel's full bottom lip until she opened for him, then Tristan surged inside.

Sweetness exploded on his tongue. He'd never tasted anything like it, like her. It was at odds with the citrusy aroma wafting from her skin. Tristan wanted more, so he took it.

He sank his hand into the wild tangle of her blonde-and-purple hair then tilted her head to get better access. Whoops and laughter surrounded them, but he ignored it all as he thoroughly explored Isabel's mouth.

Her hands tightened on his shirt, hesitated a moment, then she kissed him back. Fire spread through his body, making every inch of him hard. They needed to find a room before he ended up stripping her naked right here. Tristan calculated the distance to the nearest hotel. If they left now, it wouldn't take long to reach it.

She's human. The thought filtered through his mind. The reminder chilled his ardor as effectively as dumping ice water down the front of his jeans.

Tristan reluctantly pulled back. His chest heaved as he drew in air, waiting for his head to clear.

* * * * *

Izzy's world continued to tilt off its axis, even after he ended the embrace. Despite his frosty exterior, the man's lips were scorching. Maybe he wasn't made of ice after all.

The crowd she'd flagged down had wandered off at some point, leaving them alone. In some part of her mind, Izzy had realized that they were leaving, but for the life of her, she hadn't been able to tear her mouth away. Izzy had been kissed before. Plenty of times. But never like this.

His hands were still locked around her waist, clutching her shirt. The heat of his palms seared her flesh and made her wonder what would happen if they were skin to skin. Spontaneous combustion came to mind.

He must've realized what he was doing because he jerked his hands away and stepped back, putting some distance between them. This time when he looked at her, he scowled, banking the heat that had simmered in his mercury-colored eyes.

Was he mad at her or himself? It didn't really matter. She wasn't going anywhere with him, even if her lips were tingling and other parts of her were making unreasonable demands.

The man might be angry, but he remained fully aware of their surroundings. "If you don't come with me willingly, I'm going to pick you up and carry you."

Izzy glared at him and scrambled out of reach. "You wouldn't dare."

Before the sound of her words died, the man hoisted her over his shoulder and took off running down the street. The sudden move jarred Izzy's ribs, driving the air from her lungs. It would serve him right if she threw up on him. And she would've, had she bothered to eat.

Izzy managed to drag a breath into her body. "Put me down this instant!" She smacked his back, but the man didn't notice. "Do you hear me?"

He grunted in response but didn't slow.

"I don't know who you think you are, but you're not going to get away with kidnapping me," Izzy said.

"Who is going to stop me?" He didn't even sound winded when he spoke. "You?" he asked.

She'd stop him. Just as soon as she managed to catch her breath and quell the nausea rising inside her.

They passed several revelers on the way to Louis Armstrong Park. No one paid attention to them, even when she cried for help. The sight of a man carrying a woman over his shoulder wasn't unusual in this part of town.

The music faded as they moved farther and farther away. Soon, they'd be isolated. Izzy couldn't allow that to happen. Every investigative procedure show she'd ever watched said never leave with your attacker.

Of course, they never mentioned what to do if your attacker picked you up and carried you away.

"Put me down," she said. "I want to walk."

His thumb stroked over the back of her thigh. Every muscle inside of Izzy stiffened, while other parts melted— thanks to that stupid kiss. She pressed her lips together. She could still taste him. And an insane part of her that she refused to acknowledge wanted more.

"I mean it," Izzy said. "Put me down, or I'm going to hurl on you." She gagged to prove she wasn't bluffing.

His footsteps faltered. Guess he didn't want to be vomited on. "You cannot get away," he said.

Probably true, but it wouldn't stop her from trying.

"Let me go, and we'll forget this ever happened," Izzy said.

He shook his head, sending his long blond hair into his face. "I'm afraid that's not an option," he said.

Izzy saw her last chance to escape. She took a deep breath to scream again. The man leapt over six feet, dropping her down onto his hard shoulder. The move knocked the wind out of her again. No doubt that was his intention.

She gasped. "Jerk!" Izzy couldn't see his obnoxious smile, but she felt his shoulders shake with laughter. He'd pay for that.

* * * * *

For a human, Isabel MacDougal had a lot of spirit. Most women would be screaming their heads off by now. Oh sure, she'd tried to get help, but she hadn't fought him.

A woman afraid for her life would've ripped the hair from his head, which told Tristan that she wasn't as afraid of him as she claimed to be.

He kept running, moving them deeper into the shadows. He still sensed the Darkling's magic thanks to the lodestone around his neck, but it was fainter now.

Tristan didn't want to think about how close Isabel had come to being captured by the Darkling. He'd barely managed to reach her first.

He sniffed the air. Other than a few homeless people and some unsavory types, the park was empty. He kept moving.

With enough distance between them, they wouldn't be disturbed. Eventually Tristan stopped and set Isabel down.

She wobbled then staggered a few feet away. "What do you plan to do to me now that you've abducted me?" she asked.

Tristan arched a brow. "I'm not going to attack you, if that's what you're thinking."

"You already did," she reminded him.

His eyes narrowed. "I kissed you. It's not the same."

Her pale brow furrowed. "Why did you kiss me?"

Good question. Tristan had been wondering the same thing, since now it seemed like such a mistake. It would be easy to say that he'd been trying to keep her silent. That had been the catalyst behind his actions, but the truth was Tristan didn't care if she screamed. He would've taken her with him anyway. Then there was the kiss itself... and what happened afterward.

Not liking the direction his thoughts were taking, he glared at her. Something about her mouth captured his attention. Even now, her full lips drew his reluctant gaze. They were moist, red, and oh so soft. Even her taste had been different than he'd expected.

Perhaps she wore something to enhance their appearance, enhance their flavor?

Tristan might stretch the truth with others, but he never lied to himself. That honeysuckle flavor was all her own, and damned if he didn't want more.

His frowned deepened. That wasn't going to happen. He shouldn't have touched her in the first place. It wasn't part of his plan.

Tristan didn't need to be thinking about her lips or her succulent taste. He was here to kill a Darkling, and nothing more. If he kept Isabel alive in the process, then great, but her continued existence wasn't necessary for accomplishing his mission. At least not after she drew the Darkling out.

"I kissed you to save your life," Tristan said.

Isabel snorted in disbelief. "Right, sure you did."

"I did," he said, sounding defensive. "You're in danger."

She cocked her head and looked at him. "From who? As far as I can tell, you're the only threat to my safety."

Tristan didn't like his actions being questioned. She should just thank him and be grateful he'd arrived when he had. "Someone is hunting you."

"That didn't answer my question, Frosty," she said.

She was smart and oddly attractive despite the awful purple in her hair. "No, I didn't," Tristan said. "And my name is not Frosty."

"Whatever, Ice." Isabel rolled her eyes. "Are you always a jerk, or am I just special?"

Tristan approached her until he loomed above her. "You'd do well to remember what I am," he said softly.

She bit her lower lip.

His gaze dropped to her mouth of its own volition, and something dark rose inside of him. Her tongue darted out to wet her lips. Tristan's jaw clenched.

The memory of their kiss came charging back, and his entire body tensed to the point of pain. He curled his hands into fists to keep from grabbing her.

"I know what you are. It's not like I can ever forget," Isabel said. "I see the real you every time I look at you."

Tristan jerked his head back. He knew Sighted-Ones could see the beast lurking beneath their human forms. It was one of the things that made them so valuable to the Darklings, but it unsettled him to know a human had such ability. It would make hiding from them impossible.

The only thing that kept them from being a direct threat to the Moonlight Kin was the fact that most humans wouldn't believe them. If that were to change...then people like Isabel MacDougal would need to be eliminated.

The thought left Tristan decidedly uneasy, but he refused to look at why. Instead, he focused on her colorful hair.

"A simple thank-you would've been enough," he said.

Her brow rose at the same time as her smart mouth dropped open. "You expect me to thank you, Marshmallow? After what you did? Are you insane?" she asked.

Tristan gritted his teeth. He was not used to sparring with sharp-tongued, purple-haired hoydens who didn't know what was good for them.

As the Enforcer for the Lycanian Elders, people respected and feared him. Known for his cold countenance and unwavering tenacity, Tristan took great pride in his position. The impression he made had never bothered him until now. Of course up until now, it had never been thrown in his face.

"I am as sane as you are," he snarled, moving his face closer to hers. "The only difference is I have a stronger sense of self-preservation. You, Ms. Purple Hair, have a death wish."

Isabel put her hands on her hips and glared at him. "And you, Snowball, can suck my big toe!"

* * * * *

Did he really think she was that stupid? Only a fool would trust one of them with their lives. They were the monsters, the creatures that came out of the night to swallow you up.

Either that or he had an overinflated opinion of his kissing abilities. Izzy glanced at his harsh mouth. Okay, maybe he deserved some bragging rights on that front, but that wasn't the point.

"Listen, I'm not sure who you think I am, but you have the wrong girl." Izzy hoped he didn't notice the tremor in her voice.

"Scents don't lie," he said.

Izzy swallowed hard. "Well this time your *schnoz* is wrong. So why don't you just be a good frost giant and run along?"

His mercury eyes glistened, then he slowly blinked. "Is

there something wrong with your hearing?" He snapped his finger next to her ear.

Izzy flushed and shoved his hand away. "No, is there something wrong with *yours*?"

He stiffened. "I can hear things you never knew existed," he said through clenched teeth.

"Good for you, Snowflake, but you're still wrong about me," she said, more boldly than she felt.

The voices that had been in the distance grew louder. Perhaps if they got close enough, Izzy could scream for help. She had no doubt the giant of a man beside her wouldn't like the attention.

His silver eyes narrowed. "Don't even think about it," he hissed.

"Think about what?" she asked innocently.

"Whatever was going through your little purple head," he said.

"I didn't say anything, Whiteout," Izzy said.

"You didn't have to," he snarled.

The man raised his head and sniffed the air. The canine move startled her.

"Your pursuer has changed directions," he said after another moment.

Izzy smiled. "Great! Then I guess I'll see you around, Snow Drift."

"My name is Tristan Chevalier." He flashed astonishingly white teeth. "I suggest you remember it. You'll be hearing it a lot."

She took a step back. "I don't want to know your name."

Her confession brought out a frown, but Tristan didn't comment. "Whether you like it or not, we are stuck together." He held up a hand. "At least for the time being."

"Yeah." Izzy shook her head. "I don't think so. I'm a solo act. Besides, how do you know that I'm the one being hunted? It might be after you," she said.

"Oh, it would definitely like to kill me," Tristan said

nonchalantly. "Of that there is no doubt."

"I know the feeling, Frosty," Izzy muttered.

Tristan scowled. "But I will not give it or you the opportunity."

She believed him. Izzy couldn't imagine much taking Tristan down. "If you're so big and bad, why do you need me?" she asked. "It's not like I can help. I'm crap in a fight. Just ask my sister."

Tristan cocked his head. "There wasn't time to ask Mindy," he said.

Fear engulfed Izzy. How did Tristan know about her sister? She didn't like the look he gave her. "How do you know Mindy?" she asked, bracing for his answer.

This time his smile left her chilled to the bone. "If she hasn't already, she will soon mate with one of the Moonlight Kin."

Izzy shook her head in denial. "My sister would never marry a monster."

Tristan's smile became colder, if that were even possible. "Not all monsters are created equal. I pray for your sake that you don't learn that firsthand."

Izzy shivered and glanced away. She needed to get to a phone to warn Mindy, then she needed to get out of town.

A police cruiser rolled to a stop behind Tristan. The officers climbed out of their car. This was it. This was her chance to get away from Frosty, the crazy snowman.

Tristan raised one powdery white brow and waited for her to answer.

"Forget it," she said, then in the next breath yelled for the police.

His head whipped around too late. The officers were already approaching them. Tristan cursed loudly and glared at her.

"You're a fool," he said, then took off across the park.

Izzy watched him go. Hopefully that would be the last time she saw him. An odd sense of disappointment followed the thought.

"Jeez, girl, it was just a kiss," she muttered then approached the police. "Thank goodness you guys got here when you did. I think he was going to mug me."

CHAPTER TWO

The police escorted Izzy home and checked her apartment. As they departed, they warned her to stay away from tourists.

Izzy waved goodbye, then quickly shut the door and locked it. She wasn't safe anymore. Not that she'd ever truly been, but she thought she'd have a little more time in New Orleans before she'd have to go.

She glanced around her studio. Other than a daybed, which served as both a couch and a place to sleep, there wasn't much in the place. Her foldable table and chair were with Everly.

The blood drained from Izzy's face. Oh gawd, she had to warn Everly about Tristan. It wasn't safe for her to stay either.

Izzy tossed clothes and her essentials into her tote bag. She was in the middle of packing when someone knocked on the door. Izzy's heart jumped into her throat.

Had Tristan found her already? Maybe the police had returned? Was it too much to hope for that they'd found Tristan and arrested him?

She grabbed the bat she kept next to the daybed and

quietly tiptoed to the front door. Izzy peeked out the peephole and saw a dark-haired, handsome guy standing on her porch. She didn't recognize him. He looked young enough to be in college. Was he lost?

It wouldn't be the first time that someone knocked on her door by mistake, but after the night she'd had, Izzy wasn't taking any chances.

She checked again, this time using her gift. A swirl of darkness surrounded him, but Izzy didn't detect a beast. However, the darkness didn't bode well. She decided to ignore him and keep packing.

"Please, Isabel. I need to talk to you," he said. "I know you're in there."

He knew her name. How did he know her name?

Izzy cracked the door open, but didn't remove the chain. "Who are you, and what do you want?"

"Isabel?" he asked, as if he were unsure now that he got a look at her.

That gave her pause. "What do you want with her?" Izzy asked.

He stared at her. Like Frosty, this man was good-looking. The kind of guy most college-aged girls would welcome with open arms and open legs. Unlike Frosty, he seemed nervous.

"I came to warn you that you're in danger," he said. "Can I please come in?"

Gooseflesh rose on Izzy's arms, and she glanced behind him to make sure Tristan wasn't hiding in the bushes. The thought almost made her laugh. Almost.

"My name is..." He glanced around. "Stone," he said after a moment.

"Okay, *Stone*." Izzy emphasized his odd name so he'd know she didn't believe him. "What can I do for you?"

"It's not what you can do for me, it's what I can do for you," he said, surprising her. "I know this is going to sound crazy, but there are monsters after you."

"Monsters?" Izzy asked, trying to hide her shock. "Why would you say something like that?"

His amber gaze met hers, and he swallowed hard. "Because they're after me, too."

Izzy reared back in shock. No wonder he'd given her a fake name. He knew the truth. Stone opened his mouth to say more, but she held up a finger to stop him. "Wait." Izzy closed the door to unhook the chain then opened it again. "Please come in."

He flashed her a quick smile. "Thank you for the much-needed invitation," he said, then swept into the room.

Izzy ignored the odd churning sensation in her gut. There wasn't time to examine it. She had to get out of here.

"We don't have much time," he said, as if reading her mind. "I have reason to believe that you're being stalked."

Fear tightened her chest. She'd met her stalker already. What Izzy needed to know was if there were more of them hunting her.

"Have you seen or heard anything odd lately?" Stone asked.

Other than being kidnapped by an iceberg earlier, no, not lately. Izzy shook her head.

Stone scanned her small apartment, taking it all in with one glance. "You need to get some clothes together and come with me," he said.

Izzy wasn't going anywhere with him or anyone else. "How do you know about the monsters?" she asked.

"I sense them," Stone said. "Don't you?"

Yes, she did, but she rarely came across others like herself. Everly was the first person she'd met in years that had a true gift.

"That's why they want me so bad." Stone's head came up, and he turned toward the open door. "He's coming," he hissed. "We have to go now!"

"No," Izzy said. Although Stone seemed genuinely distressed, she didn't know this man. "I'll be okay on my own."

His eyes turned pleading. "I'm not kidding," Stone said. "He's coming. I can feel him like an itch beneath my skin."

An irritating rash... Definitely sounded like Tristan. "I feel him, too," she said calmly, though calm wasn't what Izzy felt at all. She wanted to smash the stupid butterflies flitting around in her stomach. "You should go, while you can."

Stone shook his dark head. "You don't understand the danger you're in," he said. "We should stick together."

She did, but there wasn't time to convince Stone. Izzy was well aware of what could happen to her if she let her guard down.

"The thing that's coming is a killer," Stone said.

Izzy knew that, too, since Tristan had admitted as much, though she wasn't sure how much was truth and how much was bluster. "Have you seen him?"

Stone shook his head.

"Well I have," she said. "You really need to go before he gets here."

Stone scanned her apartment. "Do you have a cell phone?" he asked.

"No." Izzy had always been afraid that the monsters would use it to track her, so she'd avoided them.

Stone pulled a cell phone out of the pocket of his jeans. He shoved the phone into her hands. "Take this. The number is in the address book, along with one where I can be reached. Once you find someplace to hide, call me and let me know that you're safe."

"I will," she said.

His gaze continued to dart toward the door. "Are you sure you won't come with me?"

"Positive," she said.

Stone looked as if he wanted to say more but instead shook his head. "I really have to go. If you run into trouble, call! I'll come and get you anywhere, anytime."

He bolted out the door before she had the chance to respond and disappeared down the street.

Izzy saw a streak of white flash by and knew exactly who was on his trail. She prayed that Stone was faster, but there wasn't anything she could do to help him. Izzy glanced back at her tote bag.

She had to get out of here before Frosty found her again. Izzy finished packing and left a note and some money on the counter for her landlord. She glanced at the small apartment she'd called home one last time, then shut the door.

Only one place she could think to go. She hoped Everly didn't mind the company. Ultimately, it didn't matter. If Tristan Chevalier found her, then he'd easily find Everly. Izzy wasn't about to leave Louisiana without warning her friend.

* * * * *

The scent of the Darkling burned Tristan's nostrils as he raced through the French Quarter in his wolf form. He was so close, he could almost taste the foul being on the air. The houses blurred as he poured on speed. The lodestone around his neck pulsed as it encountered a wave of dark magic.

Tristan shuddered and almost lost form, but somehow his great beast prevailed. He turned a corner, following the pull of the magic, and suddenly the Darkling's scent disappeared. The hair on his nape stood on end. Tristan stopped and dropped his nose to the ground.

A week's worth of city life smacked him in the face. He smelled spicy seafood, sweat, alcohol, and urine, but no Darkling. He raised his head and sniffed again, but the scent was gone. Had he opened a portal between the worlds and crossed over?

It shouldn't be possible without Tristan feeling it in the lodestone. Was this Darkling more powerful than the others? The thought left Tristan decidedly uneasy.

He circled back one more time just to make sure he hadn't missed anything, but his nose didn't lie. The Darkling was gone. Tristan growled in frustration and snapped at the air, then turned around and headed back the way he'd come.

When he'd been chasing the Darkling, he'd also picked up a familiar aroma. Isabel. Her strong scent let Tristan know that he had to have passed her during the chase or ran by her home. He retraced his steps until he encountered the honeysuckle and citrus aroma again. It was strange how quickly he'd associated the scent with Isabel.

Tristan stopped in front of a gray two-story mansion that had been converted into apartments. He put his nose to the ground and followed the sweet aroma wafting on the air until it ended at a closed door on the second floor.

Heat swept through him as Tristan allowed the change to take him. When it was over, he stood naked outside Isabel's home. He listened but couldn't hear a heartbeat inside.

Cold swept through him. Had the Darkling killed her?

Tristan's chest throbbed. He rubbed the spot, unnerved by the sudden wash of pain. He took a deep breath. Relief struck when he didn't encounter death's pungent odor.

He glanced up and down the street to make sure that no one was around. Then Tristan turned the knob, breaking the lock. He pushed the door open. It squeaked, before settling against the wall.

Tristan stepped inside and glanced around the small space. Compared to the vibrant woman who lived there, the place was lifeless. He walked deeper into the room and closed the door behind him.

There were no personal items that he saw, nothing to indicate that Isabel had ever lived here other than her scent. Two steps brought him to the daybed. Without thought, Tristan pulled the blanket off the bed and brought it to his nose.

He inhaled and smelled Isabel. He took her honeysuckle scent into his lungs and once again felt his beast rise. Tristan dropped the blanket and searched the rest of the studio apartment. The cabinets in the bathroom had been left open, indicating that Isabel had departed in haste.

Anger surged to the surface. The little fool was running from him. Didn't she know what would happen if she ran from his beast?

Tristan strode for the front door. As he yanked it open, he caught a scent of the Darkling. Fading now, but there was no mistaking the stench. A sense of urgency rose. He couldn't let the Darkling find Isabel before he did.

Thanks to her blanket, he'd be able to track her scent. Unfortunately, so would the Darkling. Tristan threw his head back as the change swept through him. Bones snapped, and his body reshaped into the perfect predator.

Isabel thought she could run from him, hide until he went away, but she was about to find out there was nowhere for her to go that he wouldn't find her.

CHAPTER THREE

No matter how fast he ran or how many false trails he laid, the white beast continued its relentless pursuit. Almost as if he were able to track his magic, which was impossible.

The Darkling had no choice but to open a portal into his realm. It was either that or fight to the death. He called out to the other side. Darkness thickened, then a tear in the fabric of this world shimmered a hundred yards in front of him.

He cursed as he ran for the entrance. The Darkling hadn't planned on returning without the female. He'd been so close. He had almost had the Sighted-One in his grasp, only to have her taken away.

The Darkling glanced back and saw a flash of white barreling toward him. He picked up speed. The houses in the French Quarter became a blur.

He passed a couple of humans stumbling down the sidewalk. His wake swept them off their feet. They tumbled into the street, their limbs tangling.

He hoped that would delay the Moonlight Kin pursuing him, but he should've known better. The wolf leapt over the downed humans and kept coming. He didn't even give them a second glance.

The Darkling frowned. This wolf wasn't like the others he'd encountered. They all cared about the humans, as if they were more than mere prey. This wolf was different. Single-minded. Dangerous.

The entrance to his perpetually dark world swirled before him. The Darkling saw the full moon glowing on the other side, illuminating the thick forest. Magic crackled in the air. Not much farther.

The white beast couldn't follow him, unless he wanted to die. The magic would take away his ability to shift into his wolf form and eventually kill him.

Only one wolf that he knew of had ever made it out alive, and he'd needed a portal rune stone to do it. His thievery had earned him a bounty on his head. Unfortunately, no Darkling had been able to locate him and claim the prize. Rumor had it he was dead.

The Darkling raced across the blackened ash that fell beneath the opening and jumped. He landed in his realm, his heart pounding in his chest, then turned to face the menace behind him.

The white wolf skidded to a halt, its nose nearly touching the entrance, and glared at him.

The Darkling laughed, but the sound came out as a shrill bark. He stood at the entrance taunting the beast, knowing full well he could do nothing about it.

Next time, he vowed, then trotted away.

Chapter Four

Izzy sat back on Everly's lumpy burgundy couch to watch the sun rise. She'd only managed to get a couple hours of sleep, which was two more than her friend. Everly had been up all night doing God only knows what in her back room.

Black candles flickered from various candelabras, highlighting the empty eye sockets of a half dozen skulls scattered throughout the living room.

One of the skulls next to a hastily erected altar in the corner looked suspiciously real. Izzy didn't say anything, since this was New Orleans and nearly fifteen percent of the population practiced voodoo. She didn't think Everly fell into that category, but she couldn't say for certain.

The scent of frankincense choked the air. Everly said it helped her think. The scent gave Izzy a headache, but she didn't complain. She was too grateful to Everly for taking her in.

Her friend came out of the bedroom and sat across from her on a beanbag. Her dark brow furrowed in thought as she picked at her chipped black nail polish. The sun peeked through the dark purple curtains. Everly scowled when a ray hit her and got up to slam them shut. Darkness once more enveloped the room.

Izzy sighed and closed her eyes.

"Tell me again how you met him," Everly said.

"Which one?" Izzy asked without opening her eyes. She felt as if she could sleep for days.

"The snowy one," she said.

"I sensed him while I was reading cards in Jackson Square last night," she said, then paused. "At least I'm pretty sure it was him."

"I remember feeling him nearby," Everly said. "It made my skin crawl."

"Yeah, mine, too," Izzy said. So why hadn't her skin crawled when she ran into Tristan later?

"He wanted you to come with him?" Everly said.

Izzy sighed. "Yeah, they both did. The strange part was they said they wanted to help me for the exact same reason."

"Weird," she said.

"I know," Izzy said. "What are the chances?"

"Too high to be a coincidence," Everly said.

"That's what I thought," she said.

"One of them has to be lying."

Izzy glanced at her. "Well, one of them *is* a monster."

Everly bit her lip. "Good point," she said. "What are you going to do now?"

Izzy thought about it, but her tired, sluggish mind wouldn't cooperate. "I don't know."

If she were smart, she'd call her sister, Mindy, but Izzy didn't want to drag her into her drama. Besides, she'd left her baby sister to keep her safe. Phoning Mindy for help would defeat the purpose.

"Do you think he was telling the truth?" Everly asked.

"Which one?" Izzy asked, giving up on getting any sleep.

Everly shrugged. "Either one."

Izzy shook her head. "I don't know." She pursed her lips. "I suppose there could be a third player in the mix that I haven't met yet. Tristan had enough opportunities to kill me if he wanted," she said. "And Stone, he looked genuinely freaked out. I've seen that look before. It can't be faked. Not that I can blame him with Frosty on his trail. To be honest, I don't trust either one of them."

Everly giggled.

"What?" Izzy asked.

She smiled. "I think it's funny that you're calling Tristan silly names. I've never heard you do that when referring to one of them," Everly said. "Normally, you just call them all monsters. Hmm..."

Izzy sat up straighter. Hard to do on a lumpy couch that sagged in the middle. "He's still a monster," she said. "If you saw him, there'd be no doubt in your mind." She pictured Tristan's handsome face and godlike body. "Okay, he might fool you for a minute, but not for any longer."

Everly arched a dark, pierced brow. "I believe you," she said. "Just thought I'd point it out. In case you weren't aware that you were doing it." She crawled off the beanbag and walked over to an unlit candle. Everly pulled a lighter out of her pocket. The candle flared to life. "If you had to trust one of them, who would it be?"

Izzy considered the question. Her mind replayed the searing kiss she'd shared with Tristan. It had stirred her more than she'd cared to admit.

"Stone, definitely Stone," Izzy said. The kiss alone had proven how dangerous Tristan could be. "His fear was real, and I didn't see a beast lurking beneath the surface when I used my gift to look at him."

"Did your skin crawl?" Everly asked.

"No," she said, then added, "but I didn't feel comfortable around him. It might've been because I'd just gotten away from Tristan. When I'm stressed, my readings aren't as reliable."

"Maybe you're right about a third player being in town," Everly said.

"Maybe."

Everly tilted her dark head, sending black hair over one eye. "You said you didn't see a beast, when you looked at Stone, but you obviously saw something that freaked you out."

"Smoke," Izzy said. "Or maybe it was shadows. Whatever it was, it obscured his features for a moment. All I know for sure is that I didn't see a monster."

Everly stared at her for a long time.

"What?" Izzy asked.

"Not sure yet," Everly said.

"Listen, I appreciate you letting me stay here last night, but more than anything I came to warn you to get out of town," Izzy said.

Everly glanced at her nails. "I'm not going anywhere," she said.

"It's not safe," Izzy said. "It is only a matter of time before they find me—and you."

Everly leveled her gaze on her. "I'm tired of running from them," she said. "Aren't you?"

Yes, she was, but what other choice did she have?

"Not sure if you noticed, but they're everywhere," Everly said, sounding as tired as Izzy felt. "If they wanted me dead, we wouldn't be having this conversation. Lately, I'm beginning to think that they aren't all bad. I ran into one at the Dungeon the other night."

Izzy gasped. "Why didn't you tell me?"

Everly shrugged. "I wasn't sure how you'd handle the news."

Izzy touched her hand. "What happened?"

Everly pulled back. "That's just it. Nothing happened," she said. "He introduced himself then bought me a drink. We chatted for a while, then he left without asking for my number."

Was it her imagination, or did Everly sound *disappointed*? "Oh God, not you, too," Izzy said. "First

Mindy, now you."

"What do you mean?" Everly crossed her arms over her chest.

"You liked him." She didn't bother to hide the accusation in her voice.

Everly's mouth dropped open. "I did not. He was just some guy."

"Liar," Izzy said. "Mindy said the same thing, then I had a vision about her and one of them. They were...let's just say I never want to see my sister doing that again." She stuck her tongue out and gagged.

Everly scowled at her. "Well you don't have to worry about that." She sounded a little sad. "They don't seem to be into Goth girls." She grinned, flashing a set of vampire fangs, but the smile didn't reach her brown eyes.

Izzy scooted to the edge of the couch. "I'm sorry, Ev."

"Don't be. I'm not," she said.

"If we were dealing with the usual kind of monsters, I wouldn't be concerned," Izzy said. "But this is something different. I can feel it."

"Me, too, but—" Everly clutched her head and her eyes widened in alarm. She opened her mouth, but nothing came out.

Izzy jumped to her feet and rushed across the small room. "What's wrong?" She shook Everly's shoulder, but she didn't respond. "Everly!" she shouted. "Help!"

* * * * *

Tristan followed Isabel's scent through the French Quarter, ignoring the steady stream of incense and spicy foods wafting on the air. He continued east, leaving the Quarter behind him.

He'd found her easily enough last night. He just hoped that she was still in the same spot.

Tristan glanced at the sun peeking through the space

between houses.

It was already warm, and the sun wasn't even high in the sky yet. He should've grabbed Isabel last night, but he'd been exhausted. She had been, too.

Her scent grew stronger as he approached a run-down mansion squatting on the corner of *seen better days.*

White paint peeled from the side of the house, exposing the yellowed layers beneath. The walkway leading to the front door had cracked and split, thanks to gnarled tree roots, and threatened to swallow anyone foolish enough to traverse it. The building looked even worse in the daylight than it had the previous evening.

Tristan inhaled. Isabel was in there somewhere. Her delicious scent perfumed the air. He trotted around to the back of the house and saw a clothesline sagging under the weight of too many items. The line had been stretched across the yard.

He scanned the line. No way would he get into those jeans. No man should. But the sweats might fit. Tristan shifted, taking human form once more. He had just grabbed the sweats off the line when a plump woman carrying a laundry basket rounded the corner.

"Well hello there." She grinned and didn't even pretend not to stare at his bare backside.

Tristan knew the kind of effect he had on human females. He pictured Isabel's sour expression. Correction, most human females. He was proud of his form—both of them. He saw no reason to rush covering himself.

"Good morning," he said, slowly stepping into the sweats. They were tighter than he would've liked, but better than nothing.

Her smile widened. "I think I liked you better without them, but I suppose you can't run around here naked. You'll cause a riot." The woman winked.

Tristan grinned at her. "We wouldn't want that," he said. "Mind if I keep these for a while?"

She chuckled. "Darlin', you can keep them as long as you like, if you promise to come back and model them sometime."

He ran a hand over his bare chest, lingering on his washboard abs.

She giggled louder.

"I just might have to do that when I'm finished with my business in town," Tristan said, making sure to stroke her arm as he brushed past her.

The woman played at fanning her face. "Ew-wee, is it hot out here."

Tristan chuckled. His smile faded the second he turned his back on the woman. He strode across the lawn to the rear door and opened it. He heard shouting coming from down the hall and instantly recognized the voice.

"Help!" Isabel said. "Somebody help me!"

The back door slammed behind him as Tristan rushed down the hall. He reached the last door on the right and kicked it in. The door cracked as it came off its wood frame and fell into the room.

Isabel screamed.

Tristan shoved it aside and ducked beneath the doorframe, expecting to see the Darkling. He crouched low, ready to fight. His gaze darted around the small space in search of the enemy, but there was none.

The only people there were Isabel and an unconscious woman. He looked at her in confusion. Isabel clutched her chest and breathed hard while she hovered over the small female.

"What are you doing?" she shouted. "Are you insane?"

He'd come in to save her, but it was obvious now that she didn't need saving. Tristan ignored the fear that had been pumping through him. When she'd screamed, he'd thought... It didn't matter what he'd thought. He'd been wrong.

He took in the situation with one glance then asked, "What happened?"

Isabel glared at him.

"I cannot help you if you do not tell me what's going on." Tristan drew closer to get a better look but didn't see any obvious injuries. "Is she hurt?"

He extended his hand to check the woman's temperature, since he couldn't smell anything due to the stench coming from the incense.

"I thought she was seizing, but now I'm sure she's having a vision," Isabel said.

Tristan jerked his hand back before he touched her. "What kind of vision?"

"Sugar plums and fairies," Isabel retorted. "You know, the usual."

He frowned in confusion.

Her expression soured, and she sighed. "Visions of any kind are rarely good. It's always about the future."

Tristan took a step back. He'd never been around anyone like this and had never experienced a Sighted-One in action firsthand. Something about the whole thing seemed *unnatural*.

"What's the matter with you?" Isabel asked.

"Nothing," he said.

"Then why are you freaked out?" she asked. "It's not like a cold. You can't catch a vision."

Tristan stiffened. "I cannot catch human diseases or illnesses," he said. "My kind is immune."

"Lucky you," she said.

His mood darkened. He'd come in here expecting to find danger, not a pissed-off woman and her unconscious friend. Tristan was used to action, not waiting around.

"What do you want me to do?" He needed to do something. Boil water. Fetch blankets. Run to the convenience store. Anything.

Isabel huffed. "Since you're here, you can help me get her on the couch." She didn't sound happy.

He picked up the tiny female.

"Be careful," she warned.

He scowled at her. "I am." Tristan gently laid her on the couch.

Isabel followed on his heels, keeping a close eye on him.

"What now?" Tristan asked.

"Now, we wait," she said.

Tristan hated waiting. He'd never been good at it, unless he was hunting.

Isabel took a seat beside her friend.

He either had to stand or... He glanced at the beanbag. Not happening. It was either that or the floor. Tristan straightened the door then jammed it in place. He glared at the beanbag, then with a long suffering sigh, sat. The bag deflated under his weight.

* * * * *

Izzy had nearly had a coronary when Tristan kicked the door in. The only thing that prevented it was her concern for Everly.

How had he found her so quickly? She'd thought for sure it would take him at least a couple days, and by then she'd be long gone.

Izzy glanced at him, trying to ignore the display of muscles that rippled every time he shifted his big frame on the bag to get comfortable.

If the situation weren't so serious, it would be comical.

Where was his shirt? And where did he get those sweats?

Heaven help her, they didn't leave much to the imagination. He caught her watching him. His expression said he knew exactly what she'd been thinking.

Izzy blushed and glanced away. She didn't like how off balance he made her feel. One minute she was attracted to him, the next she wanted to punch him in the face.

She didn't think Tristan was doing it on purpose. After all, he couldn't help how he looked, but she had no doubt he'd use his appearance to his advantage if it meant getting what he wanted.

"What are you doing here?" she asked.

"I would think that would be obvious," he said.

Izzy brushed the hair back from Everly's face. Her friend didn't seem to notice. "I told you, I'm not going with you."

"I'm afraid things have changed," he said.

"Really?" she asked. "You mean in the last eight hours?"

Tristan nodded. "Yes."

"Listen." Izzy forced herself to face him. "I'm sure you mean well in your own weird way." She had no idea if that was the truth or not, but Izzy thought it best that he think so. "But I'd rather be on my own."

His cool gaze moved past her to settle on Everly. "Then why are you here?"

Izzy thrust her chin out. "My place was getting crowded. I needed somewhere to stay," she said pointedly. "I also came here to warn my friend."

A pale brow arched. "About what?" he asked, all but daring her to admit the truth.

Izzy snorted. "I would think that would be obvious," she said, parroting his words back at him.

Tristan glared at her then slowly glanced around the room. His eyes widened when his gaze landed on the skulls. He struggled to his feet and walked over to examine them closer. Tristan lingered over the one that looked real near the altar.

"Where did she get this?" he asked, his voice low and menacing.

"No idea," Izzy said. "You'll have to ask her when she wakes up."

He continued to explore the items in the room. "What is all this?"

Izzy shrugged. "It's Everly's *collection*. She likes dark things."

He studied her friend with new intensity.

Izzy didn't like how Tristan looked at her. "She's defenseless," she snapped, moving her body in front of her friend.

Tristan balked. "You both are," he said. "You just don't realize it yet."

Everly groaned, and her eyelashes fluttered. Then she suddenly bolted upright and started to speak.

Darkness comes on silent feet. Only the light can open the door.

"What is she talking about?" Tristan asked, putting down the skull in his hand.

Izzy shook her head. "I don't know." She waved her fingers in front of Everly's face, but her friend didn't blink. "Whatever it is, it's part of her vision."

Two from different worlds will join as one. Bodies intertwined.

Izzy's eyes widened. She glanced at Tristan in time to see his lips flatten into a straight line. He looked about as happy as she felt. Surely, Everly wasn't talking about...about...sex. Was she?

"Visions can mean almost anything," Izzy said. "They aren't necessarily literal." She wasn't sure whom she was trying to convince, Tristan or herself.

As she stared at him, Tristan's mercury gaze shifted to hers. He looked straight into her soul. A shiver spread through her, and she broke eye contact.

There was no way she'd sleep with a monster. Not even a pretty one that resembled a Norse god. Not going to happen.

Trust as one you must to break the spell of darkness. For the door is open and cannot be closed until the Sighted-One crosses over, and the dead will rise to join her.

Izzy felt her face pale. That didn't sound good. Where was the door that Everly was talking about? Was it physical or metaphorical? And what would happen once Izzy got to the other side? It was one thing to see and communicate with Spirit. Quite another to make the dead rise.

Everly groaned and dropped back onto the couch. A moment later, her eyes fluttered opened and awareness returned.

"Hey," Izzy said. "You okay?"

Tristan stepped back and leaned against the wall.

Everly touched her head and winced. "I think so. How long was I out?"

"Long enough to scare the crap out of me," Izzy said. "I almost called an ambulance."

"I'm glad you didn't," Everly said. "They would've locked me up in a padded room. Help me sit up."

Izzy grabbed her hand and helped her swing her legs over the edge of the couch.

The second Everly caught sight of Tristan, her charcoal-lined eyes widened. "It's you," she said. "You were in my vision."

Tristan tensed, then pushed away from the wall and slowly walked toward them.

Everly straightened and stared directly at him.

A growl rumbled from his chest as their gazes met and clashed.

Izzy jumped, but Everly didn't even flinch.

"Knock it off, Snowman," Izzy said, not feeling nearly as brave as she pretended.

Tristan's jaw clenched, but he stopped posturing and took a seat once more.

* * * * *

The dark-haired woman should be terrified of him, but Tristan sensed no fear. She'd said she knew him from her vision. He wondered what exactly she'd seen. He didn't like being left out of the loop.

Tristan didn't know what to make of Isabel's tiny friend, but he did know one thing—there was no way in hades that he and Isabel were going to be lovers. He didn't sleep with humans. Ever! Tristan was an aggressive lover, and they were too *breakable*. They also carried inferior genes compared to the Moonlight Kin.

Of course, one look at Isabel's horrified expression and Tristan knew that wasn't something he'd ever have to worry about.

Good, he thought. *That made two of them.*

Isabel glanced at him then back to Everly. "What did you see?" she asked in a low voice.

Everly continued to stare at him. Then she slowly met her friend's startled gaze. "He can hear every word you say. Doesn't matter if you whisper. Does it?" she asked him.

Tristan stared at her. "No."

"Did you see our deaths?" Isabel asked and swallowed hard.

Everly bit her lip, and her brow furrowed. "Not the kind you're talking about."

Isabel frowned in confusion. "What other kinds of deaths are there?"

"There's true death, then there's everything else," Everly said.

Tristan inhaled. The truth...and a lie. What wasn't she telling them?

"Are you sure you're feeling okay?" Isabel asked. "You're acting weird, and for you that's saying something."

Everly's gaze slipped back to Tristan. "You're not what I imagined. In my vision you were... *taller*."

He crossed his long legs. "I am six foot five," he said.

She wasn't at all what he'd anticipated either. Something about the dark little imp made him decidedly uncomfortable. Her brown eyes held humor and knowledge. Tristan dismissed the humor, but he wanted the knowledge she hid.

There was more to Isabel's friend than she revealed, but Tristan didn't have time to uncover all her secrets. Right now, he only needed to know the answer to one.

"Introduce me," she said to Isabel, before he asked.

"You don't want to meet him," she said. "It's better if you don't know him."

Everly glanced at her. "Yes, I do. Especially now."

Isabel looked as if she were about to argue, until Everly clutched her temple again. "Fine," she said. "Everly Watts, this is Tristan Chevalier, but everyone calls him Frosty."

"Not everyone," he said through gritted teeth. Only Isabel would dare to do such a thing. He would allow no other the luxury.

Everly nodded but didn't hold out her hand.

Smart woman. Or was she simply afraid to touch him? Humans had odd ideas about his kind. Most worked in Moonlight Kin favor, but some showed nothing but ignorance. Tristan didn't think this woman was stupid. Quite the opposite. Her scent told him that she wasn't afraid.

"So where do you want to take my friend?" Everly asked, abruptly changing the subject.

"That's not your concern," he said. "Where'd you get the wolf skull?"

"That's not a wolf," Isabel said. "It's human."

"Correction," Tristan said. "He was in human *form* when he died, but he was not human."

Isabel studied the skull. "How can you tell? It looks just like the others."

"Dead or alive, I can smell my own kind," Tristan said. "Now where did you get it, Everly Watts?"

Everly crossed her arms and sat back. "I didn't kill him if that's what you're asking."

Tristan scooted forward. He had wondered if she had, but wasn't surprised that she hadn't. Female hunters weren't common, but they did exist. The east coast Alpha, Damon Laroche, had mated with one such woman.

"Then who did?" he asked. Tristan would hunt them down once he eliminated the Darkling threat.

Everly scoffed. "I'm not about to tell you that. You'd kill them," she said.

"Yes, I would." Tristan smiled, showing more teeth than necessary. That was his job, and he was very good at it.

Isabel stared at Everly. "You knew the skull came from one of them, and you kept it anyway? Are you nuts?"

"Not crazy," Tristan said, answering for her. "But not particularly bright, since my kind can smell their own."

Everly stiffened and glared at him. This time she didn't look away until Isabel shook her. "You might've mentioned his resemblance to one of the Avengers."

"It wasn't Loki, so I didn't think it was important," Izzy said.

Everly laughed. "I see why you like him."

Isabel's mouth dropped open. A plethora of emotions rushed across her face. "I don't like him. Why would you say that? He's a monster."

Tristan tensed. Humans had called him many things over the years. Nothing really fazed him anymore—or so he thought. *She's human. She means nothing to me*, he reminded himself.

Her cheeks reddened. "No offense," Isabel added hastily.

"None taken," Tristan said nonchalantly, ignoring the churning in his gut. "Your friend was about to tell me where she got the skull."

"No, she wasn't," Everly said. "So drop it."

He surged forward. "If there is someone out there hunting Moonlight Kin, then I need to know about it."

"Hunting what?" Isabel asked.

"That's what they call themselves," Everly said. "I thought you knew."

"Of course." It was obvious she hadn't.

Tristan was within striking distance. He didn't make a habit of attacking women. In fact, he avoided it whenever possible. But his loyalty was to his people, not to humans. This woman needed to be reminded of the fact.

"I'm only going to ask nicely one last time," Tristan said. "Where did you get the skull?"

Everly glowered. "It was a gift."

"For what purpose?" he asked. Getting her to respond was like pulling teeth from a mule.

She thought about the question for a moment. No doubt trying to decide whether to lie. It would do her no good. He'd scent a lie immediately.

Everly sighed. "I use it to detect your presence," she said.

Tristan's nostrils flared. That was not what he'd expected her to say. Such a thing shouldn't be possible, but the ramifications of the admission were not lost on him. This woman was more dangerous than he first thought.

Somehow she'd turned a Moonlight Kin skull into a tracking device. If the Hunters learned about it, about her, they'd go to great lengths to get their hands on her. What if she'd already shared the knowledge? He needed to find out.

"How have you used this knowledge?" If she said that she gave the information to the Hunters, then Tristan was going to have to kill her or have the local Alpha take care of the job.

He glanced at Isabel. She would never forgive him if he murdered her friend, but what choice did he have?

"The skull is for *personal* use," Everly said. "I do not share what I know. It helps me avoid your kind."

"Why didn't you tell me about this?" Isabel asked, sounding hurt. "I could've used one of those myself."

"And exactly how did you plan to get one?" Tristan asked. Had he completely misjudged her? Was she talking about killing, too?

Isabel rolled her eyes. "I'll start by melting ice."

Tristan gave her a droll look and shook his head. He should've known.

Everly touched her arm. "You need to go with him," she said.

"Okay, now I know there's something wrong with you," Izzy said. "Because the friend I know would never suggest anything so insane, especially knowing full well what he is."

Everly's dark eyes filled with compassion. "I've seen the future," she said.

"I know," Izzy said. "We heard. Though a lot of it didn't make sense, and you don't seem to be in a hurry to elaborate."

Tristan rested his elbows on his knees. "What exactly did you see?"

Everly's dark gaze landed on him. "I don't think you're ready to hear what I saw. I don't think either of you are, but it doesn't matter." She pushed her hair away from her face. "I've seen what's going to happen...to us all. You can't outrun fate. None of us can."

A shiver tracked down Tristan's spine.

CHAPTER FIVE

Izzy hugged Everly goodbye then stepped into the hall.

"You will see her again," Tristan said.

She hoped he was right, but thus far Izzy hadn't had any visions of the future. Did that mean she didn't have a future to see?

Izzy frowned.

"Come," Tristan said, but didn't reach for her.

"Where are we going?" she asked.

His guarded expression made her think he wouldn't answer, but then Tristan surprised her. "I must present myself to the Alpha of this area. He can aid us in finding shelter."

"Why do I have to go with you?" Izzy asked.

"Because you have shown that you cannot be trusted out of my sight." He smirked.

Once again Izzy had the overwhelming urge to slap the smartass expression right off his face. She'd try it if he weren't so tall.

Tristan laughed.

"What?" she asked.

"Sometimes you are so easy to read," he said.

Izzy tilted her head to get a better look at him. "I'll keep that in mind the next time I think about hitting you," she said.

"You'd only hurt yourself," Tristan said.

"Of course you would say something like that," she said, then muttered under her breath, "arrogant jerk." He was right. Hitting someone that solid would probably break her hand.

Tristan chuckled. "You mustn't be concerned about your friend's visions," he said.

Izzy stopped on the sidewalk. "I'm not. Why would you bring that up?"

He shrugged his broad shoulders. "I thought perhaps that was what you were upset about."

"No," she said. "I'm upset because you won't leave me alone and insist on disrupting my life. Hint. Hint. Hint."

"Oh," he said. "I'm glad to be mistaken. Better to be thinking that than the possibility of us having sex."

Her eyes rounded. "I wasn't thinking about having sex with you." Izzy's gaze automatically dropped to the bulge straining the front of his sweatpants. He needed to change clothes.

"Good." Tristan gave her a knowing smirk. "You can rest assured it's never going to happen."

Angry with herself for being distracted by his perfect body, Izzy rounded on him. "Damn right it's not!" she snapped. "So just get that mental picture out of your head." And she'd do the same just as soon as he got dressed.

They continued down the sidewalk toward the French Quarter, weaving their way through the growing crowds. Despite it being morning, the tourists were already out enjoying the delights the quarter offered.

"I have no idea what you're thinking, but sex with you never even crossed my mind. Nor would it ever with a *human*," Tristan said in disgust.

Izzy stopped again. "What's that supposed to mean?"

Tristan paused, his gaze scanning the people around them. "I do not sleep with inferior species," he said, giving her body a once over.

Izzy's mouth gaped. "Who are you calling inferior, Snowflake?"

His haughty expression spoke volumes. "You are human. Are you not?"

Anger rose out of nowhere. "How dare you!" Izzy shouted. "I am not a monster."

Tristan's jaw clenched, and he stepped forward until there was no space between their bodies. "Neither am I!" he snarled.

Izzy snorted. "I'm not the one who goes fuzzy once a month."

"I am *never* fuzzy!" he groused.

Izzy took one look at his affronted expression and laughed in his face. It was the wrong thing to do, but she couldn't help it. A picture of Tristan as a big, fuzzy, white dog popped into her mind, and she just could not shake the image.

"Take it back," he said softly.

"No." She crossed her arms.

"I said, take it back," Tristan hissed.

"No." Izzy shook her head. "Not until you do."

His heated gaze dropped to her mouth, and the tension between them changed in an instant. Suddenly the New Orleans heat was nothing compared to the simmering air around them. Tristan looked at her as if he wanted to eat her alive, and not in a *wolfie* kind of way.

When he stared at her like that, Izzy forgot all about him being a werewolf and saw him as a man. Their kiss came back in vivid detail. Izzy's traitorous body softened and swayed toward him, drawn by something primal.

Tristan's gaze grew hooded, and he crowded even closer. Heat poured off his body, along with a spicy scent that was unique to him alone. He unclenched his hands and reached for her.

If he touched her, she'd lose it, lose herself. *No! Don't let him kiss you again.* No matter how bad she wanted to feel his lips upon hers. Izzy's eyes widened as the insane thought struck, and she took a step back.

"We can't." She held out her hand to stop him and encountered a wall of warm marble. Izzy's fingers trembled as she pulled her hand away from his bare chest. Was it her imagination or had the color of Tristan's eyes changed? "I'm inferior, remember?"

* * * * *

Tristan took a deep breath, and his body shuddered. It took supreme effort to tear his gaze away from the temptation her mouth presented. It had been hours since he'd claimed Isabel's lips, but Tristan still tasted the honeysuckle on his tongue.

He thought about Everly's vision. She had to be wrong. There were many ways for information to be interpreted. It didn't have to be sex, though he couldn't think of any other way that bodies intertwined. And damn if that didn't make him hard.

Tristan glanced down at the front of his pants and cursed. He wasn't a little man. The snug sweats he wore hid nothing.

Isabel followed his gaze. If it were possible, her eyes widened even more. She couldn't seem to tear her attention away, which wasn't helping his current condition at all. His nostrils flared. Her warm scent filled his lungs.

She was still scared, but beneath the fear Tristan smelled something else. Something utterly enticing and overwhelmingly feminine. Isabel may not like him, but part of her desired him.

And damn if that didn't make his job that much harder.

Tristan's gaze raked Isabel. He could see the definite outline of a feminine figure underneath her long skirt and loose blouse. Hell, even if he couldn't, he'd felt her body pressed to his when he had kissed her. In that moment, whether she knew it or not, she'd surrendered.

The beast inside him roared to life. Tristan shook his head and grabbed hold of his shadow side. He couldn't afford for his beast to escape. It didn't think like he did. Didn't reason. It acted on instinct. And right now its instincts were telling it to take.

"Come," he said. "We need to hurry."

He needed to get to Pierre La Fontaine's home in the Garden District. If for no other reason than to get a break from Isabel's company and regain his footing.

She had him thinking about things Tristan rarely contemplated. Work was his mistress, not wayward females whose sense of self-preservation was questionable at best.

He led her through the French Quarter to Canal Street then hung a right. Trolleys ran down St. Charles Avenue to the Garden District, along with buses, but Tristan didn't care to wait for a bus. He preferred the open air of the trolley.

The trolley wouldn't take them all the way to Pierre's house due to the construction in the area, but it would get them close enough. Once he checked in with the Alpha, he'd retrieve his truck.

Tristan waited for Isabel to board, then he climbed on after her. There weren't any seats available, until he walked over to a couple of young men and stared at them. They suddenly jumped up and offered him their wooden seat.

He grabbed Isabel by the elbow and guided her onto the bench. She scowled at him, which was becoming an unwelcome habit. He much preferred her teasing. When she did that, Isabel reminded Tristan of his little brother, François.

He too had been a free spirit, floating through life without a care in the world. That was why it had been so easy for the lone wolf to kill him.

François had been so trusting, so innocent that when the

wolf attacked, he'd been helpless to defend himself. His death had changed Tristan's life forever—changed Tristan forever. The loss had turned him into what he was now. The cold distance kept the pain at bay.

Tristan glanced at her. Isabel and François really were so much alike that at times the similarity scared him. When that happened, he pushed her away using cruelty to make her withdraw.

He pictured his brother's mangled body. Would Isabel meet the same fate?

The thought left him feeling decidedly uncomfortable. Tristan closed his eyes and clutched the window frame of the trolley until the wood moaned beneath his grip, then he slowly released it along with the bad memories. He didn't like thinking about the past. There was nothing he could do about it, but he could change the future.

Tristan glanced out the window. "This is our stop," he said.

Isabel waited for a couple people to pass, then stood.

Tristan followed her off the trolley then indicated to the far side of the street where a massive mansion took up half the block.

"Guess you guys don't know the meaning of the word 'subtle,'" she said.

Most Alphas didn't, but that wasn't how he lived. Tristan pictured his favorite home, an adobe nestled in the foothills of the high New Mexican desert. The place was warm, welcoming, and peaceful. Perfect for relaxing and clearing his head after a job.

"When you have to house an entire pack, you need a lot of space," he said dryly.

Isabel froze on the sidewalk. Her hazel eyes widened, then widened again until they swallowed her face. "There's a whole pack of monsters inside there."

It wasn't a question, but Tristan answered it as such anyway. "Yes, there is an entire pack of wolves in there," he said. "Southern Moonlight Kin to be exact. They don't take kindly to being called monsters, so I suggest you be on your best behavior, unless you want to end up on the menu."

She blanched and swayed before his eyes.

Tristan grabbed her before she fainted. He'd meant to scare her a little, but he didn't want Isabel so scared that she couldn't function.

He didn't like her viewing him and his people as monsters, even though it was best if she did. Why it bothered Tristan so much, he couldn't say. He'd never been bothered by such a thing before.

She's human, he reminded himself. *Humans are weak. They believe they are the apex predators. They're wrong.*

Isabel turned green, and she looked as if she were going to be sick.

A pang of guilt struck. "I was just kidding," Tristan said. "I will not allow anything to happen to you."

The moment the words left his mouth, Tristan knew they were the truth. She had a smart mouth and he might want to strangle her at times, but he wouldn't let anyone harm her.

Isabel's gaze searched his face, then she glanced back at the house.

"I swear," Tristan said. He'd vow anything to take away her fear. "Now come."

He led her to the front of the mansion, where they were met by a couple of Pierre's guards. The two men stepped forward and sniffed them. Their eyes narrowed when they caught Isabel's human scent.

"I need to speak to Pierre," Tristan said.

"Who shall we say is calling?" the wolf on the left asked, watching them both closely.

"Tell him that Tristan Chevalier, Enforcer for the Lycanian Elders, is in need of his assistance."

The wolf on the right paled and took a step back. His gaze immediately dropped to the porch floor. The man on the left was slower, but he eventually followed suit.

Isabel looked at them then glanced at Tristan. This time there was confusion in her eyes.

Better that than fear, Tristan thought.

The man on the right pressed the doorbell and waited. A moment later, a short wolf dressed in an expensive suit popped his head out the door. When he caught sight of Tristan, he shoved the other two wolves out of the way and bowed.

"Sorry to have kept you waiting, Enforcer," he said. "Please come inside and bring your little..." –he sniffed and his nose wrinkled like he'd smelled something bad— "*friend* with you."

"After you." Tristan ushered Isabel ahead of him.

The second they entered the foyer, her eyes widened and her mouth dropped open. Tristan had nearly done the same thing the first time he'd seen the inside of the Southern Alpha's home.

Entering the mansion was like stepping back into the seventeen hundreds. Everything had been meticulously restored to its original grandeur.

"Tristan, my friend," a booming voice said. "What brings you to my humble abode?"

The question almost made Tristan laugh, since there was nothing humble about Pierre's abode, or the Alpha himself for that matter.

* * * * *

Izzy continued to reel from the news that Tristan was some kind of assassin. Her tumultuous thoughts were interrupted when a dark-haired man with lightly tanned skin came silently gliding down the staircase. Had he not spoken, Izzy wouldn't have known that he was there.

No, she mentally corrected. There'd be no way to miss him. His presence filled the space, adding to its opulence.

Izzy stared, unable to look away. She had never seen

anyone quite so beautiful. The man's finely sculpted face could only be called pretty. How he managed it without looking feminine in the process was a mystery.

Tristan gave her an admonishing look then glanced back to the man. "I'm sure you're aware of what has brought me to your fair city," he said.

The man stopped before them and smiled. The move seemed too practiced for her liking.

Yet, Izzy felt that smile all the way to her toes when he directed the wattage at her. Was it hot in here? She resisted the urge to tug on her collar.

"Aren't you going to introduce us?" the man asked, stepping closer to her.

Tristan looked as if he was about to refuse the request, then thought better of it. Why he cared one way or the other, Izzy didn't know, since he'd made his views on humans perfectly clear.

"Isabel MacDougal, I'd like you to meet Pierre La Fontaine, Alpha of the Southern Moonlight Kin pack," Tristan said.

So this was the biggest monster in town. Izzy stared at him until an image of his dark beast replaced his perfect features. He didn't seem to notice, or maybe he had better manners than her.

Pierre took her hand before she offered it and kissed the back of her knuckles in such a way that Izzy had no doubt he'd done it hundreds of times before. A shiver tracked down her spine, but somehow she kept her hand from trembling.

While Tristan exuded an air of ice, this man was nothing but sweltering heat and hot summer nights. He used his smoldering good looks to full advantage.

Izzy couldn't imagine many women turned him down once he crooked his finger in their direction. No doubt with one look, he could make panties drop from fifty paces.

"A pleasure," Pierre said. "I can't remember the last time

a Sighted-One graced my doorstep."

Tristan cleared his throat and insinuated himself between them, forcing Pierre to release her.

Pierre's amber gaze lit with speculation. "Perhaps, Enforcer, we should talk in private."

"That would be best," Tristan said. "What I have to say calls for discretion."

"If you don't mind waiting in the parlor, Isabel." Pierre pointed to a room off to the left. "I'll have refreshments brought to you."

Despite the polite offer, it wasn't a request. "Sure," she said. "Take all the time you need. I'll just go in there and fluff my petticoats."

Pierre frowned in confusion.

Tristan laughed. "She's a delight, isn't she?"

The Alpha watched her. "She's certainly...interesting," he said.

Izzy walked into the parlor. Two navy-blue settees had been arranged in the middle of the room, facing each other. There were wooden side tables of various sizes and shapes spaced throughout the parlor, along with several chairs and stools.

Some of the tables held board games, while others housed lamps. All were covered in lace of some type or another. Everything looked so old and expensive that Izzy was afraid to sit down.

A minute later, the man who'd met them at the door came in, carrying a tray with a pitcher of lemonade and some finger sandwiches on it. The idea that wolves served finger sandwiches struck her as funny, but Izzy didn't laugh. She didn't think he'd appreciate her sense of humor.

The man set the tray down on a small side table then turned to her. "I thought instead of breakfast that you'd prefer a sandwich. If you need anything else," he said, "just ring that bell." He pointed to a cloth lever hanging from the ceiling next to the door.

"Thanks," she said. "I'm sure I'll be fine." Izzy waited for him to leave then checked the sandwiches. As soon as she realized they were turkey and ham, she tucked into them. She hadn't eaten last night or this morning. Right now, anything looked good.

Izzy wandered around the room while she ate, a glass of lemonade in one hand and a sandwich in the other. She had no idea how long Tristan's explanation would take, but Izzy hoped they'd be out of here soon. She didn't want to be in this house any longer than necessary.

She stopped near a window and stared out at the vast lawn. The lush green space had been carefully manicured to project an image of southern refinement. If people only knew who their neighbor really was, they'd be horrified.

Izzy had just turned to retrace her steps when she heard Tristan's voice. She stopped to listen. Where was it coming from? The window was shut. She was alone in the room, and the thick walls wouldn't carry sound.

Tristan spoke again. There was no mistaking the deep timbre of his voice.

She followed the sound to a heating vent behind a nearby table. Izzy glanced over her shoulder to make sure the door was closed then moved closer.

It was wrong to eavesdrop, but Izzy was genuinely curious what he and Pierre were talking about. She grabbed a small stool and took a seat. Izzy placed her food and drink on the table, so if anyone came in unexpectedly it would look like she was enjoying her meal.

"Never thought I'd see the day that you'd be slumming it with a human," Pierre said. "Even one as attractive as her."

She stiffened but listened for Tristan's response. Whatever he said, it was too low for her to hear. Izzy scooted the stool closer.

"Have you located the Darkling?" Pierre asked.

"I almost had him, but he opened a portal and got away," Tristan said. "He's after the woman. Of that there is no doubt."

"Ah," Pierre said. "That explains why you brought her here. You know if you took away the purple streaks from her hair and changed her formless clothes, she wouldn't be bad to gaze upon."

Tristan mumbled, but his next words were frighteningly clear. "She's a means to an end," he said. "Nothing more."

"Oh," Pierre said. "I thought perhaps there was something going on between you two. There seemed to be—"

"No!" Tristan cut off whatever he was going to say. "You know I do not mix with humans. All I see is bait when I look at her. Bait to catch the Darkling."

His cold words left Izzy chilled to the bone. She shouldn't be surprised. Tristan had said from the outset that he didn't care for humans, yet somehow she'd convinced herself that the frigid exterior was just a front.

She'd been a fool.

Izzy stood. She didn't need to hear anymore. She thought of Stone's offer of help. Would it still stand? She glanced once more at the closed door.

At any moment, Tristan might return. Izzy needed to contact Stone, if for no other reason than to tell him that he was safe because the monster was with her. They *all* were.

She pulled out the cell phone he'd given her and turned it on. Izzy found the number and sent a quick text. Less than a minute later, she received a response.

I'll help you get away. Just tell me where you are.

Izzy replied. *I'm someplace you can't help me. I'll let you know if and when we leave.*

Take care of yourself. The monsters aren't to be trusted.

Izzy knew that better than most. Tristan had just squashed the tiny bit of doubt lingering inside of her. She turned the phone off and shoved it into her purse. Izzy looked at her half-eaten sandwich. Suddenly she wasn't hungry anymore.

* * * * *

Tristan sat across from Pierre in his ornate office. He'd never seen so much gilded gold outside of a Parisian palace. He didn't like the way the Alpha looked at him. It was as if he knew something that Tristan did not.

"We need a place to stay. Preferably someplace remote, so that I will know when the Darkling draws near," he said.

"No problem. I know just the place." Pierre sat back. "How does the woman feel about being used as bait?"

Tristan shrugged casually. "I hadn't planned to tell her."

Pierre watched him closely. "What if something happens to her?"

Tristan's gut clenched. Nothing was going to happen to Isabel.

"You cannot always protect bait," Pierre said. "Accidents happen."

Tristan flinched.

"Are you sure there is nothing going on between you two?" Pierre asked. "I've never seen you so wound up."

"Positive," Tristan's vehement response didn't have the effect he'd hoped.

Pierre grinned, looking positively enthralled by the whole conversation. "You say that the woman is a means to an end, yet she carries your scent."

Tristan blanched. "I had no choice but to touch her," he said. "When I first encountered her, she refused to come with me."

Pierre's face hardened, along with all the muscles in his body. "When you say touch, what exactly do you mean?"

There was one hard-and-fast rule within the Moonlight Kin. A woman could be coerced, but never be forced into physical intimacy. Doing such a thing was an automatic death sentence for any Were.

Tristan had gladly carried that sentence out a few times over the years, which was why he gnashed his teeth at the

Alpha's insinuation. "I had to pick her up and carry her someplace private so we could talk. That's how my scent got on her."

Pierre relaxed a fraction. "It seemed...stronger."

He thought about the kiss, and his whole body tensed. There was no sense in lying to the Alpha. They had ways of ferreting out information. "She forced me to kiss her."

If Pierre's eyebrows rose any higher, they'd disappear beneath his hairline. "How exactly did Isabel do that?" he asked. "Did she hold you at gunpoint?"

Tristan knew what he thought. It would be what any Alpha of the Moonlight Kin would think, when it came to him. Tristan wasn't known for being emotionally or physically demonstrative, unless he killed someone. And even then, emotions rarely played a part. He wasn't the type to keep females around.

Contrary to what they all believed, Tristan wasn't a glacier and he wasn't gay. He had needs just like any other male. He just rarely acted upon them.

Instead, Tristan focused on the job. It took a special breed of wolf to hunt down your own kind and kill them without mercy. It wasn't something he enjoyed, but Tristan was exceedingly good at the job. There were a few other Enforcers, but none were better.

Pierre continued to stare at him until he squirmed in his seat.

"She wouldn't shut up," Tristan said, trying to make the Alpha understand. "When she wasn't threatening to scream, she tore into me. Since I didn't have a gag, I improvised. That was all. The kiss meant nothing." The lie slipped out before he could stop it.

Pierre's amber eyes glistened. "That's some improvisation on your part. I would've never thought you had it in you."

"It's been a while, but kissing is not something one forgets how to do," he said mockingly.

"Wish I could've been there to see that," Pierre said.

"What did she do when you kissed her?"

Tristan's mind blanked. "I don't understand the question."

Pierre's lips canted, and his eyes crinkled in amusement. "Did Isabel smack you? She would've had every right to do so, since I have no doubt you kissed her without permission."

Tristan hesitated. Where was Pierre going with this line of questioning? "No, she didn't strike me, though Isabel did look like she wanted to," he said.

Why hadn't she hit him? She'd had plenty of opportunity. Tristan hadn't exactly been as unaffected by the kiss as he claimed. He wished the Alpha wasn't so amused by the situation, but Pierre had always had an annoying sense of humor.

"Did she scream or try to run away?" he asked.

Tristan shook his head. "No, she didn't do anything like that."

"Hmm..." Pierre said. "Interesting." He leaned forward. "I have one final question."

"Then ask, so I can put us both out of our misery," Tristan said impatiently.

Pierre chuckled. "Did she kiss you back?"

Yes, the word whispered through Tristan's mind, leaving confusion in its wake.

He straightened in his seat. "You don't know her. Isabel may look soft and tempting, but her tongue spews acid," Tristan said. "I am lucky to have flesh left on my bones."

A grin parted Pierre's face. "So she *did* kiss you back. Fascinating, don't you think?"

"Did you not hear what I said?" Tristan ran a hand through his long white hair. "There is nothing interesting about this situation," he said. "Isabel can be utterly infuriating, when she wants to be. Which is most of the time, I might add."

"Yes, I can see that," Pierre said. "Isabel." Her name rolled off his lips.

The seductive tone made Tristan's hackles rise. "That is her name," he said.

Pierre carefully blanked his expression. "It is indeed. Perhaps I need to speak with Isabel once more. I feel that I prematurely formed my opinion of her."

Tristan's muscles flexed as he gripped the arms of the chair. "I've told you everything," he said.

The Alpha gave him a knowing look. "I have absolutely no doubt, but women can be quite elusive when they want to be," he said. "There's obviously more to Isabel than meets the eye."

Something akin to panic struck. Pierre was renowned for his charm and his many conquests. Women of all ages responded to his devilish good looks. Isabel hadn't been immune. Tristan had seen her pupils dilate and heard her pulse jump when she looked at him. He didn't want the Alpha anywhere near her.

"I assure you that she will show you no respect whatsoever," Tristan said, trying to dissuade Pierre. "You are wasting your breath."

"If you don't mind, I'll be the judge of that." Pierre rose from behind his desk.

Tristan stood, too.

"Please, have a seat," he said. "This shouldn't take long." Pierre winked at him. "Or perhaps it will. One never knows what kind of mischief one can get up to in the parlor."

A deep growl rumbled out of Tristan as his wolf surged to the surface.

The Alpha stopped and gave him a hard look, one that all but dared him to continue.

Tristan clenched his hands at his sides.

"Sit, Enforcer," Pierre said. "Or I'll make you sit."

For one insane moment, Tristan considered challenging the Alpha. The thought must've shown on his face because

Pierre's amber eyes widened.

"I won't harm her," he said.

Tristan wanted to stop him, but he couldn't forbid the visit without starting a major incident. He'd never wanted to be Alpha. Tristan didn't want the responsibility of caring for so many wolves. So what had gotten into him? Isabel's face flashed in his mind. He knew she was trouble, and this proved it.

Pierre laughed, and then the Alpha stepped into the hall.

It took every fiber of Tristan's being to nod and sit back down.

Pierre made sure to shut the door behind him, so there would be no chance of Tristan hearing what was going on. That didn't stop Tristan from trying to listen. He'd give the Alpha ten minutes. If he didn't return within that time, then Tristan would go after him.

* * * * *

The door opened behind Izzy. She turned, expecting to see Tristan, but instead found the darkly handsome Pierre La Fontaine staring at her. He noted the missing sandwiches on the platter.

"I trust they were to your liking," he said, indicating to the food.

"They were fine. Thanks," Izzy said, rubbing her arms. Where was Tristan? She wanted out of here. Now!

"I'd like to have a word with you before Tristan joins us. Which I have no doubt will be very soon." Pierre grinned.

What was so funny? Izzy hoped Pierre skipped the niceties and got straight to the point. He didn't know that she'd heard them talking, so if he lied, she'd know.

"Please, have a seat." Pierre pointed to one of the expensive-looking settees.

Izzy hesitated then perched on the edge of the seat. Instead of taking a seat opposite her, Pierre sat down next to her. Izzy immediately scooted away.

She checked to see if the move had insulted him, but his smile only widened. Izzy angled herself in such a way that she kept him and the door in sight.

Pierre noticed but didn't comment though for a second Izzy thought she heard him laugh. The sound was there and gone before she could be sure.

"What did you want to talk about?" she asked to hurry things along. She knew exactly what the monsters had planned for her.

"What do you think of Tristan?" Pierre leaned back and draped his arm over the back of the settee.

Izzy blinked. The question surprised her so much that it took her a full minute to answer. "What do you mean?"

This time Pierre did laugh. "I'm just curious what you think of him. Feel free to speak candidly. You are safe within these walls."

Yeah, but what would happen when she left the house?

"He's fine," she said noncommittally.

"You can do better than that," he said.

"Okay, he's bossy and thinks he knows everything." She had no idea what Pierre was after, and until she figured it out Izzy wasn't about to be too direct.

"So the kiss wasn't that good," Pierre said.

Izzy's eyes widened in shock. Heat spread from her face to the rest of her body. Why had Tristan told Pierre about their kiss?

She sputtered as words clustered in her mouth and tangled on her tongue. "I-I-I." Izzy cleared her throat. "I'm not sure what that has to do with anything."

Pierre took pity on her. "I've known Tristan Chevalier for years. He's never been one to play with..." –he paused— "anything."

Play? What did he mean by that? Izzy had no clue, but it hardly mattered since she'd heard exactly what Tristan had planned for her.

"Perhaps he's trying to soften me up before he delivers bad news," she said.

"Perhaps," Pierre said. "But I've never known Tristan to care about such things."

"I'm not sure what you want me to say," she said.

Pierre tilted his head. "You are a unique woman," he said, surprising her once again. He rose from the settee and walked to the door, where he paused. "Contrary to his appearance, Tristan wasn't always made of ice. There was a time when he was a lot like you."

Izzy couldn't imagine Tristan ever being like her.

"Thank you for..." Pierre's brow furrowed, and his voice trailed off.

"What?" Izzy asked, more confused than ever.

"For thawing him a little," Pierre said, then opened the door.

Tristan stood in the hall, his hand raised to knock on the parlor door. He had an unreadable expression on his face.

Pierre grinned. "Right on time I see."

As if on cue, Tristan scowled. "Let's go, Isabel," he said. "I have the keys to the cabin. Thank you again for your assistance, Alpha. I will let the Lycanian Elders know of your aid."

Pierre laughed. "You do that."

Izzy waited until Tristan climbed behind the wheel of his silver F150 pickup truck and pulled out into traffic before she confronted him. She hadn't planned to bring the subject up, but Pierre's questions had rattled her, and Tristan had been acting distant ever since they'd left the house. Frankly, the whole situation pissed her off.

Tristan had no right to be angry or pouty or however snowmen acted when they got their carrot noses out of joint. Izzy was the one being taken advantage of. She wasn't the one in the wrong. He was.

"So," she said, itching for a fight. "How exactly do you plan to use me as bait?"

To his credit, he didn't flinch, but his glacial features tightened.

Didn't think I knew about your little plan, did you?

"Did Pierre tell you that?" he asked.

"Does it matter how I found out?" Izzy wasn't about to let him know that she'd eavesdropped on their conversation. There was confessing and then there was *confessing*.

Tristan exhaled. "The Darkling wants you. We have to give it what it wants," he said. "There is no other way to draw it out."

Izzy crossed her arms. The move pushed her breasts up. "Do I get a say in any of this?"

He glanced at her chest, then his expression hardened. "No," he said then returned his attention to the road.

He doesn't care about you, remember?

"Well I'm sorry to rain on your party, Snowflake, but you're just going to have to find the monster without me," she said. "Because I have no intention of helping you."

Izzy might've helped him, if he'd bothered to ask, but he hadn't. Instead, he'd planned to deceive her.

"The Darkling doesn't want me," Tristan said. "It wants you. It followed you here from Oregon. It knows you're here. It won't give up until I stop it."

"Sounds like you need me more than I need you," Izzy said. "That must suck for you."

Tristan laughed, but the sound sent shivers down her spine. "It matters not," he said. "You *will* help me."

"I will not," she parroted.

Izzy stared out the window. She didn't like anyone giving her orders. She'd had her fill of them when her parents had her locked up in the asylum.

"You either help me or everyone you love will die," Tristan said. "Just like your friend, Celina Gibson."

Her head whipped around in surprise. At the same time, a wave of pain struck. Mindy had told her about Celina's death. Told her about Slade, the man who'd killed her. Izzy had already known that her best friend had passed because she'd caught a glimpse of her spirit shortly after her death.

Izzy didn't like having the incident thrown in her face. And she damn sure didn't like being threatened. She'd done everything she could to lead the danger away. It just hadn't been enough.

She glared at Tristan. She'd known he was stubborn and beyond uptight, but Izzy hadn't thought he was capable of killing innocents. She'd really read him wrong. Or perhaps, she'd read him right the first time. He was a monster after all.

A strange calm came over her. Izzy loosened her seatbelt to face him. "Don't threaten my family," she snarled. "I may not be as strong as you, but I will find a way to stop you."

Tristan's hands clutched the wheel until his knuckles turned white. "It's not me who is threatening their existence," he said.

"Then who is?" she snapped. "Because it sure as hell sounds like you talking."

"The Darkling," he said with impatience.

"Is that supposed to mean something to me?" Izzy asked. He'd mentioned she was being hunted. Why differentiate the Moonlight Kin from the Darklings? All monsters were the same, weren't they?

Izzy had lied when she'd told Mindy that the monsters were just like humans. They weren't. They were far worse.

Her sister had mentioned something about a Darkling. What did she say? The music had been so loud and Izzy had still been reeling over Celina's death, so she hadn't asked a lot of questions. Now she wished she had.

"Yes, the word should mean something to you," he said through gritted teeth.

"Well it doesn't," she said just to aggravate him. "Right now the only person threatening me and my family is you."

She faced the window once more. Izzy had to get away from Tristan. It had been a mistake to think she was in any way safe around him. Tristan might claim he'd protect her, but after that statement there was no way she'd ever trust him. They were no longer just talking about her life.

"Where are we going?" she asked, so she could tell Stone. At this point, he was her only hope of getting out of this mess alive.

If Tristan thought she'd put herself in danger to help him kill someone—to help him period—he was wrong. Izzy had no intention of getting in the middle of this monster war. Let them wipe each other out. It would make her life much easier if they did.

She glanced at Tristan and pictured him covered in blood. Instead of relief, the thought brought only sadness.

He put his blinker on and took the Barataria Boulevard exit toward Jean Lafitte Park. The traffic thinned as he continued down the road.

Eventually, Tristan turned right. It looked as if he were driving into the woods, but it turned out to be a poorly maintained gravel road. The truck bounced as it hit the potholes, jarring Izzy.

Trees scraped the side of the doors as they squeezed their way along the unmarked road. Izzy heard Tristan curse under his breath as a particularly large branch scratched his truck.

So he did care about one thing, she thought. Typical guy.

Tristan turned left onto a game trail. It certainly wasn't a road. The overgrowth was even worse, though she didn't know how that was possible given what they'd just driven through. Tristan drove over downed limbs and squeezed his way through the woods. At one point, he had to cross a murky stream.

His curses grew louder. Most were aimed at Pierre.

Izzy said nothing. Instead, she paid attention to the route they were taking. Somehow she'd have to explain to Stone where they were located. It wouldn't be easy without street signs. Hopefully he was from around here and would know what she meant. Because as far as Izzy could tell, they were in the middle of the woods next to the swamp, which in Louisiana could be just about anywhere.

* * * * *

Tristan had said what he'd said to anger Isabel. If she were angry with him, then she'd keep her distance. The spot in the center of his chest ached. Tristan ignored it. What he was doing was for the best—for both of them.

She was human. He was Moonlight Kin. Their worlds were never meant to intertwine.

He thought about Damon Laroche and Aidan Fortier. Both Alphas had taken human females as mates. They'd even managed to breed true, but that didn't mean the Lycanian Elders and the rest of the packs wanted consorting with humans to become habit. Aidan's parting words to him came rushing back.

Once the wolf makes its decision, there's nothing you can do to change its mind.

Tristan shuddered. It would not happen to him. He'd make sure of it. Contrary to what the Alpha believed, Tristan controlled his wolf, not the other way around.

The cabin came into view, or at least what was left of it. Like a lot of structures built in and around New Orleans, this one had been lifted off the ground to protect it from flooding. Too bad the move didn't protect it from the elements.

There was no paint left on the walls, except a thin strip of haint blue around the windows and on the front door. He'd bet his fur that the front porch roof had also been painted the same aqua blue color. Something clinked in the tree beside him. Tristan glanced at the branches. They were covered in bottles.

Like the haint blue painted on the house, the bottle tree was there to ward off evil spirits. It was a Gullah tradition, but obviously the Kin saw no need to get rid of it. Tristan stared at the blue bottles covering the tree and shook his head. He'd never been superstitious. He should remove them, but they could use all the help they could get.

Tristan turned off the engine. A frown marred Isabel's soft features as she stared at the shack.

"I'm sure it looks better on the inside," he said, hoping it was true. Wolves were used to roughing it. In their beast form, indoor plumbing and lighting wasn't a concern.

Isabel glanced at him. "Doesn't matter. I won't be here

long."

What did she mean by that? He wanted to ask, but was afraid of her answer.

Just like on the night Aidan warned him about his wolf, Tristan felt as if someone walked over his grave.

His wolf snarled inside him. Tristan ignored his beast and opened the truck door. He climbed out and immediately sank two inches into the mud. Lovely, he thought, then raised his nose to the wind.

Tristan wanted to get a good scent of the area so he'd know the second something entered his territory. He smelled stagnant water, along with fresh. The rich aroma of green plants and lurking predators came next.

His gaze moved through the trees to the water beyond. Beneath that surface lurked at least one gator, quite possibly a few. He glanced at Isabel.

"Stay away from the water," he said, then grabbed his bag and hers from behind the seat and headed for the cabin.

The place looked as if a strong wind would bring it crashing down upon their heads. Izzy didn't want to think about how many creepy crawlies had made their way inside.

Did it even have a bathroom?

The thought of having to traipse into the woods to do her business left her uneasy. Tristan may be a woodland creature, but Izzy was not.

He climbed the stairs. The sweats molded to his tight butt like a second skin. There wasn't an inch of fat on him. Everly was right. Tristan did resemble one of the Avengers.

Izzy sighed. It would be so much easier if he were an eyesore. As much as she wanted to hide out in the truck, she had to go inside. Tristan opened the front door and disappeared into the dark interior.

She waited, but he didn't come back out. Izzy pulled her phone out of her purse and quickly dialed Stone. The phone rang and rang, but he didn't pick up.

"Where are you?" she muttered. Her eyes remained

locked on the front door.

Izzy saw a flash of white and quickly turned the phone off and put it away. She didn't want Tristan to know that she had it. No doubt he'd take it away. She'd just have to try to get in touch with Stone later, when Tristan wasn't around.

That thought brought her up short. What if he was serious about not letting her out of his sight? It didn't matter. He had to go to sleep sometime or take a shower. Izzy would figure something out.

She shoved the door open and climbed out of the truck. Izzy tiptoed through the mud, though it didn't do her or her shoes much good. She glanced at the mud covering the toes and scowled.

When she reached the front door, Izzy slipped her shoes off and turned them upside down. At least if something crawled inside them, it would fall out when she lifted them up. She hoped.

Izzy pulled the screen door open and stepped inside. Tristan was right. It did look better on the inside than on the outside, but it was still only a one-room cabin.

A large quilt-covered bed had been shoved against the back wall. At the foot of the bed sat a small table with two chairs. The opposite wall held a couch. Perched beside it was an overflowing bookshelf. Whoever lived here liked to read, which surprised her.

A kitchenette, which consisted of a stove, a sink, and a couple of cabinets, had been tucked in a corner next to a small fridge. Izzy scanned the space, but didn't immediately spot a bathroom.

"Don't worry." Tristan pushed what she thought was the back door open. "The bathroom is in here. The place has a generator and its own well."

Good to know, Izzy thought.

"I'm going to take a shower," he said. "If you're hungry, Pierre keeps the kitchen fully stocked."

"I'm fine. I'll just..." –Izzy searched for a quick

distraction— "read a book."

He hesitated then shook his head. "I'll be out shortly. Try not to get into any trouble."

Izzy waited until she heard the water come on, then slipped out onto the front porch. She pulled her cellphone out and called Stone again. This time, he picked up.

"Isabel?"

"It's me," she whispered. "You told me to call once we settled into a spot. I don't have long. The shifter is in the shower. I'm in a cabin in the middle of nowhere. I need you to get me out."

"Describe it," he said.

"Woods, mosquitos, and swamp," she said. "There weren't any road signs once we turned off."

Stone grew quiet. "I'm going to need a little more info."

Izzy glanced over her shoulder, but the bathroom door was still closed. "We turned right before we got into Jean Lafitte Park, then took a road that was barely visible. We made one or two more turns, then crossed a creek. I'm sorry. I've always had a bad sense of direction, especially when there aren't street signs."

"It'll be okay," he said. "We have time. He's not going to hurt you as long as you're of use to him. You've given me enough information. I'll be able to find you. Just stay put. You did the right thing by calling me."

Before she could ask when he was coming, Stone disconnected. Izzy turned the phone off and dropped it into her purse. She came back in the cabin as the bathroom door opened and Tristan stepped out.

Water dripped down his bare chest, and his hair was slicked back away from his chiseled face. He'd wrapped a towel around his trim waist, which only accentuated his rippling muscles. For a moment, she forgot how to breathe.

Tristan scanned the cabin. "Who were you talking to, Isabel?" he asked as he finger combed his long, white hair.

Izzy flinched but managed to keep her composure. "No

one," she said. "Why do you ask?" Her voice squeaked.

Tristan's silver eyes narrowed. "I heard you speaking to someone. I'm a wolf, remember?"

Oh God! How much had he heard? Izzy didn't know and couldn't ask. Maybe he just suspected and hoped she'd confess. She needed to stay calm.

He stalked forward.

Izzy's heart skipped, and her mouth went dry. She couldn't seem to tear her gaze away from his moist flesh. This close she could smell the soap he'd used.

Tristan stopped in front of her and sniffed the air, then his expression darkened. "You're lying," he said. "Who was here?"

The accusation snapped her out of her momentary fascination. "No one," Izzy said, which was the truth. As far as she knew, they were alone. "I doubt there's another soul around here for miles."

Tristan walked past her and stepped out onto the porch. His skin glistened in the afternoon light, making him appear even more ethereal. His head lifted and he inhaled deeply, taking in the scents from various directions. When he finished, his shoulders relaxed, but Tristan's expression remained impassive as he came back inside.

A water droplet slipped down the center of his chest then glided over the ridges of his abdomen before seeping into the towel around his hips. Izzy licked her lips, suddenly thirsty.

It took her a moment to pick up on the silence. When she did, Izzy glanced up. Tristan's body was rigid. He didn't appear to be breathing at all. The heat in his mercury eyes looked hot enough to melt steel.

Izzy cleared her throat. "You should probably get dressed," she said.

Tristan took a step forward. "Who were you talking to, Isabel?" She'd lied when he'd asked her the first time, but he didn't know why. He couldn't sense anyone nearby, but that didn't mean they weren't there. When you were dealing with magic, you couldn't be too careful.

The heat from her body increased as he closed the distance between them. So did his. Isabel shouldn't look at him like she wanted to eat him up. She shouldn't be admiring his appearance at all. But she had been. There was no mistaking the hunger in her gaze or the longing.

Tristan crowded her until she backed against the front door. The pulse jumped in her neck. He slapped his hands down beside her head, caging her. If she weren't human, he would strip her and take her right here. But she was.

His chest brushed hers. Tristan felt her nipples pebble just like they had last night when he'd kissed her. Isabel's rich scent grew stronger. He wanted to roll in it—or at least his wolf did. His nostrils flared. Her desire wrapped around him, hardening every inch of his body.

"Tell me the truth," he said. He made sure they continued to touch, even though it was sheer torture.

Tristan had meant to intimidate her into telling the truth. He had always been good at holding himself separate from his duties, but Isabel's sweet citrusy scent was doing strange things to his head.

She glared at him. "I was talking to myself. Okay?" Isabel put her hands on his chest and pushed, but she didn't put much power behind the move. Instead, her fingers lingered on his hot skin and stroked across his pecs.

Tristan quivered. Did she realize what she was doing? He wasn't sure, until she did it again.

Isabel's eyes widened in surprise as his body responded to her caress. The woman was playing with fire. Her hands moved over to his arms, encircling his biceps.

It wouldn't take much effort to rip the clothes off her. Even now, Tristan tried to work out the easiest way to bare her.

She stroked the length of his arm.

Tristan froze, torn between wanting more and moving out of reach. It had been a long time since he'd taken a woman to his bed. Too long, given his state of arousal from a simple touch. Maybe later he'd go out and find a willing she-wolf to take the edge off.

"What are you doing?" he asked.

Isabel's mouth opened then closed. "I don't know. I just couldn't stop myself."

That was the truth. Tristan didn't need his wolf to know it. "If you keep touching me like that, you're going to end up flat on your back in that bed," he said.

Isabel yanked her hand back as if she'd been burned.

Tristan told himself that he wasn't disappointed, but the damn ache in the middle of his chest told a different story.

Chapter Seven

Izzy had managed to distract him—and herself. She had no idea how long it would last. Tristan struck her as the tenacious type. Why had she touched him?

Sure, when he wasn't scowling, Tristan was quite handsome in a god-like way. Not all women went for that type of guy. She glanced at his bare chest and wide shoulders. Okay, only someone blind wouldn't notice all those muscles.

When he'd cornered her, she hadn't been able to see anything but his beautiful chest. With the heat pouring off him and his muscles right in front of her face, she just couldn't resist.

Once she touched him, Izzy hadn't been able to pull her hand away. His skin was smooth like marble but hot to the touch. When he'd trembled beneath her fingertips, she'd thought she had imagined it. Izzy had touched him again to be sure.

The second time, he'd quivered and that rich spicy aroma of his skin had increased. She'd actually grown dizzy. Or maybe she'd just forgotten to breathe.

Izzy had gone on dates with good-looking men, but none

had anything on Tristan. He was in a category all his own.

Tristan may not care for humans, but some part of him was attracted to her. If Izzy had needed any more proof, her doubts evaporated when she caught sight of the towel around his waist. There was no denying the hard ridge of arousal lifting the front of it.

It took every fiber of her being to tear her gaze away, but not before she saw Tristan's pained expression. "I'll give you some privacy to get dressed," she said.

He nodded and waited for her to leave.

Izzy stepped out onto the front porch and pressed a hand to her head. It had been so long since she'd touched anyone in a sexual way.

Mindy thought she was wild and slept around, but Izzy hadn't done that since her late teens. Even then, it had been out of rebellion and self-loathing.

Those days were long behind her, but that didn't mean she was dead inside. Even though she didn't want to, Izzy found herself responding to Tristan. Her physical reaction to his nearness had nothing to do with logic and everything to do with primal need.

How could you hate someone and want them at the same time?

She didn't know, but Izzy couldn't deny the truth any longer. She may not like Tristan, but part of her wanted him. A part of her that she hadn't allowed to surface for a long time.

Izzy glanced at the closed screen door but didn't spot Tristan. She hoped they didn't have to spend too much time here. She had no idea what would happen if they did.

Scratch that. Izzy knew exactly what would happen if they were trapped together for too long. It was the same thing that almost happened a minute ago.

They might hate each other and themselves afterwards, but they'd eventually give in to the physical attraction simmering between them.

Izzy thought about the hard ridge under that towel and felt her body moisten. He'd been so big and so beautifully formed. Such a waste.

She closed her eyes and sent up a silent prayer that Stone found her before she and Tristan did something they'd both regret.

* * * * *

Tristan's hands shook as he pulled on a shirt and a pair of shorts. He couldn't believe how close he'd come to taking her. He decided to back off from his line of questioning, at least until he had himself together. Tristan walked into the small kitchenette and opened the cupboard.

Cans of various items filled the shelves, along with flour and everything else needed for baking. He pulled items out and placed them on the small counter.

"What are you doing?" Isabel asked as she came in from outside.

"Making an early dinner," he said.

She frowned.

"What?" Tristan asked.

Isabel shrugged. "I just never imagined you in a kitchen cooking."

Tristan laughed. "Why? Because I'm a guy?"

She came closer. "No, that's not it. I just thought..."

His brow arched. "Thought what?"

"That you'd become fuzzy and go out and catch a rabbit or something," she said.

He balked and went back to organizing the gumbo ingredients to make sure he had everything he needed. "Would you prefer to eat rabbit?"

His wolf rose in an instant, eager to get her what she wanted. Shocked by its behavior, Tristan shoved the beast back down.

Isabel leaned against the table. "No."

Tristan went back to prepping. It bothered him that she had such bad impressions of his kind, of him. Sure, he hadn't helped change her views, but given her experiences throughout life, she should've known better.

He opened the refrigerator to find it fully stocked like the cabinets. Tristan pulled out chicken, green peppers, onions, and carrots, then found a cutting board. He made quick work of dicing the chicken.

"Do you need any help?" Isabel asked.

Tristan glanced at her but kept cutting. She thought he was such a wild beast that he'd simply shift into his other form and go catch fresh meat. Why should he let her help?

Helping may loosen her tongue.

"Do you know how to make biscuits?" he asked.

Isabel shook her head. "I'm not really much of a cook," she said.

"Check the drawers to see if there's a peeler. If you find one, then start in on the carrots," he said.

She did as he asked. A moment later, she found a peeler and picked up the bundle of carrots. Isabel grabbed a paper towel then went and sat at the table. There she peeled the carrots.

Together they worked in silence until everything was prepared, then Isabel stepped back as Tristan browned the chicken in a pot. Once he finished, he tossed in the diced onion, peppers, and carrots. He found chicken broth and Cajun seasoning in the cupboard and added them to the mix.

"This needs to cook for a while," he said. "Thanks for your help."

He opened the refrigerator and pulled out a beer. "Want one?" he asked. Thanks to his fast metabolism, Tristan couldn't get drunk, but he did like the taste.

Izzy nodded. A beer sounded good.

Tristan grabbed another bottle and placed it on the table in front of her. Before she touched it, he twisted off the cap.

"Thanks," she said. This whole thing struck her as

surreal, especially seeing him in a vintage rock T-shirt and shorts.

Izzy had never imagined Tristan dressed so casually or cooking anything. The act was so...so...*normal*. It was another reminder of how little she knew about him. She picked up the beer and tipped it into her mouth. It wasn't her beverage of choice, but at least it was cold and wet.

"Where did you learn how to cook?" she asked when he took a seat across from her.

Tristan stared at her.

For a minute, Izzy didn't think he was going to answer.

He took a drink of his beer then set the bottle down. "Mom taught me and my brother, when we were young."

Why she was surprised that he had a mom and a brother, Izzy didn't know. It wasn't like monsters were hatched from eggs. She guessed she'd never given their origins much thought.

"How old is your brother?" she asked.

Tristan's expression darkened. "Who were you speaking with earlier, Isabel?"

The change in subject gave her mental whiplash. If Tristan didn't want to talk about his family, then he shouldn't have brought the subject up.

"I told you. I was talking to myself," she said and glanced away.

"You're a terrible liar," he said. Before she responded, he added, "I have to stir the gumbo."

Izzy took another strong pull off her beer. This time the taste didn't burn as bad. She waited for Tristan to return to the table, but he didn't. Instead, he put the spoon down next to the pot and walked out the front door.

She sighed. It was only late afternoon. There was no way they were going to make it all night if they kept going like this. Izzy pushed the chair back and followed him.

She shouldered screen door and stepped out onto the porch. "What are you doing?" she asked.

Tristan didn't look at her. "I'm making sure our location hasn't been compromised."

Izzy tensed then forced herself to relax. "I doubt anyone could find us here. Wherever here is," she said.

His sharp gaze didn't miss a thing. "Not without help anyway."

She put her bottle down, so he wouldn't see her hands tremble. "Are you from around here?"

Tristan slowly pulled his gaze away from her and went back to scanning the woods. "No, but I come here often enough to be familiar with the area."

"Pierre called you an Enforcer," she said. "What does that mean exactly?"

Tristan's shoulders tensed. "I'm sort of like a cop," he said. "I hunt people who break the law."

"Hunt?" she asked. "Like a bounty hunter?"

He nodded. "Yes," he said. "But there are no bounties involved."

"So you take them to jail?" she asked. Izzy didn't know werewolves had a prison.

This time Tristan did look at her, and he slowly shook his head. "No jail."

"Then what—" Izzy's eyes widened. "You kill them? All of them?"

"I am an Enforcer for my people. It is my job to protect them from exposure and threats," he said. "I am very good at my job."

He'd insinuated that he was going to kill the Darkling, but Izzy hadn't really believed him. Deep down she didn't want to because that would mean that the person she was attracted to was a heartless killer.

"It sounds like you're an assassin, not a cop," she said quietly. Please let her have misunderstood.

"There is not a distinction between the two with the Moonlight Kin," he said, then turned his back on her.

Tristan hated seeing that disappointed look in her eyes.

He'd never lied to Isabel about what he was. She'd known from the start he hunted the Darkling. But seeing the disbelief, the disillusionment, then eventual acceptance of the truth shattered something inside him.

He wasn't ashamed of what he did. His job was important, even if she didn't fully understand their ways. Tristan stared at the woods, unseeing. He still smelled her, but her sweet, delicious aroma had soured.

It's for the best, he told himself.

Tristan surveyed the area one last time then walked past her. He didn't look at Isabel. He couldn't. Tristan didn't need to in order to know what she thought. To her, he was, and always would be, an uncaring, unfeeling monster.

* * * * *

They ate dinner in tense silence. The second she finished her bowl, Isabel jumped to her feet. "I'm going to get ready for bed."

She took her bowl to the sink and rushed off to the bathroom before Tristan could respond. A moment later, he heard the shower come on.

Tristan finished his meal then walked into the kitchen to clean up. As he washed the dishes and put the leftover gumbo in the fridge, he heard splashing.

Despite his best efforts, Tristan couldn't help but picture Isabel standing naked under the spray. Her firm breasts and supple thighs covered in water. Her wild blond hair with purple highlights slicked back. Would her skin still hold the warm musky scent that perfumed the air every time he drew near?

Tristan felt his body harden again. It had been doing that a lot around her. He needed to figure out a way to stop it, especially after their last conversation. Isabel would never understand him or his people. She was too human.

Another sound came from the bathroom. His ears perked.

Was she singing?

Before he knew what he was doing, Tristan moved closer to the bathroom door. He listened to the off-key warbling and couldn't help but smile.

Did Isabel always sing in the shower? He'd like to think that she did. He pictured her using her hand as a microphone as she wailed out the latest pop song. It was...cute.

The singing stopped and the shower ended. Tristan hurried back over to the sink. He wasn't about to be caught lurking outside the bathroom door. Even he knew that was creepy. He went back to cleaning the last of the dishes.

Five minutes later, the bathroom door opened and a cloud of steam came out. Isabel followed, wearing nothing but a long T-shirt. The shirt left her firm thighs and pink painted toes visible. It also left little to his already strained imagination. As he watched, her nipples crinkled. He could see the rosy outline through the front of her white shirt.

He'd been right when he'd guessed that the baggy clothes she wore hid some serious curves. Isabel was built like a wet dream. She was soft where she needed to be soft and full where it counted.

The plate in his hand cracked under the force of his grip. "You aren't going to wear that, are you?"

Isabel glanced down at the front of her shirt, then back at him. "Everything is covered."

Not everything. Not nearly enough.

"Don't you have sweats or something you can put on?" he asked.

She put her hand on her hip, which only emphasized her trim waist. "Don't know if you noticed, but there's no air-conditioning here. It's too hot to wear sweats," she said. "If you don't like what I'm wearing, you don't have to look."

Oh, but he did. That was the problem. Tristan couldn't help but stare at her. There was too much bare skin visible for him to ignore. He tossed the broken plate in the trash and turned in time to see Isabel stop at the foot of the bed. Her shoulders stiffened, and her sweet scent curdled.

"What's wrong?" He scanned the bed to make sure a spider hadn't crawled onto it.

"Um..." She glanced over her shoulder at him. "We need to talk about the sleeping arrangements."

Tristan hadn't thought about there only being one bed. Pierre had conveniently forgotten to mention the fact. He'd have to have a word with the Alpha before he left town. The lumpy couch was too short for his large frame, but he couldn't exactly make her sleep there.

"I'll take the couch," he heard himself say.

CHAPTER EIGHT

Tristan knew it was going to be a long night as he listened to Isabel toss and turn, trying to get comfortable.

He wondered, not for the first time, if she had trouble sleeping because he was so nearby. He certainly was having trouble, and it only got worse, when he pictured Isabel in that sheer T-shirt.

He punched his pillow and turned over toward the window. If he sat up, he'd have a good view out to the front of the cabin. Not that he needed it. His incredible hearing had already picked up the gators sloshing around in the water and a few deer passing through.

Tristan closed his eyes and forced himself to sleep. He needed to get some rest. He'd just dozed off when Isabel whimpered. Tristan shot to his feet, prepared to face whatever had disturbed her, but he found the room empty.

He glanced over at Isabel. She thrashed against the covers, her limbs tangling in the sheets. A thin layer of sweat glistened on her pale skin. She whimpered again then let out a bloodcurdling scream.

Tristan leapt across the room, landing next to the bed. Isabel bolted upright and stared out the window. Her eyes were wide, but her gaze remained unfocused. His beast rose and he scanned the darkness, but didn't spot anything.

He watched helplessly as tears streamed down her cheeks. Tristan didn't know what to do.

"It's okay," he said awkwardly. "I'm here. You're safe. I'll be right back."

He bolted outside and quickly circled the house to ensure there wasn't a threat. When Tristan was sure they were alone, he went back in.

Isabel glanced his way, and her brow furrowed in confusion. "Did you find it?" she asked.

"Find what?" he asked.

"The monster," she whispered, then glanced out the window and screamed again.

Tristan rushed to her side and pulled her into his arms. There wasn't anything there, but he searched again to ease her fears.

"Please don't let it get me," she begged.

"Shh... You're safe," he said, lowering his voice. "I won't let anything harm you."

Isabel fought his hold for a minute then slowly relaxed. She blinked a couple times, and her eyes cleared. A moment later, she frowned. "Tristan?"

"I'm right here," he said, gently rocking her.

"What are you doing?" she asked.

"You were having a bad dream," he said. At least he hoped that's all it was. Tristan glanced back out at the darkness and felt his wolf pace restlessly inside of him.

Isabel ducked her head, but not before he saw her face blossom with color. "Sorry I woke you," she said. "I should've warned you that I have a lot of nightmares."

"It's okay." Tristan wished he could go into her dreams and slay the monsters plaguing her, even if they looked exactly like him. "You all right now?"

She nodded.

Tristan slowly released her and rose off the bed. Before

he took a step back, Isabel grabbed his wrist.

"Don't go," she said, her panicked gaze searching the darkness. "Not yet."

Tristan hesitated. She was awake now and aware of her surroundings. He should just go back to the couch. "I'll be right over there." He pointed.

"Please," she added. "Can you just stay for a little while?"

He sighed and put his knee back onto the bed, then sank down beside her. "I'll stay until you fall asleep."

"Thank you," she said.

Instead of turning her back to Tristan, she cuddled up next to him. Isabel's body fit perfectly against his larger frame. He felt every curve, every indent beneath that thin T-shirt.

Tristan tried to relax, but it was impossible lying next her. He remained rigid as she snuggled even closer and her breathing evened out. He had no idea how much time had passed. Tristan was about to slip off the bed and return to the couch when he felt tears hit his forearm.

Had he somehow woken her? It wasn't until he caught a glimpse of Isabel's blotchy face that he realized she was crying in her sleep.

A crack formed in his icy exterior as her tears fell. Tristan brushed her tangled hair back and made soothing sounds. The kind of sounds he hadn't made since childhood.

He couldn't bear to see Isabel like this. He wanted her fighting, yelling at him, anything but scared. Until this moment, Tristan had no idea she was in so much pain.

More and more of him thawed as the minutes ticked by. He continued to coo until her tears dried. As he stared at her, Tristan's control wavered.

He shouldn't touch her. It would only complicate things. Isabel didn't really want to be comforted by him, but that didn't stop him from pulling her into his arms. She snuffled, let out a long sigh, and relaxed.

Tristan held her tighter as something inside him broke. The wave of emotion that struck would've knocked him off his feet had he been standing. The emotion wasn't anything as superficial as lust. Though he definitely felt that, too. This was deeper and more profound.

Isabel's warm scent tickled his nostrils. Tristan waited for her breathing to even out, then he buried his nose in her hair. There it was again. Honeysuckle. Just like the night they'd met.

He would never admit it, but Tristan loved the scent. Loved that she smelled like summer and blooming flowers. It reminded him of his childhood. His grip on her tightened, as he wondered if she smelled like that *everywhere*.

He forced himself to relax. He didn't want to accidentally hurt her. Isabel nestled closer, and her hand brushed his shaft. Every muscle in Tristan's body tensed, and he groaned. She made it difficult to remain detached.

Despite his resolve, Tristan felt a bond forming between them. A bond that shouldn't exist and would only get in the way of his mission. His gaze shifted to the window. The Darkling was hiding somewhere out there.

Isabel was a distraction he could not afford. Tristan would need all his wits if he were going to defeat his enemy.

* * * * *

It had taken hours, but he'd eventually picked up on the Sighted-One's scent. The small cabin sat in the middle of the swamp like a fat toad on a log. There was no light shining from any of the windows, but she was in there.

They both were.

The wolf's stench clogged his nostrils, filling him with disgust. There was no way to get to her without going through him.

He circled the cabin, taking care to keep to the shadows. It wasn't hard given that he and the shadows were as one. He thought about burning them out, but couldn't take a chance that the woman might be harmed.

Waiting wasn't his strong suit. Heat rippled over his dark fur. The Darkling had felt the sensation before. He knew what it meant. The beast was watching.

He hadn't spotted him yet. If he had, there was no doubt in the Darkling's mind that he would've confronted him. After all, he'd chased him through the French Quarter, unconcerned that they'd attracted attention.

The Darkling lifted its nose and smelled the air. The muscles in his body tightened. Why were their scents entwining? He sniffed again to make sure he wasn't mistaken, but the odd mingling hadn't changed.

That shouldn't be possible without close contact. It would take more than being in a cabin together to create the aroma. Even a cabin that small. What was going on?

The possibilities that flitted through his mind left the Darkling enraged. There was a fine line between attraction and hate, but surely it hadn't been crossed so soon.

If that wolf had laid the Sighted-One, then he'd do more than kill it. He'd make that Kin suffer like no other. In the end, the wolf would beg for death.

* * * * *

Izzy awoke to find her nose buried in Tristan's neck. His arms were around her, holding her tenderly, and his chin rested on top of her head. To make matters worse, she'd snuggled up against him with her arm wrapped around his waist.

His breathing was even and relaxed, which seemed at odds with the hard ridge resting next to her hip. There was no way she could extricate herself without waking him.

She tried to remember how they'd gotten like this. A dream flashed in and out of focus. Izzy remembered tears... and asking him to stay. Tristan hadn't wanted to from what she recalled, but he'd done so anyway.

So he hadn't been the one to instigate this situation. She had. That just made everything worse. Izzy pulled the covers up over her head. The movement disturbed Tristan.

He dipped his nose to her hair and inhaled, then sighed loudly. A second later, his hips rocked, and she felt every inch of his morning erection.

Izzy closed her eyes and groaned.

Tristan stiffened beside her.

"Don't worry, you didn't disturb me. I was already awake," she said.

He pulled his arm out from under her, and her head dropped to the bed. A second later, he was off the mattress and halfway across the room. She stared at him from beneath her lashes. Tristan scrubbed a hand over his shadowed jaw.

"I'm going to catch a shower," he said. "Unless you want to go first."

Izzy pulled the covers down to her waist but couldn't meet his gaze. Instead, she focused on his shoulder. "That's okay. You go ahead."

Tristan gave her a curt nod and grabbed his tote. "When I get out, we'll grab something to eat, then get out of here."

"Where are we going?" Izzy thought for sure they'd spend their days hanging in the swamp, waiting for the monster to come.

"Into town," he said as if that were obvious. "We want to make sure the Darkling catches your scent."

Izzy didn't reply. What was the use? He'd told her yesterday that he'd planned to use her as bait. One night spent in his arms wasn't going to change his plans.

She waited for the door to close behind Tristan then wandered into the kitchen. Izzy put on some coffee and found a box of cereal. She pulled out two bowls and a couple of spoons. She left one out for Tristan, then filled hers and wandered back to the table.

Izzy slipped on some shorts. She felt too exposed in her

T-shirt. Which was weird, since she hadn't felt that way last night. She thought about the moment she'd woken, wrapped in Tristan's strong arms.

For a few seconds, Izzy had forgotten all about monsters and being hunted. She'd forgotten all about being stuck in a cabin with a man who hated humans. She'd just been a woman, lying in a man's arms. And it had felt...*nice*. For once in her life, she had actually felt safe.

Izzy should've known the moment wouldn't last. Life as she knew it was a never-ending nightmare. Tristan's arrival wasn't going to change that.

* * * * *

Tristan couldn't seem to get her scent off his skin. It was like he'd absorbed part of her essence overnight. He scrubbed harder, but he still felt her warmth in his arms. He glanced down at his hard shaft and cursed under his breath.

This wasn't good.

He jerked the nozzle to cold and stood under the pelting spray. It helped with his body's physical response but did little to alleviate his growing need.

Damn her!

Tristan shut the water off and wrung his hair out. He didn't dare go out there in his current condition. He heard Isabel crunching on something and smelled the aroma of freshly brewed coffee wafting on the air.

He couldn't hide in the bathroom all day. Eventually he'd have to face her. It was best to do so head on before she got the wrong idea about them—about him.

Tristan pulled on a pair of jeans and a clean navy T-shirt, then yanked his hair back and tied it at his nape. He shaved quickly, while glaring at himself in the mirror.

Last night, he'd come close to doing something he'd absolutely regret. He'd have to make sure the opportunity didn't arise again because he wouldn't be strong enough to turn it down a second time.

CHAPTER NINE

The French Quarter bustled with tourists by the time Tristan parked his truck. He hadn't said much on the drive into New Orleans, and for that Izzy was grateful.

She was so embarrassed about last night that she'd rather pretend it didn't happen. Izzy unhooked her seatbelt and climbed out.

"What now?" she asked.

Tristan adjusted his sunglasses. "Now we mingle, so the Darkling has a chance to catch your scent."

"What happens if he does?" she asked, hoping there was more to the plan than that.

"It'll draw him out and allow me to get close to him," he said.

Izzy glanced around at the crowded sidewalks. "Tell me your plan isn't to kill him in front of all these people," she said.

Tristan snorted. "Hardly," he said. "I'll track him back to his lair, then I'll kill him."

Izzy rolled her eyes.

"What?" Tristan asked.

"Frosty, you make him sound like a Bond villain," she

said. "I'll follow him back his lair." Izzy rubbed her hands together and cackled maniacally.

Tristan's expression eased.

For a second, she thought he might laugh, but then the moment passed.

"There's something really wrong with you," he said.

"At least I'm not a talking snowball," she said, then wandered down the sidewalk.

Tristan crossed his arms over his chest. "Where are you going?"

Izzy shrugged. "You said to wander. I'm wandering."

"I'll be close by," he said.

Her footsteps faltered. "You're not coming with me?"

"He won't approach you if I'm by your side," Tristan said, then disappeared in the crowd. Quite an impressive feat given his size.

Izzy hesitated then kept walking. Being bait sucked! As she window-shopped, she thought about last night. She hadn't expected Tristan to be so caring. When she'd woken up and thought she'd seen a monster outside her window, Izzy had expected him to ask her if she was okay, then go back to the couch. But he hadn't.

Instead, Tristan had climbed into bed beside her and held her until she fell asleep. Izzy didn't want to think about how good his arms had felt wrapped around her. Part of her hated that he'd made her feel safe. It only made his absence worse.

She kept walking. A couple times Izzy thought she caught a glimpse of Tristan in the window's reflection, but when she'd checked, he was nowhere to be found.

Izzy wandered another two blocks. The heat was already beginning to make her sweat. Most natives knew to get inside in the afternoon. Only the tourists were dumb enough to soldier on.

She turned a corner, and the skin on her nape prickled. Izzy allowed her senses to flare. The power she brushed against didn't feel like her snowman's. Was it the Darkling?

Izzy slowly scanned the area. What did a Darkling look like? Did it resemble a werewolf? A person? Or something altogether different? She should've asked.

She casually glanced at the faces around her, searching for some sign that would let her know that they weren't human. When that didn't yield anything, Izzy opened her power of Sight. The second she did, she saw Spirits fleeing from the next street over.

What could've frightened the dead? Izzy fought the urge to run with them.

She needed to find out what was going on. Izzy passed a couple of houses but didn't see anything unusual. She took a deep breath and kept going. Where was Tristan? Izzy crossed between two more houses. One of the homes had a massive trellis attached to the side of it. As she stepped past a trellis of honeysuckle, someone grabbed her.

Izzy opened her mouth to scream, but a palm came down over her face before she could. Fear stabbed her and her skin crawled. She struggled to break the man's tight grip. Everything inside of Izzy told her to get away.

"It's Stone," a low voice hissed. "Don't scream." He waited for her to nod, then he quickly pulled his hand away.

Izzy found Stone standing behind her. "What are you doing?" she whispered. "I thought you were—" She cut the words off before she finished the sentence. Izzy wasn't going to get into a conversation about a creature she knew nothing about. "You scared me to death," she said instead.

"Sorry." He scrubbed a hand through his disheveled hair. He'd shoved his wrinkled shirt into one side of his jeans, leaving the other half to flap on the outside. His red eyes showed just how little sleep he'd gotten. "I couldn't take the chance that the monster would hear you."

Izzy understood all too well the need for caution, given a wolf's keen senses. "Are you okay?" she asked, attempting to read him. She encountered a wall of darkness. "You look..." Tired. Wrecked. Stressed. None of those words properly described his current state.

"I'm fine." Stone frowned at her. "What are you doing? Why are you giving me that funny look?"

She'd been busted. "I tried to read you."

Stone became unnaturally still. "And?"

"I can't," Izzy said. "Why is that?"

Some of the tension in his body eased, and he scanned the sidewalks around them. "I've learned how to block people like us and the monsters. No one can sense me unless I want them to. If we had more time, I'd teach you how to do it."

The idea was beyond tempting to Izzy. What would life be like if she didn't have to worry about the monsters sensing her? It seemed like a fantasy...yet if what Stone said was true, then perhaps it was possible.

"Then how did you know I was here?" she asked in confusion.

Stone blinked. "You called me. Remember?"

"Oh, right," she said. Izzy had forgotten all about phoning Stone. She'd told him about the cabin, but how did he know she'd be here?

"You still want my help, don't you?" he asked.

His question interrupted her thoughts. "Yes, of course," she said.

Stone smiled. "Good," he said. "I thought for a minute that you'd changed your mind." Something about the grin reminded her of a shark.

You're seeing monsters everywhere now, she chastised.

Izzy hadn't changed her mind about getting away from Tristan. She thought about it. No, definitely not. Though leaving didn't seem nearly as urgent as it had yesterday afternoon.

"I've parked a few blocks over," Stone said. "If we can make it to my car, I think we can get away from him. The last time I saw him, he was several blocks away."

Izzy followed a few feet then stopped. *How did he know where Tristan was?* She didn't even know where he'd wandered off to.

"How did you see him without him knowing that you were there?" she asked.

Stone glanced back. "What?"

Izzy repeated the question.

His brow furrowed. "I told you. I'm able to block myself. Even if I hadn't been able to, I spotted his blond head above the crowd and went the other direction before he saw me."

It was possible. She'd managed to avoid Tristan, but not for long. "Where are we going?" she asked.

"I have an apartment on the other side of town," he said. "We'll be safe there for a little while, but it's merely a temporary solution. There's only one sure way to get away from the monster for good."

"Do you mean blocking him?" she asked.

Stone stopped. The look he gave her sent a chill down Izzy's spine.

Her steps faltered. "What exactly are you referring to?"

"If you want to protect yourself, protect me, protect your friends, and your family, there is going to come a time when you have to choose sides. It's either us or the monsters."

Izzy stumbled back a step. "Are you talking about killing Tristan?" she asked, horrified by the notion.

Stone shook his head. "No, I'm talking about killing the monster before it kills us."

"I—I can't kill Tristan," she stuttered. "I can't kill anybody." But especially not him, even though Tristan had behaved like a careless jerk.

Stone gave her a hard stare. "We may not have a choice. You need to be prepared for that possibility," Stone said.

How could she prepare for something she couldn't comprehend? In all the years that Izzy had been running from the monsters, it never occurred to her to fight them head on. She pictured Tristan's face, pictured the concern that had been on it last night when he'd crawled into bed beside her. The idea of killing him left an odd ache in her chest.

"We have to go now," Stone said. "He's getting closer."

* * * * *

The first pulse from the lodestone around his neck nearly drove Tristan to his knees. It was like taking a direct strike from lightning.

The fact that it was so strong told him that the Darkling was nearby. His head whipped around, but Tristan didn't see Isabel.

Where had she gone?

He'd put enough distance between them to draw it out, but perhaps it had been too much. Fear embraced him as Tristan realized he might not reach her in time.

You can't always protect bait... Pierre's parting words struck deep.

Failure wasn't allowed to enter his mind. Just the thought of losing Isabel gutted him. Tristan didn't want to look too closely at why.

He followed the pulse of magic around the next block, but Isabel was nowhere to be seen. The lodestone throbbed like a toothache. Tristan turned left and ran another block.

As he rounded the corner, he saw a flash of purple hair in the distance. Isabel. He'd just taken a step toward her when he caught another movement. She wasn't alone. The man disappeared out of sight, and Isabel chased after him. Tristan's beast nearly burst from his body as he watched her run away.

* * * * *

Izzy followed Stone's brisk pace. Every step she took got heavier and heavier. It was as if her body didn't want her to leave, which was insane, since she'd been trying to get away from Tristan since they met.

She may not like Frosty, but she didn't want him dead. The thought made her heart hurt. As she ran, Izzy wondered just how many monsters Stone had killed. Suddenly, she wasn't sure going with him was the right thing to do.

He knows how to block them. Block you. If you could learn how to do that, it would change your life. Hell, it would give you back your life.

As much as she disagreed with his methods, Izzy had no choice but to go with him, at least until Stone taught her how to block. Then they'd part ways. Izzy wasn't a monster slayer and had no desire to be.

"How much farther?" she asked.

"We have another block and a half to go," Stone said, then his eyes widened. "He's right behind us. Run faster!"

Izzy turned to see Tristan sprinting toward them. He had a murderous expression upon his face. She glanced back to check on Stone, but he was long gone. So much for saving her.

* * * * *

Tristan's heart stopped. Fear had crippled him at first, but he'd been determined to reach her. When Isabel saw him and ran, Tristan's fear turned to anger. An unexpected wave of hurt followed his fury.

"Isabel, stop!" he shouted, easily closing the distance between them. There was no way a human could outrun one of the Moonlight Kin.

She skidded to a halt.

"What are you doing?" he asked. "Who was that man you were with?" He demanded answers. This time he wouldn't allow her to deflect the questions.

"He's just a friend," she said.

Tristan's beast didn't like the idea of another male hanging around her. "If he's just a friend, then why did you run?" he asked.

"He's like me, okay?" she said, defensively.

"Like you how?" Tristan asked.

"He's Sighted," Isabel said.

Tristan had never heard of a male being a Sighted-One, but he supposed it was possible. "What were you doing with him?"

Her brow furrowed. "Um..."

"Isabel?" He didn't bother to hide the warning in his voice.

She rounded on him. "If you must know, I was running away."

"From me?" Tristan reeled back. He'd wanted an honest answer. He just wasn't prepared for what he got.

"No, I ran from the other monsters," she said sarcastically.

His scowled deepened.

Isabel glared at him. "Can you really blame me, when it's obvious you don't care about anything but your mission?" she asked.

Tristan jerked as her words lashed him, scoring deep. He'd been so frightened for her. So scared he wouldn't reach her in time. He'd been a fool.

The warmth that had encased them last night evaporated. Tristan felt the cold inside of him return and openly embraced it. This was familiar. This was what he needed. He should've known there was no place for warmth, no place for her in his life.

"Thank you for the reminder." His words froze the air between them. "I'd temporarily lost sight of what was important."

Isabel blanched, and her color drained. "I didn't mean—"

His hard gaze stilled her words. "Yes, you did. Now let's go."

Izzy felt horrible. She'd purposely hurt him, which was something she never did to anyone. It was like Tristan brought out the worst in her. She stared out the truck window as they drove to the cabin.

Time only added to her sense of guilt. She hadn't really meant what she'd said to him. Izzy had been so shocked by Stone's suggestion and her reaction to it that she'd lashed out.

She glanced at Tristan. His stony expression never altered. She didn't think there was anything she could say that would make things better.

* * * * *

He didn't speak to her for the rest of the night. The silent treatment got on her nerves so bad that Izzy decided to head to bed.

She didn't know what time the vision struck. Izzy felt danger drawing nearer. She pushed back the haze that normally clouded her visions and gazed deeper. Izzy wanted to see what—or more appropriately who—was coming.

Her sense of dread grew. In her vision, Izzy saw trees all around. Trees with thick undergrowth. Trees that shook as the danger closed in on her. Hands parted the bushes.

Izzy turned and ran...straight into Tristan.

His hands closed around her arms.

Izzy glanced behind her, but there was no one there. Tristan's normally cold eyes shimmered like warm mercury. Before she could ask him to release her, his mouth claimed hers.

She remained tense in his arms for all of a minute, then Izzy's body melted. The heat between them flared even hotter as he deepened the embrace.

Tristan released her shoulders, and his hands dropped to her waist. He pulled her closer. Close enough for Izzy to feel a hard ridge. She gasped, and his tongue swirled around her mouth.

Izzy's heart stuttered, but this time it wasn't from fear. This time it came from desire. She pressed her hands to his chest then slid them up around his neck.

Tristan groaned and his fingers bit into her waist.

She couldn't seem to get close enough to him. Izzy stripped his clothes off. Her hands trembled as she made contact with his bare skin.

"Do you want me?" he asked against her lips.

"Yes," Izzy hissed.

Tristan nipped her bottom lip, then grabbed her T-shirt with both hands and tore it off her body. Izzy gasped as the rest of her clothes followed.

Within seconds she was naked and standing before him. Her body quivered as he cupped her sex to test her readiness.

"I will be here soon," he rasped. "It's only a matter of time before you welcome me inside."

What was he waiting for? She was naked and ready now. Izzy couldn't be more welcoming if she tried.

"Take off the rest of your clothes," she said.

Tristan smiled and shook his head. "Not yet," he murmured, nuzzling her neck. "You're not ready."

The moisture pooling between her thighs said otherwise. Izzy felt the brush of his lips, then sharp teeth scored her skin. Her nipples hardened, and she grew restless in his arms.

"I want you," she said, all but begging him to take her.

Tristan licked the spot at the base of her neck where it met her shoulder. "You only want this part of me." He guided her hand to the front of his jeans and left it resting on his erection.

Izzy shook her head. "No, you're wrong," she said. "I want all of you."

He pulled back just enough to look her in the eyes. "All of me?" he asked. "Are you sure?"

Izzy would swear to it, if it meant he'd get undressed. "Yes."

Tristan smiled at her, revealing his extended canines.

It took a second for Izzy's desire-fogged brain to register

what she'd glimpsed. The moment she did, she jerked away.

Tristan's hard laugh filled the silence. "Told you," he said softly. "I won't touch you until you want all of me," he said, then turned to go.

"Wait!" Izzy shouted as the vision faded.

She blinked into the darkness, wondering if she'd spoken aloud. Her body was so aroused it ached. *Please be asleep.* She sent the silent prayer up into the ether.

Izzy turned her head toward the couch and found Tristan staring directly at her. His silvery eyes glowed in the dark. She inhaled sharply and caught a hint of her desire wafting on the air. If she smelled it, then it was a good bet that Tristan could, too.

The question was would he act upon it?

And if he did, would she stop him? The answer she received left Izzy blindsided.

Tristan continued to stare at her.

I want you, a little voice inside of her whispered.

He stiffened as if he'd heard her thought then slowly turned over, leaving her to stare at his pale back.

Izzy punched her pillow while cursing her visions. Normally they came true, but in this case, the chance of that happening was slim to none.

CHAPTER TEN

"Today we'll try again," Tristan said, taking a bite of bacon. "But this time I'm going to stick by your side, since you've made it clear that I can't trust you."

"I thought you said your presence would keep the Darkling away," she said.

He glanced at her, but his expression remained hard, unyielding. "There are other ways to draw it out. Ways I've avoided until now because of the discomfort they'd cause."

Discomfort? Izzy didn't like the sound of that. She stared at him across the kitchen table. "What exactly do you have in mind?"

"If it's worried that it's going to lose you to another wolf, it'll become desperate to grab you," he said.

"I don't understand." There was no warmth in Tristan's slate eyes.

He pushed his breakfast aside and walked around the kitchen table. He stopped in front of her.

"What are you doing?" Izzy craned her neck and scooted back, but there was nowhere for her to go.

He grabbed a fistful of her shirt and yanked her off her feet. Tristan's lips came down upon hers in a searing kiss.

The kiss left Izzy breathless and shaken.

It took her a moment to recover and pull herself together. "What was that for?"

"To give you a taste of what's to come," he said, his voice hard and raspy. "Try to play along. It'll be more convincing that way." Tristan returned to his seat and finished eating his breakfast like nothing had happened.

Pain sliced Izzy. How could a kiss heat her to her toes and leave her so cold? Whatever softness she had witnessed from him the other night was now long gone. Tristan was back to being all business, and she was to blame.

She thought about Stone's warning again... *It's either them or us.*

Would this hunt come down to life or death? Izzy sure hoped not. What would happen if it did? The question left her nauseated.

Izzy shoved her breakfast aside. No longer hungry.

* * * * *

Tristan still felt her lips pressed against his. His anger had subsided, but not the hurt. He wanted to hurt Isabel back. Show her what it felt like. Glimpsing her pained expression, Tristan was confident he'd succeeded.

You did what you had to do, a little voice said.

So why did his actions feel so wrong? And why in hades did she always feel so right in his arms? If that kiss got any more convincing, they'd end up on the bed.

Tristan shoved his food away as Isabel stomped off to the bathroom. The second the door closed behind her, he ran a trembling hand through his hair. This whole situation was getting out of hand. Maybe he needed to call in another Enforcer to take over. There weren't many, but there were a few.

Even as the thought flitted through his mind, Tristan wouldn't do it. Just the idea of another wolf staying in the cabin with Isabel had his hackles rising.

"Get your head in the hunt," he muttered.

Thirty minutes later, the bathroom door opened and Isabel stepped out. "Ready," she said.

One look at her in that strappy purple sundress and the air rushed out of Tristan's lungs. She couldn't go out like that. Isabel couldn't go anywhere dressed that way.

The sundress plunged just low enough to give him and every other man a tantalizing view of the soft mounds filling the front of it. The dress nipped in at her waist, emphasizing how small it was, before flaring out at the hips.

Tristan's gaze traveled down before reversing direction.

The material ended just above her knee, showing off her shapely legs. Isabel was quite literally stunning.

It took Tristan a moment to recover. "What are you wearing?"

Isabel glanced down at her dress. "I would think that would be obvious," she said.

He clenched his jaw and tried again. "Why are you wearing that dress?" he asked.

Her blond brow arched. "You said we were going in town to draw the Darkling out. You said we were going to pretend to be a couple, or at least you implied as much," she said. "We can't really make someone jealous if we're dressed as slobs."

"I never dress like a slob," he said, insulted by the insinuation.

"Okay." Isabel rolled her eyes. "Maybe not sloppy, but definitely casual." She walked deeper into the room. "We won't attract attention if we're dressed like all the other tourists. We need to stand out."

She had a point, but Tristan didn't have to like it. He stared at her, trying to ignore the curves that were no longer hidden beneath baggy clothes. It was impossible. Without effort, Isabel had just turned a hard day into sheer torment.

"Give me a minute to change, and then we'll get out of

here," he said.

* * * * *

The tension continued to build on the drive into town. Izzy caught Tristan admiring her legs a couple times and wondered if he even knew he was doing it.

The look on his face when she'd stepped out of the bathroom was one she wouldn't soon forget. Izzy had heard of people being stunned speechless, but she'd never witnessed it firsthand. And she'd certainly never expected to cause such an event.

Part of her felt unduly pleased that she'd been able to surprise him. That hadn't been Izzy's intent when she'd put the sundress on, but it was a nice byproduct.

They parked just off the French Quarter near Louis Armstrong Park then strolled toward Jackson Square. When they reached the square, Izzy spotted Everly's dark head near the west end.

Tristan scanned the people with quiet intensity.

"Mind if we stop at Everly's table?" she asked.

"I'm surprised she's up so early," he said.

"She probably hasn't been to bed yet," she said.

Tristan slipped his hand in hers. It should've been awkward, but for some reason the fit seemed natural.

"Lead the way," he said.

They walked hand and hand over to Everly. Her dark eyes widened when she caught sight of them and widened some more when she saw their joined hands. Her pierced brow arched.

"It's not what you think," Izzy said.

"Yes, it is." Tristan raised her hand up to his mouth and kissed the back of her knuckles.

She felt his tongue snake out to taste her. Heat spread from Izzy's hand down her arm before rocketing through her body. If it got any hotter, she'd have a heat stroke.

"What are you two up to?" A smile played across Everly's face as she indicated for them to sit down.

They took the seats in front of her table. To an outside observer they'd look like a couple of tourists getting their cards read. Only she and Tristan knew the truth.

Everly shuffled the tarot cards on her table then turned them over slowly. Her gaze focused intently on what they revealed.

"What are you doing?" Izzy asked, growing alarmed as the cards fell. She didn't want a reading, especially in front of Tristan. Goodness knows what the cards would say.

Everly grinned. "Thought it would be fun to see what's really happening here."

Izzy's jaw set. "I already told you," she said.

"You and I both know just how deceptive appearances can be." Everly stared at Tristan.

Izzy couldn't see his eyes narrow, but she felt his body tense and the grip on her hand tighten.

"You say one thing. He says another," Everly said. "I don't think either of you know the truth."

"What do you see?" Tristan asked, showing more teeth than necessary.

Everly flipped another card. The Lovers appeared. She tapped the card with her index finger. "That's the same thing I got in my vision," she said.

"But you *can* be wrong." Izzy heard panic and desperation in her voice. Seeing the card reminded her of the vision she'd had last night.

Everly glanced at her. "Sure, I can be." She paused. "But not twice."

"We are not sleeping together," Izzy blurted.

Tristan released her hand and placed his palm on the small of her back. His thumb made small circles at the base of her spine. If he was trying to relax her, it wasn't working.

"Now honey," he said, nuzzling her, "what starts in the bedroom, stays in the bedroom."

Two women passing by snickered and gave Tristan a once- over that made Izzy want to poke their eyes out. Couldn't they see his hand on her? Was she invisible? Didn't they notice her sitting next to him?

Before the next thought struck, Izzy stilled. Was it possible that she was *jealous*? How could that be? She didn't even *like* Tristan.

Everly kept turning the cards over, ignoring them both. The Devil card appeared. She frowned and flipped a few more over for clarification, but it only frustrated her more.

The Devil didn't necessarily mean something bad. It also indicated drastic change depending on the other cards around it.

Everly flipped the last card. Death.

Izzy gasped. Like the Devil card, the Death card didn't mean that someone was going to die. It could be the death of an old way of thinking or the death of an old way of life. It wasn't always literal...except it was next to the Devil card.

Everly's gaze met hers. "You have to be careful. Evil is nearby."

Nearby or sitting next to her, Izzy thought.

She glanced at Tristan. Frosty may be a pain in the rear with a questionable job, but as far as she could tell, he wasn't evil. This whole situation would be easier if he was bad, but Tristan wasn't. She'd been around him long enough to ascertain that much. Evil didn't fix omelets. Evil didn't hold someone in the middle of the night after they'd had a bad dream.

No, Snowflake wasn't evil, but his behavior left much to be desired. Perhaps that was what Everly picked up on.

"Thanks for the reading." Izzy pushed her chair back. She'd seen enough.

"I didn't do it just for you," Everly said. "What are you guys *really* doing here?"

"I wanted to make sure you were okay and to let you know that I was all right," Izzy said. "I also wanted to ask you again to get out of town."

Everly shook her dark head. She'd dyed the strands so black they appeared blue in the sunlight. "I told you before, I'm not going anywhere." Her gaze darted to the cards in front of her.

"Frosty says there's something worse than the monsters running around town." Izzy touched her hand. "Be careful, okay?"

Everly laughed. "Frosty?"

"Don't call me that," Tristan said.

"But it's okay if Izzy calls you that?" Everly asked.

Tristan's jaw tightened. "That's different," he said.

"I just bet it is." Everly laughed. "Don't worry, I will be careful," she said. "I think you're the one who needs to watch out. Trouble could be closer than you think." She gave Tristan a pointed stare.

Izzy snorted. "Tell me something I don't know."

"Okay," Everly said, taking her statement as a request. "You cannot change your fate on this one."

Gooseflesh prickled along Izzy's skin, despite the growing heat.

"Neither can I," Everly added softly. "When the time comes, remember that."

The resolve in her voice worried Izzy. She'd never heard that tone from Everly before. They needed to talk. There had to be something they could do to get out of this mess.

"Ready to mingle?" Tristan asked, kissing her cheek.

The move distracted her from her dark thoughts. "As I'll ever be," Izzy said.

* * * * *

Tristan tried not to show any reaction when the tarot cards were turned over. He didn't believe in those kinds of things, but Everly wasn't a normal reader. She was a Sighted-One, so he couldn't dismiss her findings out of hand.

It bothered him that she saw him and Isabel as lovers. Not because he couldn't imagine it anymore, but because he could. She'd worked her way under his skin and Tristan had no idea how to get Isabel out.

He touched the lodestone around his neck. Thus far, he hadn't felt even the slightest pulse. Perhaps the Darkling had left New Orleans. Wishful thinking on his part, since it hadn't gotten what it had come for.

Tristan glanced at Isabel. Her fair skin glowed in the sunlight. It was a stark contrast to her purple sundress, yet somehow as a whole it worked. Too well for his peace of mind.

Human males walked by with their necks craning to get a better look at her.

A growl rose from Tristan's chest before he could stop it. Isabel didn't seem to notice the men, but she certainly heard the growl. Her gaze cut to his, and her hazel eyes narrowed.

"What are you doing?" she whispered.

Tristan stared at her for a moment. "Making sure people mind their manners."

"What?" she asked in confusion.

She had been totally unaware of the attention. Isabel really didn't know what kind of effect she had on men, had on him. Tristan clasped her hand and tugged.

"This way," he said. They'd take a stroll along the river then circle back into the Quarter. He wanted to make sure Isabel's scent permeated the area and that she was highly visible. In that dress, he wouldn't have to worry about the latter.

Heads continued to turn as they strolled along the Mississippi River bank. Tristan tried to relax, but it was impossible with so many males sniffing around. Inside, his beast bared its teeth and snarled. Outside, Tristan pulled Isabel into his arms and kissed her often enough to send a message to the men around her.

Every time he kissed her, Isabel's gaze grew unfocused, and her luscious scent deepened. If only she weren't human. It would be far too easy to get used to this, get used to having her in his arms.

Tristan needed to think of something else, something to distract him and his beast from the urges pummeling his body. "How long have you known Everly?" he asked.

"Not long," she said. "I met her when I first hit town a month ago."

"She should leave," he said.

Isabel gave him a sad smile. "I know, but she won't. She told me she's tired of running," she said, her voice weary. "Can't say I blame her. It gets old."

"You sound tired, too," Tristan said.

"I am," she said. "But there's not a lot I can do about it. I'm more concerned with Everly's vision."

He was, too. Tristan tried to imagine what it would be like moving from place to place, knowing that you were constantly being pursued. The beast in him rose to the surface and growled.

Isabel laughed at him. "What's up with all the growling?" she asked.

"Sometimes my beast likes to voice its opinion at inopportune times," he said.

"Do you have conversations with it often?" she asked.

Tristan shook his head. "Not really. We rarely disagree with each other."

"Interesting," she said. "Where do you live?"

The change of subject surprised him. "I have homes in many places," he said. "My favorite is in New Mexico."

"Wow," she said. "I wouldn't have pictured you in the Southwest."

"Why?" His fingers lingered on her bare shoulder after he brushed her hair away from her face.

Isabel shrugged and casually stepped out of reach. "I don't know. You look more Nordic than Navajo," she said.

"I do have a Nordic heritage, but I prefer the sunshine and warmth over the cold and gray skies," he said.

"You don't look like you get a lot of sun," she said.

"I don't tan easily," he said wryly.

Isabel laughed.

"What's so funny?" Tristan asked.

She put her hand over her mouth to hide her smile. "I just pictured you in Bermuda shorts and a Hawaiian shirt, sitting on a turtle float in the middle of a pool."

"Is that so hard to imagine?" Tristan asked, liking the sound of her laughter, even if it was at his expense.

Isabel's shoulders shook. "Yes, it is, Frosty."

He laughed with her. "I must do a better job of distracting your smart mouth."

She flinched.

"What's the matter?" Tristan asked, unsure of what he'd said or done to cause the reaction.

"That's the first time I've heard a real laugh from you," she said. "I was beginning to think you'd never learned how to laugh."

"And you find the sound frightening?" he asked.

Isabel shook her head. "Just the opposite. It's quite nice and unexpected."

Tristan wasn't sure how to respond, so he didn't. He held her hand as he led them down to a docked riverboat.

"One of these days I'm going to take that ride." Isabel pointed to the boat.

Tristan had the sudden urge to get her tickets. *You're not here for fun.* For a moment, Tristan had forgotten why they were here. He'd been so caught up in touching her, kissing her, and holding her that he'd lost focus.

"Mind if we do it some other time?" he asked.

"You want to go, too?" she asked, surprised again.

Tristan glanced at the boat. He would enjoy the ride, if she were with him. "Sure," he said, then turned right so they were heading back into the quarter.

"How will we know if this works?" Isabel asked.

"He'll make a move." Just the thought of the Darkling trying to rip Isabel out of his hands made his beast snarl.

"You're doing it again," Isabel said.

"Sorry," Tristan said. "I didn't mean to. The necklace around my throat detects the Darkling's magic. I'll know he's coming long before we see him."

"Magic? As in Harry Potter or watch me pull a rabbit out of my hat?" Isabel pulled her hand out of his and stopped.

"Neither," he said.

"But you're telling me that magic is real," she said.

Tristan debated how to respond. He decided to be honest with her. "How else would you explain your abilities or what I'm able to become? The powers might be different, but they're nothing short of magic."

"But." She rubbed her forehead and took a deep breath. "I guess I never looked at it that way."

"I'm not surprised," he said. "You've spent your life running from us monsters. When you view an entire species that way, it's hard to see beyond your preconceived notions."

He was right. Izzy knew he was right, but it was a lot to take in. Her world had been filled with humans and monsters without anything in between. Now he was telling her there was even more to the world than she'd imagined.

Izzy had never once asked herself what was behind the ability to shift. She'd simply assumed they were all evil and left it at that.

Magic... just the word conjured all kinds of images in her mind.

She glanced at Tristan. "If you're magic, then why don't you feel your power pulsing in the necklace?"

Tristan opened his mouth and closed it again. "I'm not sure you're ready to hear the answer to that question," he said.

"Try me," she said.

"Like humans, there are both good and bad Moonlight

Kin. We have far more gifts than humans could ever imagine, but we also have a shadow side," he said. "A very dark shadow side."

"You turn into wolves and the Darklings?" She took a step back. That would be bad. Very bad. Izzy wasn't sure what she'd do if Tristan said yes.

"No! Never that," he said. "I told you the truth when I said that the Darklings are from another world. Our shadow sides reside in another world. They do not belong here. Every time they've crossed into this world, they've caused bloodshed and conflict between humans and the Kin. Most humans don't distinguish between monsters. When pushed, they want to kill them all."

Guilt made Izzy look away, but she had to know more. She needed to know everything. "That doesn't explain why you can wear the necklace without it reacting."

He pursed his lips, and darned if he didn't look cute. She bet he made that same face when he was little. The look made her want to rise onto her tippy-toes and kiss him, but that would be inappropriate after what he'd just shared.

"Moonlight Kin magic is part of this world. This lodestone is designed to pick up the magic of creatures from other worlds," Tristan said. "Including our shadow side."

"If they're part of you, why can't you make them stay in their own world?" she asked.

"Can you make your shadow stop following you?" he asked.

Izzy looked down at her shadow. "I suppose not."

"Neither can we," he said.

Izzy's stomach rumbled.

Tristan grinned. "Hungry?"

"Sounds like it," she said. "I know right where to go."

Izzy led Tristan to St. Peter Street. She didn't stop until they reached Yo Mama's Bar & Grill.

"What's this place?" he asked, staring warily at the front of the building. "It looks..."

"Like a bordello?" she finished for him.

Tristan nodded. "I was going to say dive bar, but it resembles that, too."

"The décor is a bit of both, but it has the best burgers you'll ever eat in your life," she said.

They climbed the stairs and settled at a table near the small bar. Instead of sitting across from her, Tristan sat next to her, his leg brushing hers.

Every time he spoke, he leaned in close to her ear and brushed her sensitive lobe. At first Izzy thought he was doing it because the music was so loud, but he did it no matter what was playing on the jukebox. Was this part of their performance?

His actions left her feeling antsy and unsure. She tried to separate reality from make-believe, but the line blurred in her mind. It didn't help that Tristan played his role so convincingly.

Their burgers arrived, and they tucked into them. Izzy scarfed down half her burger before she noticed Tristan staring at her.

"What?" She wiped the ketchup off her fingers and hoped she didn't have more on her face.

"I love that you like to eat," he said. "Most human females don't."

Izzy put her napkin down. "That's not true. Most women *love* to eat. They just don't for fear of getting fat."

He laughed. "You don't have to worry about that."

"I do," she said and grinned. "But my fear doesn't outweigh my love of food."

"I don't like skinny women," he said so low that Izzy almost missed the comment.

She wondered if Tristan even knew he'd spoken aloud.

"Can I have a bite of your burger?" he asked.

Izzy never shared her Yo Mama's burgers, but she couldn't bring herself to tell him no. "Sure." She put her burger down and waited for him to pick it up.

He didn't.

"I thought you said you wanted a bite," she said.

"I do," Tristan said.

Then what was he waiting for? Surely he didn't want her to feed him. Did he?

Izzy picked up her burger and brought it to his mouth. Ketchup and mayo dripped down her fingertips.

Tristan grinned and took a big bite. "It's good," he said after swallowing.

Izzy put the burger down and picked up her napkin, but before she used it, Tristan captured her hand. He brought her fingertips to his mouth and sucked on each one, licking them clean.

Every suck and every lick triggered a reaction in another part of her body. By the time he finished cleaning her hand off, the spot between her thighs was throbbing and Izzy was squirming in her seat.

"Thank you," she croaked.

Tristan's eyes sparkled. "Anytime," he said, his voice rough.

It wasn't until later, when they'd left the French Quarter, that Izzy remembered that there'd been no one in the bar to see their performance.

Chapter Eleven

Izzy walked through town with the monster. They were holding hands and whispering into each other's ears like lovers.

Had she taken the wolf to her bed? Just the thought of her lying in the beast's arms made Stone crazy. What was she thinking?

The monster released her hand then slid his palm down to rest on the small of her back. It was a cozy act. The kind of act that implied intimate knowledge.

Fury filled him. Why would she beg him to take her away, then throw herself at the white beast? It made no sense. They laughed, then the monster leaned in and kissed her.

Stone waited to see what Izzy's reaction would be. He hoped for anger, but got breathlessness and fluster instead.

Was she setting him up?

Stone had thought her desire to escape was genuine, but watching them now, he wasn't so sure. He pressed the pre-programmed number on his phone.

Izzy didn't pick up. He hung up and tried again, but she didn't answer. She was too busy hanging on the beast's arm and flirting.

He couldn't let her do this. Not when he was so close. One way or another, Stone would have to stop the beast by her side. Failure was not an option.

* * * * *

Izzy's phone vibrated when she turned it on, indicating that she had a message. She'd kept the phone off after Stone had left her yesterday. She'd expected him to call eventually but hoped he'd take more time to come to his senses.

She glanced at her watch. It was still relatively early. The sun wouldn't go down for several more hours. She thought about how she and Tristan could pass the time. Instantly, a carnal image flashed in her mind.

Izzy glanced at Frosty. He hadn't said much since they'd gotten back to the cabin, but she had caught him looking at her a couple times. As per usual, she hadn't been able to read his expression. The man should play poker.

Her phone vibrated again. Izzy needed to deal with one problem at a time, starting with Stone. "I need to use the bathroom," she said.

Tristan glanced up from the paper he read. "Okay," he said.

Izzy picked up her purse and walked into the bathroom. They'd had such a nice day that she didn't want to do anything to ruin the mood. She shut the door and pulled out her phone, expecting to see a missed call. Instead, there were at least a half dozen text messages from Stone, each one angrier than the last.

Saw you in town today. What were you doing?

You said you wanted help getting away. Didn't look like you needed help to me.

How could you bring yourself to kiss a monster? What's wrong with you? He had his hands all over you and you looked like you loved every minute of it.

It's us against them or have you forgotten?

Makes me think you've been setting me up all along. Have you? I only wanted to help you. Why would you do something like that? Do you want the monsters to catch me?

You'll be sorry, if I find out that's what you've been doing all along. You don't know who you're messing with.

Is that why you didn't leave with me yesterday? You were too busy screwing a monster. Sick! Now I know why you didn't want me to hurt him.

I can no longer trust your judgment. Who knows what kind of magic he's worked on you. For your sake, I hope you're not around when I take out your boyfriend.

Wouldn't want you to get hurt by accident.

Izzy felt bile rise in her throat as she struggled to get control of her fear. She turned on the water, so Tristan wouldn't hear her texting Stone back.

I don't have to explain myself, but I will because you're obviously mental. Everything you saw today was... It wasn't what you think. The whole thing was an act.

But it hadn't felt like an act. A few times when Tristan had kissed her, it had actually felt real.

The whys are not important—just know that it was. Tristan is not my lover.

Everly's reading came rushing back to her. She saw them as lovers. Heck, even Izzy had seen them together in her vision. That didn't mean it would happen. It couldn't. Izzy's certainty wasn't nearly as strong as it had been in the beginning.

The more time she spent with Tristan, the easier it was to imagine them together. It would never last, but Izzy could no longer deny that she wanted him. If only for a night.

Stone's response was swift. *Looked like he was working his magic on you.*

Tristan had mentioned something about magic, but he'd made it sound like his was nothing special. Had he lied? The thought that he might have worried her. Worried her enough that Izzy was going to have to ask.

Izzy typed another message. *I believed that all monsters were the same. I was wrong. So are you.*

Tristan wasn't like any of the others she'd met over the years. In hindsight, most had left her alone. It had been her who'd run away, and only when she'd received a psychic warning.

You should go ahead without me. Get out of town while you can. I'll leave once I'm finished here.

Stone's response was immediate. *I am not going anywhere without you. Got it? So get your things packed. I'll be there soon.*

Izzy didn't need his help. His militant insistence frightened her. *I've changed my mind. I no longer want to go. Please, Stone, just leave.*

If you won't save yourself, I'll have to be the one to save you from yourself.

Stone's message made Izzy shiver. What was she going to do? His heart might be in the right place, but it was obvious that he wasn't stable.

Izzy felt sorry for him. She knew what it was like to feel like the only sane person in the world. Stone had been on his own for too long. Maybe he just needed time to cool off? Once he did, perhaps then he'd listen to reason.

She turned the phone off and dropped it back into her purse, then flushed the toilet. Izzy splashed some water on her face then walked back into the main room.

Tristan set his paper on the table, when she came out. "Everything okay?"

"Yeah," she said, hoping it was the truth.

* * * * *

Tristan noticed the change in Isabel's complexion. Despite the moisture clinging to the side of her hair, she looked pale. Certainly paler than she'd been when she walked into the bathroom.

He inhaled, catching a sharp scent that indicated fear. What had her so upset? He'd thought the day had gone as well as could be expected. She'd seemed fine a moment ago. Tristan pulled her into his arms as she walked past.

Isabel yelped. "What are you doing?" Her body remained tense for a moment, then she relaxed.

What was he doing? Sure, he wanted to know what was wrong, but he also had gotten used to touching her whenever he felt like it. There was no one here to see them, no one to perform for, but Tristan wasn't ready to stop the *act*.

"I know today was stressful," he said, rubbing his thumb along her spine, soothing the tense muscles.

She shrugged awkwardly. "It wasn't so bad," she said. "After a while I forgot we were pretending."

So had he.

"Toward the end, I thought we were actually having a good time," she said.

Tristan agreed. "Thanks for introducing me to Yo Mama's Bar and Grill," he said. The burgers had been delicious.

Isabel smiled. "I figured you'd like the hamburgers."

"I did indeed." He leaned in close to her ear. "We might have to do it all again tomorrow, including the lunch break."

Her scent changed subtly, growing warmer, richer, more intoxicating. Isabel probably wouldn't admit it, but she wasn't as adverse to the idea of pretending they were a couple as she'd been earlier.

Neither was Tristan.

Her delicious scent made him wonder exactly where she'd draw the line. Before he had the chance to change his mind, Tristan framed Isabel's face and kissed her. He made sure to linger over her lips, savoring her flavor.

At first, she was too shocked to respond, then her fingers sank into his hair and Isabel kissed him back. Tristan's whole body hardened beneath her. A sound rumbled out of his chest, and he pulled her even closer, deepening the embrace.

Their tongues brushed, then swirled, tasting, teasing, and delighting in the kiss. Tristan's hands dropped away from her face and slid down her bare arms, pausing only long enough to scrape the sides of her breasts.

Isabel gasped but made no move to stop him. Encouraged, Tristan continued his exploration. He kneaded his way down her arms before grasping her lush bottom.

Tristan squeezed and massaged until her luscious scent permeated the room, then he lifted her higher so she could straddle his thighs. The move made her sundress bunch around her waist.

The material presented no barrier when he rocked his hips against her core. Isabel moaned and wiggled to get closer. Her blunt teeth latched onto his lower lip, and she tugged.

It was Tristan's turn to groan. Wolves loved to bite, especially during lovemaking. And there was no doubt that's where they were headed if he didn't put the brakes on. Tristan thought about it for half a second then surrendered to his beast.

He'd wanted to sink inside her since he first laid eyes on her photo back in Oregon. He'd told himself that she was human, that he should stay away, but despite appearances, Tristan wasn't a glacier. In fact, if he got any hotter, he'd melt the polar ice caps.

Tristan hooked Isabel under her legs and stood. He waited for her eyes to open and her vision to clear. "If you don't want this, you need to tell me now," he said.

Indecision crossed her face for a moment. "You know this isn't going to last," she said.

"I know." He ignored the pain that knifed his chest.

"Before I say yes, I need to know one thing," she said.

"What?" he asked, distracted by the feel of her in his arms.

"Are you using magic on me?" she asked.

"Why would you think that?" The question cooled some of the desire coursing through Tristan's veins.

Isabel took a deep breath and met his gaze. "I just wondered if that was why I wanted you so bad."

Tristan felt as if he was being ripped in two. On the one hand, he was angry that she'd accused him of doing something to her to get her into bed. On the other, he was elated to know that she wanted him.

"The only magic in this room is the kind conjured between a man and a woman," he said.

It took her a moment to understand, but when she did, her eyes widened and she kissed him.

It wasn't exactly the declaration Tristan hoped for, but it would have to do. He strode the short distance across the room to the bed. Tristan juggled Isabel in his arms and pulled the covers back, then he laid her down.

For a moment, all he could do was stare at her. Isabel's wild hair had fanned out around her head, and her purple sundress was wrapped around her waist, revealing a matching satin thong. Tristan smelled the moisture gathering between her thighs. The beast in him drooled.

This was a bad idea, but Izzy's body didn't care. All day long, she'd endured Tristan's gentle touches, his long drugging kisses, and his intimate nuzzling. By the time they'd left the Quarter, she'd been wound so tight she thought she'd burst.

Stone had accused her of taking Tristan as a lover. She hadn't lied, but she also hadn't told him the whole truth, which was that Izzy had been thinking about it. Thinking of little else. Now it looked like her wait was over.

Tristan grabbed his shirt and pulled it over his head. Muscles rippled in his arms and over his chest as he tossed it behind him onto the couch.

He truly was incredible. Izzy was pretty sure she'd never seen anything like him and doubted she would again. His fingers dropped to the front of his jeans. With a flick of his wrist, the button opened and his jeans split, revealing bare skin.

Izzy swallowed hard. He wasn't wearing underwear. Her imagination went wild as Tristan slid his zipper down. The hiss filled the silence, then his hard shaft spilled out of his pants.

How he'd kept it inside them was beyond her. It shouldn't have been anatomically possible to squeeze something so big into material so tight.

Tristan chuckled and slid his jeans down before kicking them aside. Naked, he stared at Izzy until she grew self-conscious. She wasn't ashamed of her body, but she was well aware she wasn't built like a god.

Izzy covered herself with her hands.

"No!" Tristan snapped. "I want to look at you. I've been imagining what you would look like with your dress hiked up around your waist all day."

The admission surprised her. "Really? But you don't like humans."

"And you don't like monsters," he replied, his gaze soaking her in.

"You're not a monster," Izzy murmured softly.

Tristan's dark gray eyes widened then quickly shuttered to hide his emotions. "You have no idea how beautiful you are, do you?" he asked. "Men were falling over themselves trying to catch your attention. It was very hard not to respond."

"As I recall, you growled at them," she said.

"For me, that counts as no response," he said.

Izzy laughed and sat up to untie the straps on her shoulders.

"Let me," he rasped. Tristan's hands trembled as he untied first one side of her sundress, then the other.

The material dropped, but the dress stayed in place—thanks to her ample chest. "There's a zipper in back," she said.

"I know." Tristan leaned over her and kissed her. Another hiss filled the air as her zipper came down.

Izzy had not felt his hand move. She'd been too busy trying to uncurl her toes. She hadn't worn a bra, since the dress had built in support. Now that the material pooled around her waist, Izzy wished that she had.

Tristan pulled back from the kiss to look at her. He shuddered. "Beautiful," he said, his attention locked on her engorged nipples. "Stay just like that." Before she could figure out what he was going to do next, Tristan dropped to his knees in front of her.

The position put him between her legs, but he couldn't get any closer without climbing onto the bed. He clasped her hands and tugged her forward, then he latched onto her nipple.

Fire shot through Izzy, spreading at an alarming rate. The flames leapt higher with each pull of his mouth. Tristan sucked her deep, laving her until Izzy thought she'd scream. She squirmed to get closer, but he wouldn't let her.

With infinite care, Tristan released the swollen bud then sucked the other one into his mouth.

Izzy clutched his head. She pulled his hair when the sensations got too much, but he didn't seem to notice or to mind. Every time Tristan swirled his tongue, she felt an answering flick between her thighs. Moisture trickled between her legs, soaking her thong. It wasn't enough. She needed more.

"Tristan," she gasped and tried to yank his head back.

He growled and kept feasting.

The pressure continued to build inside her. The steady throb left Izzy teetering on the edge of oblivion. "That's it," she said. "Just like that."

Right before she toppled over, he stopped.

Izzy growled in frustration.

Tristan's silvery gaze met hers, then he licked his lips.

"You taste delicious. I can't wait to taste the rest of you." He slid his hands under her body until he got a hold of her dress, then tugged. The material slid out from under her, leaving Izzy in her thong.

"That's better," he said, scooting her closer to the edge of the bed. "Just one more thing." Tristan threaded his fingers into her thong and snapped the material in half. He pulled it aside and threw it onto the floor next to his jeans.

Izzy couldn't remember how to speak or to think. The look in Tristan's eyes left her breathless. She'd never had a man look at her the way he was right now. His gaze held so much hunger, so much passion—so much need.

"What now?" she croaked.

His lips tilted. For a second she saw a flash of extended canines poking out the side of his mouth. She should be frightened, but fear was the last thing on her mind.

"Now I savor," he said and slowly lowered his head between her thighs.

The first swipe of Tristan's rough tongue sent Izzy spiraling over the edge. Her fingers sank into his shoulders as she tried to ride out her orgasm.

It had been so long since she'd allowed any man close enough to touch her, much less make love to her. Izzy forgot how wonderful it could be.

Tristan lapped up her juices then dove in with gusto. His tongue swirled and teased, flicking her swollen flesh until it filled with blood once more.

"I can't," she gasped.

Izzy's thighs trembled and she tried to shut her legs, but Tristan wedged his shoulders between them to stop her.

"We're not done yet," he said, his chin moist from her release. "Not by a long shot." He licked his lips. "Mmm."

Tristan drove his tongue inside Isabel's tight channel. He'd never tasted anything so delicious, and it scared him that he might never again. He ate her, nibbling her flesh, until she writhed on the bed once more.

He sucked the bundle of nerves into his mouth and worried it with his sharp teeth, then plunged two fingers inside her. Her body clamped down on him. Isabel let out a harsh cry, then flew apart in his arms.

Tristan licked her, not wanting to miss an ounce of her juices, as her second release rippled through her. When the fluttering in her channel lessened, he slowly pulled his fingers out. Tristan waited until he had her attention, then he stuck them in his mouth and sucked them clean.

Isabel shuddered again, and her eyes clouded.

He rose to his feet. "You are everything I imagined and more," Tristan said. His shaft was so hard and engorged that it curved under the weight. Tristan wrapped his fist around his erection and stroked.

Isabel's gaze followed the movement, and she licked her lips.

Tristan traced her mouth with his finger. "I can't wait to feel you taking me here." He tapped her lower lip. "But first, I have to take the edge off." Tristan grabbed onto her waist and pulled Isabel fully onto the bed, so he could join her.

He dropped onto the bed. "Open for me," he said, his voice so gruff that he barely understood the words.

Isabel's legs dropped open. Moisture covered her swollen sex. He couldn't get over how responsive she was or how delicious she tasted.

Tristan settled between her thighs, letting her get used to his weight. Their gazes met and locked. He couldn't turn away if he wanted to. Tristan kissed her tenderly then positioned himself at her entrance.

As much as he wanted to thrust hard and bury himself inside her, Tristan didn't. Instead, he took it slow, giving Isabel's body time to adjust to his large size.

She was so tight, so blissfully snug that he wondered when she'd last been with a man. Just the thought of her being with another male, brought his beast surging to the surface. Tristan clamped down onto it, but it continued to stare out through his eyes.

If Isabel noticed, she didn't say anything. She also didn't look away. The move goaded his beast, challenging its dominance. He growled deep in his chest. Isabel ignored the threat and stroked his jaw. Tristan's control shattered and his hips rocked, sending him deeper inside of her.

Isabel gasped, and her body tightened.

"Sorry," he said.

"It's okay," she murmured. "It's just been a while for me."

Tristan gritted his teeth. "Me too."

She blinked in surprise.

"Is that so hard to believe?" he asked, trying to keep still when everything inside of him wanted to thrust.

Her brow furrowed. "I guess not." Isabel's body relaxed, allowing him to sink even deeper.

Between the warmth, the moisture, and the growing pressure, Tristan was in heaven—and hell. The scariest part of all was that he didn't want to leave.

* * * * *

Izzy felt stretched beyond her limits. Tristan was even bigger than he'd appeared, which was saying something. He rocked his hips, and pleasure shot from her core through her entire body.

"Do that again," she said.

"And again," he responded, then thrust harder.

Izzy moaned and wrapped her legs around his waist. Tristan must've taken it as encouragement because he began to move steadily in and out of her. The delicious motion spread through her entire body, leaving her aching for more.

Tristan stroked her jaw and kissed her. The ice in his mercury-colored eyes was gone. Now they shimmered with undisguised heat.

His hand slid down, then he hooked his arms under her

knees. The move lifted Izzy's legs even higher and spread them at the same time. From this angle, Tristan bored straight into her soul.

Izzy mewed. Each thrust merged them together, taking him directly over the hidden bundle of nerves. He ground himself into her as he impaled her again and again. Tristan drove her body harder and harder until pleasure blinded her. She cried out from the overload and tried to wiggle out of his grasp.

Tristan's hands locked onto her shoulders, and Izzy saw his eyes shift to wolf. A growl rumbled from his throat right before his teeth locked onto her shoulder.

"I'm not going anywhere," she murmured, but she wasn't sure Tristan heard her.

His thrusts became more primal. His hips bucked, and he pounded into her.

Izzy thrashed as the pressure built inside of her. She couldn't stop the moans from escaping or the nonsensical pleas for release. Tristan licked her shoulder and let her go.

"Don't hold back," he snarled. "I want to hear you scream my name. Want to see your body flushed with passion. What to feel you embrace every inch of me." His speed increased.

Izzy unraveled in his arms. The pleasure was unlike anything she'd ever experienced. When she came, it was like a detonator went off inside her head. Everything exploded. Colors burst behind her eyes, and Izzy screamed Tristan's name. The world faded as the blast sent her tumbling over the edge.

Isabel's scream rang in his ears, and her tight sheath gripped him like a vise until Tristan could barely move. When had sex ever been like this?

Never, a little voice whispered.

He gazed upon her. She was perfect. Tristan felt his body tighten as her core continued to pulse. He didn't want the moment to end. This might be the only time they slept together. He rocked his hips to draw out her orgasm. Once the spasms eased, Tristan sought his own release.

He surged inside of her and felt his sac rise. Tristan built up a steady rhythm. He wouldn't last long. A ripple of pleasure struck, taking his breath away. He'd had sex plenty of times and never experienced anything like it.

Tristan stoked faster, reaching for completion. The pleasure inside him increased to the point of pain. Something was wrong, but he couldn't seem to stop. His movements became frenzied, and Tristan began to swell.

What were those stories he'd heard about Damon and Aidan, when they'd found their mates?

Realization dawned. It couldn't be. Horrified, Tristan tried to pull out of Isabel, but he couldn't. His shaft was too big. He rocked his hips back, but only managed to move an inch.

No! No! No! He wouldn't allow this to happen. Tristan tugged harder, but he didn't budge.

Isabel moaned and raked her nails down his back, oblivious to the physical changes taking place in him.

Tristan hissed at the mixture of pain and pleasure, then felt his canines lengthen. She was human. This couldn't happen to him. He was stronger, more focused than the others. Determined to outsmart fate, Tristan jerked his head to the side and bit his own arm.

Blood filled his mouth, but he didn't care. As long as he didn't bite her, he could get through this. All he had to do was achieve release.

Tristan locked a hand onto Isabel's hip and thrust harder. Pleasure erupted inside of him, and he swelled even more. Fire raced down Tristan's spine, leaving him gasping for air.

The flames spread, and he bellowed. The first white-hot wave struck, and Tristan's body convulsed. His release went on forever and ever. Every time he thought his beast had finished, he'd spurt again and groan in blissful agony. Tristan had never experienced this level of blinding pleasure in his life.

Was this what sex would be like every time with Isabel? If so, he'd never survive.

Bondmate, the word echoed in his mind.

Tristan shook his head in denial. She couldn't be. He waited for the swelling to ease then quickly pulled out. Isabel's eyes were closed, but she had a smile on her face. He didn't want to ruin the moment, but Tristan was too shaken by what had occurred to stay in bed.

"I need to use the bathroom." He practically leapt off her.

Isabel cracked an eye open. "You must have to go bad."

He caught a glimpse of the hickey on her neck and stopped short. Had he broken the skin? Please goddess no. Tristan ran his tongue over his teeth, but didn't taste anyone's blood but his own.

"How's your shoulder?" he asked, hoping he hadn't hurt her.

"It's a little tender, but I'll live," she said.

"Don't worry, I didn't break the skin," he said.

"I wasn't worried. It kind of felt good." Isabel's lashes fluttered open all the way. Her smile slowly faded as she caught sight of him. "Are you okay? Your arm is bleeding."

Tristan put on his social mask. He wore it anytime he needed to avoid emotional entanglement. "It's nothing," he snapped and shoved his arm behind his back.

"Doesn't look like nothing to me, Frosty." She rolled onto her side to get a better look.

Tristan gritted his teeth. "I said it's nothing. Leave it alone."

Isabel's brow rose, but she didn't say anything else.

Tristan rushed into the bathroom.

He felt like an ass. He never rushed out of a woman's bed, but tonight he'd had no choice. Tristan stared at his reflection in the mirror. His wolf stared back.

"What were you thinking?" he muttered.

The wolf snarled and bared its teeth.

Tristan turned the water on and splashed it over his face. The cool liquid wasn't enough to diffuse the panic. He reached for the shower nozzle instead. Once he had the shower set to cold, Tristan took off the lodestone necklace and set it on the side of the sink, then stepped beneath the spray.

The water took his breath away but did little to ease the tension inside of him. He'd read the reports about Damon Laroche and Aidan Fortier. He'd even gone to check on them in person.

He'd been so certain that choosing humans for mates was due to their bloodline that he'd dismissed the cases as anomalies. But there'd been no mistaking what had happened with Isabel.

From all the reports Tristan had read and the wolves he'd interviewed, he knew that the only time a wolf locked inside a woman was when it found its mate. He liked Isabel. How could he not? But she was human. And humans weren't meant to mate with the Moonlight Kin. It was a fact his wolf would have to accept.

* * * * *

Izzy hadn't expected flowers or for Tristan to fix her dinner, but she'd thought he'd at least be polite enough to stick around for a few minutes after they'd had sex.

She pulled the blanket around her, feeling chilled despite the heat. Izzy didn't feel used. She'd entered into this with her eyes wide open. But she did feel cheap. Tristan must've thought the same. He'd barely been able to look at her. When he had met her gaze, he'd appeared positively panic-stricken.

It was obvious he had more than a few regrets about what they'd done.

The worst part was Izzy didn't. The sex was beyond a doubt the best she'd ever had. She'd tried to hold part of herself back, while keeping lust at the forefront, but it hadn't worked.

Despite her best efforts, feelings had worked their way into the equation. Unwelcome feelings. Feelings that would only end up hurting her, when it was time to walk away.

When did she start caring about him? She couldn't care about him. They weren't even the same species. For some reason that didn't seem to matter to her stupid, stupid heart.

Izzy had to get out of here. She couldn't face Tristan, not after what just happened.

His opinion of humans wasn't going to be changed by great sex, and she wasn't dumb enough to believe that what had occurred was anything other than a roll in the sack.

She listened to the shower. The sound sent pain slashing through her. It was as if he was washing the whole event away, washing her away. Maybe he was. If she were smart, she'd do the same.

Izzy glanced out the window. It was still daylight, but it wouldn't be for much longer. She slipped off the bed and quickly got dressed in a pair of sweats and a T-shirt.

Her gaze shot to the bathroom door. It was still closed, and the shower was still going. Izzy grabbed her purse. She quickly found her phone and hit the pre-programmed number.

The phone rang...outside the front door of the cabin.

Izzy looked up and found Stone standing in the doorway, glaring at her.

"Looks like I got here just in time," he said.

Chapter Twelve

Izzy grabbed her tote bag and threw what little clothes she had inside it. "We need to hurry," she said. "Tristan will be out any minute."

"The car's unlocked," Stone said. "You go ahead. I'll be right out."

"Are you insane?" she asked. "Come on."

"Just go!" Stone snarled.

Izzy cursed under her breath and rushed outside. She threw her tote into the backseat of Stone's car and waited. When he didn't come out right away, she went back in.

"What are you doing?" she hissed.

"Taking care of the problem once and for all," he said.

The blood drained from Izzy's face. "You can't hurt him." Just the thought of Tristan being hurt left her feeling adrift.

"Yes, I can," Stone said.

Izzy grabbed his arm and swung him around to face her. "I didn't mean it like that. What I meant was I don't want you to hurt him." She didn't want to stay with Tristan any longer. It would just cause too much pain. But she darn sure didn't want to be part of any plan to hurt him. "Let's go."

His amber gaze hardened. "You wouldn't be saying that if you hadn't slept with him."

"How did you—"

Stone yanked her hair to the side.

Izzy slapped his hand away. "What are you doing?"

"Looking for bite marks," he said.

"Tristan didn't bite me," she said. At least not hard enough to break the skin. "He's not a vampire."

"That hickey on your neck says otherwise," Stone said. "You're a lucky lady. If he had bit you, there'd be no getting away from him."

What did he mean by that? And why didn't the idea frighten her more? "I don't know what you're talking about," Izzy said, glancing at the bathroom door. "Time to go." If Tristan found Stone in the cabin, there would be bloodshed.

"Go to the car, Izzy," Stone said.

She wasn't going anywhere.

"I don't want you to get hurt," he said.

Izzy put her hands on her hips. "I won't, if we leave now."

Stone's gaze locked on hers. "I have to slow him down so we can get away. If I don't, he'll be on us immediately."

"And just how do you intend to do that?" Izzy asked.

"I'll think of something." Stone glanced at the small knife rack in the kitchen.

Izzy followed his gaze. "Don't even think about it," she said.

"Wait in the car."

"If you're not out in one minute," Izzy said. "I'm leaving without you. I mean it."

* * * * *

Tristan stayed in the shower until his skin pruned. He couldn't hide in here all night. He'd have to face Isabel eventually. Better to do it sooner rather than later. He would simply go out and tell her that they'd made a mistake—that he'd made a mistake.

He shut the water off and grabbed a towel. He was drying himself when his head swam. Tristan clutched the sink and rubbed his temple. What was wrong with him? He didn't get sick. Ever.

Tristan glanced at the lodestone next to his hand. It glowed bright as a star. He cursed and picked it up. The Darkling had to be close. Really close. Tristan pulled the necklace on over his head. He instantly felt better, but the magic in the stone would only protect him for so long. He secured the towel around his waist then reached for the doorknob.

"Isabel," he called out.

There was no answer.

Maybe she'd fallen asleep. It wasn't late, but he had kept her busy for well over an hour.

"Isabel," Tristan said, then inhaled. The scent of dark magic filled his lungs. Fear enveloped him as he felt his muscles weaken.

He had to get out there and protect Isabel before the Darkling drained him completely. Tristan called to his wolf, but he couldn't shift. Not with the Darkling controlling his power. He tried again and managed to grow some claws.

Those deadly weapons and the lodestone around his neck would have to be enough until he got to his sword. Tristan shoved the bathroom door open and rushed out.

He saw the Darkling stumble as he drew nearer. Tristan didn't see Isabel. Where was she? Had it harmed her? He managed to rake the Darkling with his claws. Tristan heard a loud yip then saw a cast-iron pan coming at his head. He didn't have time to duck.

Colors exploded behind his eyes as the pan smashed into him. Tristan dropped to the floor. He tried to rise, but the Darkling hit him again. This time the colors dancing in his vision faded to black, along with the world around him. His only regret was that he hadn't been able to save Isabel.

* * * * *

Izzy heard a loud bang and rushed back into the house. She came through the door in time to see Stone approach Tristan. He had a butcher knife in his hand. Tristan was on the floor. Blood pooled around his head, and he wasn't moving.

How had Stone overpowered him so easily? She didn't think it was possible.

Stone raised the knife over his head and prepared to plunge it into Tristan's bare back.

Izzy rushed forward and shoved him aside. "What are you doing? Can't you see that he's down? He's not going anywhere." Perhaps ever. Tears filled her eyes. All Izzy wanted to do was get away, so she wouldn't have to face the emotions Tristan stirred inside of her.

Rage filled Stone's amber eyes. "If I don't kill him, he'll just keep coming after us."

"You said you just wanted to slow him down," she said. "Was that a lie?"

His jaw clenched.

Izzy knelt down beside Tristan. "You told me that we were better than the monsters," she said, trying to swallow past the lump in her throat. He was still breathing, but his breaths were shallow. She hadn't meant for any of this to happen.

"We are," Stone said, yanking her to her feet.

"Then prove it!" Izzy shouted. "Come with me right now. If you don't, I'll know you're no better than them."

She glanced down. There was so much blood. It soaked his blond hair, turning it crimson. Izzy's stomach lurched.

"I'm going to be sick." She stumbled to the door, half faking and half telling the truth.

Stone swore loudly and dropped the knife. He grabbed her by the elbow and shouldered the screen door open. He led her down the stairs and over to the car.

"You're an idiot," he said. "You know that?"

"We need to call an ambulance," she said. "This whole thing has gone too far."

"You're not calling anybody. That's not a human in there. It's a monster." He shoved her in the passenger seat and slammed the door behind her. Stone ran around the front of the car and climbed behind the wheel. "Buckle up."

He threw the car into drive and mashed his foot down on the gas pedal. The car lurched and the tires spun, sending mud flying into the air.

Izzy scrambled to get her seatbelt on. "Do you think Tristan will be okay?" she asked.

Stone glared at her. "I sure as hell hope not," he said.

Her heart sank. "We need to call for help," she said.

"I told you no. Do you want to get the paramedics killed?"

"No," Izzy said. Would Tristan harm an innocent person? Normally, she'd say no, but there was nothing normal about this situation. Wounded animals often lashed out at the people trying to help them.

"Sit back and be quiet," Stone said. "I need to think."

Izzy just couldn't shake the image of Tristan lying on the cabin floor. "Pull over," she said. "I need to go back. I have to make sure he's okay."

"No," Stone said. "You need to calm down and think. What do you think would happen if you went back there right now?"

"I'd be able to check on him," she said. "Make sure he didn't have a concussion."

"Then what?" he asked. "You'd wait around until he figured out that you called me?"

She had called him. Izzy had only wanted help with getting away, but would Tristan see it that way once he recovered—if he recovered?

Izzy thought about what Tristan had told her about his job. He was paid to eliminate any and all threats to the Moonlight Kin. This move certainly put her in the threat category. Tristan didn't strike her as being very forgiving.

Perhaps the Death card had been referring to her death after all. Izzy pictured Tristan's cold slate eyes and felt fresh tears burn her eyes.

Stone looked at her. "Now you finally understand why I wanted to kill him."

Izzy glanced at him. "Just because I understand your reasoning doesn't mean that I agree with you," she said, angrily wiping the tears away before they could fall. "My name is Izzy, not Buffy. This isn't the movies. We're not Slayers."

His amber eyes narrowed. "Speak for yourself," Stone said, then clutched his head and groaned.

"Are you okay?" she asked.

"I'll be fine once we put more distance between us and the monster," he said.

She pointed to his bloody shirt. "Tristan wouldn't have done that to you if you hadn't attacked him."

"Stop giving the monster a name," he said.

"I didn't," Izzy said. "That is his name."

"You just couldn't keep your legs closed. Could you?" he asked in disgust.

Izzy's face flamed.

Stone hit the steering wheel with his fists. "I should've killed him when I had the chance."

He might already be dead. A wave of pain followed the insidious thought.

"Listen, I don't know what happened to you before we met, but I can tell that you're carrying a lot on your shoulders," she said.

Izzy had thought she and Stone were alike, two lost souls trapped in a world full of monsters. Now she knew that wasn't the case. Something had pushed him over the edge long before tonight.

She'd have to live with what she'd done to Tristan. If it turned out that he was dead, then she'd accept the consequences of her actions, even if that meant her death. If Tristan was still alive, then she'd cross that bridge when she got to it.

"I appreciate you getting me out of there, but I think when we get to town we should split up."

Stone yanked the car over to the side of the road. "We aren't going into town," he said.

Izzy's stomach pitched. "Where are we going?"

"To my house to lay low for the night," he said.

"I thought you said that you lived in an apartment in town," she said.

He glanced out the window. "That's what I told you at the time because I didn't know you." *Didn't trust you,* was left unsaid.

They drove to one of the wards that had been devastated by Hurricane Katrina. There'd been so many that Izzy wasn't sure which one they were in. Most of the people who'd lived in this one hadn't returned. The houses were still boarded up, and spray-painted signs covered many of the outer walls. It reminded Izzy of a warzone.

Stone drove down the deserted street to the last house at the end of the lane. He pulled into the driveway. Unlike the other homes they'd passed, this one's lawn was neatly trimmed, and plywood didn't cover the windows.

Flowerbeds lined the home's foundation, and the shutters around the windows were painted bright lavender. Stone didn't strike Izzy as a lavender kind of guy, but she didn't know him well.

"We should be safe here until tomorrow night," he said, killing the engine.

"What happens tomorrow night?" Izzy asked.

Stone looked at her. "We leave town for good." He

swayed on his feet when he climbed out and had to catch the side of the door to steady himself.

"You sure you're okay?" she asked. "Do you want me to take a look at that wound?"

"I said I'm fine," he snapped, then moved toward the door.

The stench of death punched Izzy in the face the second she stepped out of the car. She nearly dropped her tote in an attempt to cover her nose.

"What's that?" she asked.

Stone's confused expression cleared. "Oh, an alligator wandered into the backyard. I had to kill it."

"Is it lying in the backyard now?" she asked. "Because that will only draw more of them. They can smell decomp from quite a distance."

"No, I shoved the corpse into the shed until I can dispose of it properly," he said, then continued toward the front door.

"Don't you mean carcass?" Izzy asked.

Stone hesitated. "Yeah, sure," he said, then added, "Stay out of the backyard. There might be more of them hanging around."

Izzy stayed by the car.

He noticed she wasn't beside him. "You coming?" Stone asked.

She looked at the decrepit neighborhood. It was almost dark. At first glance, it appeared abandoned, but that didn't mean there weren't gangs roaming around the area. And apparently alligators.

Stone waited for her next to the door.

Tonight, she was all out of options. Izzy hoisted her tote higher onto her shoulder and walked to the house. Stone stepped inside before she reached the porch and dropped his bag next to the door. He walked into the kitchen when Izzy reached the doorway.

The feminine touches on the outside carried on in the interior. Pink and lavender filled the small space, from the frilly curtains to the lace tablecloth. Photos of a blond woman and a fair-haired, freckle-faced little girl covered the walls.

Izzy walked over to one of the photos to take a closer look. "Who are they?" she asked.

Stone glanced at the photo. "My sister and her kid," he said.

"Really?" Izzy asked.

Both of the females had fair hair and blue eyes. Their features were soft, almost delicate. Stone had dark hair and amber eyes. Nothing about him gave Izzy the impression of soft.

"Yes," he said. "Your room is at the end of the hall on the left." Stone pointed down the only hall in the house.

"Thanks," Izzy said. She glanced one last time at the picture then walked down the hall. The home only had two bedrooms and a bath. She wondered where Stone's sister and her daughter were. Would they be coming back soon?

The thought of involving a child in this mess didn't sit well with Izzy. It was dangerous enough as an adult. She opened the door on the left and stepped into...a child's room.

The walls were a light pink like the curtains framing the window. The bedspread on the twin bed held the latest cartoon princess's likeness. Next to the bed sat a small dresser that doubled as a bedside table. On top of the dresser was a lamp and another photo of the mother.

A small child-sized white desk was pushed against the opposite wall. Beside it was a trunk. Izzy assumed it was full of toys, since there wasn't a single one on the floor.

She stepped inside, shut the door, and rested her back against it. Izzy didn't like taking a child's room away from her. She needed to find out when they'd return. As long as it wasn't tonight, it wouldn't matter, because Izzy planned to be long gone tomorrow.

Izzy unzipped her tote and took out a wrinkled shirt to wear in the morning. Maybe if she hung it up overnight, the wrinkles would release. She opened the closet to get a hanger and found it bursting with clothes.

She shut the closet door and walked over to the dresser. Izzy opened each drawer to check inside. The drawers held socks, underwear, pajamas, everything a child would need on a trip.

In the bottom drawer, she even found a well-loved, stuffed brown bear. The kind of stuffed animal that a child kept with them at all times. Maybe they were coming back tonight after all.

Izzy closed the drawers and walked out the bedroom. "Stone?"

"In here," he said. Stone was bent over a pot on the stove. The contents were bubbling and hissing from the high heat.

Izzy couldn't tell what he was cooking, but it smelled funny. "Are your sister and niece coming back tonight?" she asked.

He shook his head. "No, why do you ask?" Stone picked up a spoon and stirred the contents of the pot. He brought the spoon up to his mouth and licked it. His eyes closed in ecstasy at the taste.

Izzy tried not to gag. "When do you expect them back?"

Stone's mouth tightened. "I don't know. In a few days," he said. "We'll be out of their hair by then, so stop worrying."

Their return wasn't what worried Izzy. It was the fact that it didn't look as if they'd left.

"Do they have another house?" she asked. That would explain not needing to pack.

"No," Stone said. "Not that I know of."

His response gave her pause. This was his sister he was talking about. Surely he'd know if she owned more than one property.

"Are you sure she doesn't mind us staying here?" Izzy asked.

Stone dropped the spoon into the pot. It hit the liquid with a *kerplunk* and sent droplets onto the stove. He turned to face her. "What's this all about?" he asked. "If I didn't know better, I'd say you weren't grateful that I rescued you."

"I—I am," she stammered. "I mean, I do appreciate it."

He looked as if he didn't believe her. "It's getting late. Unless you want something to eat, you should probably get some rest," he said.

Izzy smelled the food again. The odor seemed even worse than before. "No thanks. I'm not very hungry."

"Your loss," Stone said, then took another spoonful.

She had no intention of eating it, but she was curious. "What is it?" she asked.

Stone grinned at her. "Game," he said.

His response didn't exactly narrow it down, but it didn't matter. "Enjoy," Izzy said, then wandered back to the little girl's room.

Before she entered the room, Stone called her name. Izzy turned to find him standing at the entrance of the hall. "I'll stand guard in case the monsters find us. If you need anything, I'll be right outside the door."

Suddenly Izzy didn't feel as if she'd been rescued. She felt like a prisoner whose guard would be stationed at her door. Izzy didn't know what to say, so she nodded and stepped into the room.

The second she was out of sight, Izzy opened her mind to her gift. She needed to figure out what was happening. She closed her eyes and inhaled deeply. Her gift flowed out of her straight into something solid.

Izzy's eyes flew open. Something was blocking her, blocking it. Stone said he had the ability to block the monsters and people like her, but Izzy had only wanted to check in with the other side. She should've been able to get through to her spirit guides. Weird...

Maybe she was just tired. It had been a long evening, and she'd been through a lot. Izzy would try again later once she'd gotten some sleep—if she managed to sleep at all.

Chapter Thirteen

Tristan stepped out of the darkness. His mercury eyes glowed silver as his gaze swept over her. He was naked like the last time she'd seen him and gloriously aroused. Izzy licked her lips and scooted across the bed to make room for him.

"I'm so glad you're okay," she said. "I was worried that you wouldn't be."

"You've been a bad girl, Isabel," he said.

"I'm sorry that I left you," she murmured, meaning it. "I was just freaked out after... I don't expect you to understand. We both knew sleeping together was a mistake."

"You shouldn't have run from me." He stopped next to the bed.

Izzy patted the bed beside her. "If I could take it back, I would."

He smiled, flashing long canines, and took a seat. The bed dipped beneath his weight. "What am I going to do with you?" he asked.

"You can start by holding me," she said, unable to meet his gaze.

"Is that what you truly want?" he asked.

"Yes." Izzy nodded.

Tristan slid into bed beside her and pulled Izzy into his arms. His strength made her feel safe. He ran his hand down the side of her body and kissed her, lingering on her lips until her toes tingled.

"Open for me," he said as he pulled her under him.

Izzy did as he asked. She was so grateful that he was alive that she'd do anything to please him, even if that meant feeling foolish in the morning.

Tristan climbed between her thighs.

Izzy grasped his shoulders as he nudged her entrance.

She felt him swell even more. He'd done that the last time they were together. At the time, Izzy had been too far gone to take notice, but now she was fully aware.

"Is that normal?" she asked.

Tristan smiled. "For me it is." His teeth were even longer now and so sharp they could slice through steel.

"Maybe we should talk first," Izzy said. "I need to explain."

"A minute ago, you told me that you wanted me," Tristan said. "What's the matter, Isabel? Change your mind already?"

There was no warmth in his eyes when Izzy met his gaze. Only the cold stare of a killer.

"You betrayed me, Isabel." Blood began to drip down Tristan's face. "You left me to die," he snarled.

"I'm sorry." Tears welled in Izzy's eyes as blood hit her cheek. She tried to wipe it away, but there was too much.

Blood covered Tristan's white hair and obscured his features. "Do you know what happens to people who betray me and my kind?"

She shook her head.

His lip curled flashing his sharp teeth, then Tristan attacked.

Izzy awoke screaming. Her limbs thrashed as she struggled to get away. She reached for her throat, expecting to find it torn open. It wasn't. Her heart continued to thunder. She scanned the darkness for Tristan, but nothing looked familiar. All she knew for sure was that he was gone.

The door hit the wall, knocking a hole in the plaster. The light from the hallway temporarily blinded her. Stone rushed into the room, carrying a bunch of knives in his hand. By the time Izzy was able to focus, the knives were gone.

"Are you okay?" he asked, frantically searching the room.

"I'm fine," she said, quickly wiping her tears away. "I had a nightmare."

"Is that why you shouted the monster's name?" he asked.

For a second Stone's eyes glowed, but the flash was there and gone so fast that Izzy couldn't be sure her sleep-fogged brain hadn't invented the light.

She didn't remember calling out Tristan's name, but she did remember the horrible dream. "Sorry I woke you," Izzy said.

"You didn't," Stone replied. "Want to talk about it?"

She did, but not with him. Izzy plumped her pillow. "I'm really tired. I think I want to try to go back to sleep."

Stone looked as if he wanted to argue. "Sure," he said instead. "See you in the morning."

The moment he shut the door, Izzy curled into a ball, and hugged herself. She should never have left Tristan. The dream or vision proved it. Now more than ever she needed to know if he was okay. There had to be some way she could find out. Izzy couldn't leave town until she did.

The dream had allowed her to admit a hard truth. The feelings she had for Tristan weren't going away. She'd eventually have to face if she wanted to move on with her life.

In the dream, there'd been so much blood. He had to be all right. "Please be all right," she murmured.

"Izzy, did you say something?" Stone asked from the other side of the closed door.

How had he heard her?

Izzy closed her eyes a second before the door to her bedroom opened. She felt Stone's gaze upon her. Izzy kept her breathing even and didn't move. Her pulse throbbed in her throat, but there wasn't anything she could do about it. He stood in the doorway for what felt like an eternity, before he eventually closed the door.

It wasn't until she heard the click that Izzy released the breath she held.

* * * * *

Tristan groaned and rolled onto his back. He came to with his head pounding and a vague memory of being attacked by the Darkling. He tried to sit up and immediately fell back down. What had the Darkling hit him with, a truck?

He opened his eyes, and the first thing Tristan saw was Pierre's face. The Alpha stood over him with a concerned expression.

"*Mon ami*, I'm so glad you're back with us," he said. "You had me worried." Pierre held out his hand to help Tristan up. "You look like hell, by the way."

"Feel worse." It was a testament to how bad he felt that Tristan accepted the Alpha's assistance. He glanced around the cabin and noticed the darkness outside the window. How long had he been out? "Where's Isabel?" he croaked. The bed was still in disarray from the earlier lovemaking, but her things were gone.

Pierre's expression suddenly blanked. "I am sorry, my friend, but we haven't been able to find her. There were no signs of a struggle," he said. "But my wolves will continue to search."

No signs of a struggle? That would mean that Isabel had left voluntarily. Why would she do such a thing? Tristan thought about how he'd behaved after they'd made love and had a sinking feeling. The Darkling didn't have to take

Isabel. Tristan had driven her away—straight into his enemy's arms.

He swallowed the bile rising in his throat. Its bitterness was nothing compared to the taste of shame. "The Darkling has her."

"Then why aren't you dead?" Pierre asked.

"Good question." Tristan had thought for sure the creature was going to kill him. It had to have been Isabel who saved him. It wasn't in a Darkling's nature to show mercy.

Pierre sniffed. "I don't mean to point out the obvious," he said. "But why does the cabin smell like sex, *mon ami*?"

"I don't have time for this crap," Tristan said.

Pierre grinned. "So you sleep with her. I thought as much," he said. "I just needed confirmation. Had it been the Darkling, you wouldn't be so defensive."

Tristan froze. Until that moment, it hadn't even crossed his mind that the Darkling might take Isabel against her will in that way. At least not until they'd crossed into his realm. He pictured her horrorstruck face and felt his lungs squeeze until he could barely breathe.

Not since he lost his brother had Tristan experienced terror on this level. The unwelcome emotion drove home just how much the little hoyden meant to him.

He rushed across the room and lifted the sheets to his nose. The musky scent of well-loved woman filled his lungs, along with the earthy aroma of Kin. The scent soothed his beast for a moment, but Tristan knew the emotion wouldn't last.

Pierre shook his head and gave him a sad smile. "The fact you are smelling that sheet in your hand proves she means something to you. I hope for your sake we are able to get her back."

Tristan's beast growled. The sound made Pierre and the young wolf who'd just entered the cabin freeze. Tristan felt his control weaken and his other push to the surface.

Pierre's eyes glowed as he faced Tristan. "This will not help," he said. "Get control of yourself."

White fur rippled over Tristan's arms, and claws sprang from his fingertips, as he struggled to cage his beast.

The Alpha growled, and black fur spread over his skin. "I understand what she is to you, even if you're not ready to admit it, but you must keep it together. You won't be able to save her if you don't."

Tristan yanked hard on his beast's leash. It reluctantly gave way, but not before it snapped at him. The fur faded back into his skin and his claws retracted. "Let me just gather my things."

"You might want to put on some clothes," Pierre said. "Can't exactly walk through town like that."

Tristan glanced down. The towel he'd been wearing was lying on the floor where he'd fallen. He shrugged and pulled on a pair of jeans, then grabbed a shirt. Tristan glanced around the cabin. He didn't want to leave, because there was always a chance that Isabel would return, though it was unlikely.

He packed his tote and gathered his weapons. He tucked the sword he'd named Selene into its sheath then glanced at Pierre. "What if—"

"One of my wolves will stay here just in case," he said, cutting Tristan off. "For now, let's head back into town to regroup and recover. You are in no condition to fight tonight."

Tristan hated to admit it, but Pierre was right. He just hoped the Darkling was in bad shape, too. Being near Selene had affected him, but to what degree?

"Can you drive?" Pierre asked.

Tristan scowled at him.

"I had to ask, since I have no idea how long you've been out," Pierre said.

Tristan glanced at the clock and frowned. He'd been out for several hours. That wasn't good. It said a lot about how powerful the Darkling was.

"Why did you come here?" he asked, wondering how Pierre knew he was in trouble.

Pierre hesitated. "I sensed the evil and felt your strength wane."

Tristan's brow furrowed. "How? I'm not one of your wolves."

Pierre grinned. "You don't have to be mine for me to detect you," he said. "You of all people should know that, Enforcer."

Tristan nodded, but the truth was he hadn't known that Pierre could do such a thing. Perhaps the Darkling wasn't the only creature cloaking its powers.

"I'll follow you," he said.

"Do keep up," Pierre said, then headed out the door.

Tristan spent the night tossing and turning at the Alpha's house. Normally when wolves surrounded him he slept well, but tonight sleep evaded him.

He kept picturing Isabel's face as she came apart in his arms. He'd never seen anything so beautiful in his life. He tried not to think about how hurt she'd looked when he'd fled to the bathroom.

Ashamed by his cowardice, Tristan sat up and scrubbed a hand over his face. Where was she? Was she still in this world or had she already slipped into the other? Wherever Isabel was, Tristan wanted her back, wanted to know that she was safe.

He should've taken her blood when he had the chance. If he had, Tristan would be able to track her anywhere. But if he had taken her blood during sex, he would've bound her to him. The thought should've disturbed him, but for some reason it didn't. He wanted to go back to that moment and do what he should've done from the start.

Tristan didn't think Isabel would've appreciated waking up to find herself bound to a werewolf, but that connection would have damn sure come in handy now. New Orleans was a big place, even bigger when you factored in all the parishes outside of the city proper. Then there were the swamps...

He lay back down and closed his eyes. With his Lycanian Elder job, Tristan had accepted long ago that he'd never have a mate. He'd vowed to stay clear of humans after Aidan and Damon had bound them and bred true. Now...well, nothing had really changed.

Even as the thought filtered through Tristan's mind, he knew that it wasn't true. He'd give his life to get Isabel back safely. If that Darkling was as powerful as he suspected, that might be what it took.

Chapter Fourteen

Izzy awoke to the sounds of birds chirping and a shower running. She turned over, expecting to see the cabin. Instead, she came face to face with a popular princess.

She pushed the covers away and glanced around. It took her a moment to remember where she was and how she got there. As soon as she did, her hopes fell.

Izzy had never been one for regrets, but when it came to Tristan Chevalier, she had more than a few. She wondered again if he was okay. There was no way of knowing for sure. The dream flashed in her mind. It had been horrific, but at least he'd been alive. Izzy clung to that aspect. She had to. It was either that or fall apart.

She threw the covers back and rolled out of bed. Izzy listened for the shower. It was still going, so she slipped out of the room. She found a pot of coffee sitting next to the stove.

For one crazy minute, Izzy considered stealing Stone's car, but she didn't think she could take it and get away before he caught up with her. She still had the phone he'd given her. Her best bet was to call Everly.

Izzy poured herself a cup of coffee and walked to the

back door. A small porch had been attached to the rear of the house. The screened-in area held a couple of chairs and a small table. She turned the knob, expecting to find it locked, but the door opened.

She glanced down the hall, but the bathroom door remained closed and the water continued to run. Izzy stepped out onto the porch and shut the door behind her. She'd just pulled the phone out of her pocket when the breeze shifted and the stench hit her.

Izzy gagged. She'd forgotten all about the dead alligator. She blindly reached for the doorknob to go back inside, but an inner voice told her to stop. Izzy always listened to those voices. They rarely steered her wrong.

She peered into the yard. Like the front lawn, the back was well cared for and lined with flowerbeds. Other than a few birds, she didn't spot any movement. She'd never seen an alligator up close.

Curiosity got the best of her. Izzy shoved the phone into her pocket and put her coffee down on one of the chairs. She glanced back at the door and listened for footsteps, but didn't hear anything.

Izzy pushed the screen door open and took the two stairs down into the yard. The odor was stronger now. She checked to make sure the stench hadn't attracted more alligators.

She didn't see anything, but that didn't mean they weren't there. They were masters at hiding in plain sight.

Her inner voice urged her forward. The odor made her eyes water, but she kept going. When she neared the shed, her instincts screamed at her to stop. Izzy hesitated, but it was too late to turn back now. She was outside the door.

The tin structure was no more than ten by twenty in size. Rust covered the sides of two walls, thanks to the high humidity. The door to the shed was the kind that slid open. It would make a horrendous noise the second she touched it, alerting Stone.

Izzy stared at the door, studying it for what felt like an

eternity. "Just open it," she muttered under her breath. "It's just the alligator." Why was her heart pounding? Why was she hesitating? Was it because Stone had told her to stay out of the backyard? Or was something else directing her?

She glanced one last time at the house. There was no sign of Stone, but he had to be done with his shower by now. Would he think that she was still asleep? He'd know she wasn't when she opened the door.

Izzy took a deep breath and grabbed the handle. The door screeched as she wrenched it aside. The shed's interior was dark. Sunlight barely penetrated the glom. Izzy waited for her eyes to adjust then scanned the space.

At first, all she spotted were tools for doing lawn work. She didn't see an alligator or anything else that would explain the gut-kicking, nausea-creating stench.

She looked again. The second time, she spotted a lump on the floor. The pile was too small to be an alligator and too large to be rags. It took a moment for Izzy's brain to register what her eyes were showing it. When it did, bile rose in her throat, choking her. She took one step back and vomited, then like a driver passing a bad car accident, Izzy looked again.

The woman's esophagus had been ripped out, and scratches covered the front of her body, leaving deep furrows in her clothes and flesh. Beside her was a smaller mass.

"No," she murmured. "Please no."

But her denial didn't change the facts. The smaller bundle resembled the little girl she'd seen in the photographs—or what was left of her. She'd been wrapped in a pink blanket, but the cloth didn't conceal the fact that half of her body was missing.

Not missing, Izzy thought. *Eaten. She'd been eaten.*

Izzy backed out of the shed and collided with a hard chest. Her legs nearly collapsed beneath her, and she let out a loud scream that was cut off by Stone's hand.

"You've been a bad girl, Izzy," he said. "I told you to stay out of the backyard. You should've listened."

Pain knifed through Izzy's chest, and she couldn't seem to breathe. She gasped and gasped until Stone grabbed her by the neck and led her to the middle of the yard.

The second he stopped, Izzy dropped to her knees. "What have you done?"

"What do you mean?" he asked, sounding genuinely perplexed.

"Stone, you need help. Serious help," she said. "This woman and her child weren't a threat." Had he somehow mistaken these two for werewolves? If so, he was further gone than she'd anticipated. "Why did you kill them?"

"I got hungry waiting for you," he said so matter-of-factly that it took Izzy a moment to comprehend.

"What?" Izzy glanced up at him. She couldn't have heard him correctly.

"Don't knock human flesh until you try it, Izzy," he said. "It's quite tasty, especially the young ones. They're tender and sweet." Stone stepped around her until he stood near her head. "I offered you some last night, but you were too good share a meal with me."

Izzy gulped. "That's what was cooking in the pot? A child?" Her stomach lurched, and she vomited again.

"You make me sound like I'm a monster," he said, his disgust evident.

"If you're capable of doing that to a defenseless woman and her child, then you are," she said, wiping her mouth with the back of her hand.

Stone glared at her. "You have no idea what I'm capable of," he said softly. "You'll change your tune once we get to my home."

Izzy staggered to her feet. "You said you lived here."

His lip curled. "You know I don't. I believe that's obvious now." He glanced over her shoulder toward the bodies. "I wouldn't live in this world if you paid me."

Her mouth watered and she swallowed hard, fighting the urge to throw up again. "This world? What are you talking about? Stone, let me get you help."

"You're not very bright," he said. "Doesn't really matter. I didn't fetch you for your brains. As long as your other parts are working, that's all that matters to my people."

Izzy scrambled back, searching for a way to escape. "What do you mean by *your* people?"

"Don't bother trying to run," Stone said. "I will catch you. I'm very fast, when I need to be."

Cold enveloped her, until Izzy felt oddly calm inside. It was the kind of calm that came when someone knew they were going to die and accepted the fact. "What do you plan to do with me?"

"I told you," he said. "I'm taking you to my world."

His words finally registered. "You're the Darkling that Tristan has been hunting," she said.

Stone laughed. "Finally she gets it."

Izzy shook her head. "You said you were like me."

"I lied," he said.

"But that doesn't make sense," she said.

"Why?"

"Because I can detect evil and see hidden beasts," she said. "It's part of my gift. You should've set off my internal alarms the second I got close to you."

"Ah, yes, your gift." Stone glanced around the yard. "I'm sure the fact that my magic is stronger than your 'gift' is unsettling. It's always a tough lesson to learn that your power isn't as strong as you thought it was. Don't feel too bad. Soon all humans will know that they are not the be all and end all of existence."

"What does that mean?" Izzy asked.

"It means we're coming," he said. "Soon this world and the women in it will be ours."

"You're insane." She took another step back. "Tristan is going to come for you," she said.

"I'm sure he will if he's still alive. I hit him pretty hard. Thanks again for helping me get close to him," Stone said.

Guilt over what she'd done swamped her. Izzy had been so stupid.

"By the time Tristan recovers, you and I will be long gone." He glanced up at the bright morning sky and winced. "You should probably enjoy the sunshine while you can. It doesn't exist where we're going."

The thought of living in constant darkness terrified her. Izzy would rather die than be trapped somewhere like that.

Stone sighed. "I know what you're thinking."

Did he or was this another lie? "You can read my mind." Izzy tried to clear her thoughts.

"I don't need to be able to read your mind. The look on your face told me that you were thinking about doing something stupid," he said. "Don't! Or I'll have to tie you up for the rest of the day."

"We're not leaving right now," she said. There was still time for her to escape. Izzy made sure her hope didn't show.

"No." Stone shook his head. "We'll leave tonight as planned." He took a step toward her.

She skittered back.

"Izzy, I may not have read your mind a minute ago, but that doesn't mean that I can't," Stone said. "Try to keep that in mind as you make your escape plans. Now come along. Looks like I'll have to tie you up after all."

"No," she said. "I won't go with you. There has to be someone in this neighborhood that will help me."

"The people in this neighborhood learned a long time ago to mind their own business and only count on themselves when there's trouble," he said. "You can scream if you want, but know this: if someone does come to your rescue, I'll kill them. Their death will be on your head. Do we understand each other?"

All too well, she thought. Izzy couldn't endanger anyone else. Stone had already proven that he could kill without remorse. One more death wouldn't matter.

He waited for her to answer.

"Yes," she said reluctantly.

"Good," Stone said. "Now come inside like a good little breeder and let me tie you up."

"What if I promise not to try to escape?" she asked.

Stone smiled at her. "We both know that would be a lie."

* * * * *

Tristan shifted into his wolf. He hadn't gotten much sleep, certainly not enough to recover from his injuries, but the shift would change all that.

Within seconds, he was back in his human form and heading to the shower. He stepped under the spray, and memories from the last time he'd been in the shower returned.

Tristan had been hiding from Isabel, unable to face her and the emotions she'd dredged up after they'd made love. At least now he accepted the fact that they had made love. As much as he wished otherwise, it wasn't just sex.

If only he hadn't run away, then none of this would've happened. Guilt assailed him. It joined the weight he carried from the past. Tristan couldn't do anything about those mistakes, but he could affect the future. At least he hoped he could.

Tristan closed his eyes and pictured Isabel lying on the bed, her multi-colored hair spread out around her head. Her lips had been swollen from his kisses, and she'd had the sleepy-eyed expression of a woman well loved. The satisfied expression vanished, the second he ran into the bathroom.

He ducked his head under the water, hoping it would wash away some of the regrets, but water was only so strong. It didn't have the power to cleanse one's soul.

Tristan hurried through his shower. He was done hiding from life. It was time to accept both the pain and the pleasure that came with this existence. He just hoped he had another chance to feel some of that pleasure with Isabel before it all ended.

The moment Tristan stepped out of the bathroom, he encountered Pierre's assistant. "The Alpha has issued an invitation for you to join him for breakfast in the sunroom," he said.

"I'll be right down," Tristan said.

Five minutes later, Tristan sat across from Pierre La Fontaine as the Alpha's hired help served them breakfast in the enclosed veranda.

Ceiling fans churned the air lazily over a small four-seater table. It was set for two, letting Tristan know that the Alpha wanted this to be a private conversation.

Pierre waited for the staff to load up the plates in front of them and pour the coffees. "Feeling better?" he asked, after the staff exited the room and shut the door behind them.

Tristan shrugged. "I'm fit enough to take care of what needs to be done."

"For your sake, I hope so. What do you plan to do?" Pierre asked, taking a bite of blood sausage. Like most Weres, the Alpha preferred a high protein diet.

Tristan took a sip of his coffee. A hint of chicory hit his palate, and he nearly groaned in ecstasy. This town could do coffee. He'd give them that.

"I'm going after them," he said. He owed the Darkling for hitting him upside the head and nearly crushing his skull.

"That's a given," Pierre said, then took another bite. "What I want to know is where are you going to start your hunt?"

Tristan thought about it. He had to narrow the search area down. If he didn't, he'd never find them in time. If the Darkling managed to drag Isabel into his world, then there'd be no getting her back. The spot in the center of his chest throbbed. He rubbed it absently.

Pierre watched him but said nothing.

"When I first met Isabel, she hung out with a friend in Jackson Square," Tristan said. "The woman is also a Sighted-One."

Pierre's eyebrows shot to his dark hairline. "Why didn't you tell me? I could've had her picked up or at least watched."

"I've had my hands full," Tristan said.

The Alpha grinned. "Yes, you have."

Tristan growled.

"Knock it off," Pierre said. "Does the Darkling know about Isabel's friend?"

"I don't know," he said. "It depends on how long he's been stalking her. He didn't strike me as being very patient."

Pierre sat forward. "We can't let him get his hands on another Sighted-One."

"I agree," Tristan said. "But I don't think it's smart to grab Everly. If she's able, I do think Isabel will try to contact her. I need her to be there to get that call."

"That's a huge risk you're taking," Pierre said.

"I know," Tristan said.

"What if she leaves town?"

He shook his head. "Everly's not going anywhere. Isabel tried to warn her to get out of town, but she refused to leave."

Tristan pictured Everly. The fiery Goth with a Moonlight Kin skull in her house was hardheaded like Isabel, but she was also loyal. If it were possible, Everly would be the first person Isabel contacted. What if Isabel was injured and wasn't able to contact her? He couldn't think about that or he'd go insane.

"I don't like the idea of another Sighted-One running around town unprotected," Pierre said.

Tristan picked up his fork and played with his food. "I don't either," he said. "But Everly is stubborn."

"You said the same thing about your human," Pierre said.

"She's not *my* human," Tristan replied.

"The sheets in the cabin say otherwise," he said.

Tristan ignored the Alpha's bait. "Even if Isabel hasn't been in contact with her, Everly still might be able to help. From what I've seen, her gift is quite powerful. Possibly more powerful than Isabel's," he said. "Putting your wolves on her won't do any good. She'd know they were there. Everly has power objects in her home. Things that protect her and mask her presence."

"What kind of power objects?" Pierre put his fork down.

"It's not important," Tristan said. He needed Pierre's cooperation. If the Alpha found out about the skull, he'd pull his assistance and scoop up Everly immediately.

"Let me decide what is and is not important in my territory," Pierre said.

"I'll be more than happy to have this discussion once we get Isabel back," he said, letting his frustration show.

"I will not forget."

"You never do," Tristan muttered.

Pierre picked up his coffee cup and took a drink. "What makes you think Everly would help you?"

"She wouldn't, if it was just me asking," Tristan said. "But she'd definitely help Isabel. Of that I am certain."

Pierre sighed. "What can I do to help?"

"Have your wolves continue their search for Isabel's scent, but if they haven't found it by this evening, then call them in," Tristan said. "The Darkling will make his move tonight. That's when he's most powerful."

"Do you think you can take him?" Pierre asked, setting his cup down.

Tristan had the utmost confidence in his abilities, but he'd never encountered a being as powerful as this Darkling. He wasn't sure if he could beat him in a fight, even with his sword, Selene. "I may not be able to take him, but I will stop him. One way or the other."

Pierre's lips twitched. "Do me a favor," he said.

"What's that?" Tristan asked.

"Try not to get yourself killed," he said.

Tristan laughed. "I'll do my best."

"When are you going to approach the other Sighted-One?" he asked.

Tristan glanced at a clock on the wall. "Not for a few more hours. From what I gathered, she likes to stay out all night with the wannabe vampires."

Pierre's brow furrowed. "The what?"

Tristan picked up a piece of bacon and popped it in his mouth. "You know, the people who put in fake fangs and pretend to drink blood."

"This is a friend of Isabel's?" Pierre asked, his disgust evident from his expression.

"Yes," Tristan said. "Everly's definitely odd, but her concern for her friend is real."

Pierre dabbed the side of his mouth with his napkin. "I hope you know what you're doing," he said.

Tristan did too.

CHAPTER FIFTEEN

Izzy pulled against the extension cord Stone had bound her with, trying to break it. She only succeeded in cutting off her circulation. He'd tied her up in the little girl's room, so she had a constant reminder of what sat out in the shed.

The sun moved across the sky fast. It was only a matter of time before he came for her to take her to his realm. She had to get out of here. Izzy yanked, and pain shot through her wrists.

She wondered where Tristan was. Wondered if he was even alive. Stone had thanked her for helping him. Izzy's head dropped back and hit the wall with a *thunk*. How could she have been so stupid?

If Tristan was alive, the chances of him forgiving her were slim to none. She might not have helped attack him, but she had been in contact with Stone the whole time.

Please be alive...if for no other reason than to avenge me.

Izzy yanked at the cord again. It stretched, but held. Stone would have to untie her when he moved her. Wouldn't he? What if he didn't? Izzy needed to have her hands free in order to fight.

He's a werewolf, a little voice reminded her.

No, he was something far worse than the creatures she'd encountered over the years. Izzy racked her brain trying to remember what Tristan had told her about Darklings. Unfortunately, it wasn't much because she hadn't wanted to listen.

She had to think. There had to be a way out of this situation. She wasn't a damsel in distress. Okay, maybe she was, but there was no way Izzy would let him drag her anywhere. She'd rather die. At least if they found her body, her sister Mindy would know what happened to her.

The door opened. Stone stepped into the room holding... Izzy squinted. Was that a sandwich?

She thought about the little girl in the shed, and her stomach twisted. "I'm not hungry," she said.

"You have to eat something," he said. "The crossing is rough on the body. It's especially difficult for humans. Don't want you dying before you get there."

"Perhaps you didn't hear me. I said I wasn't hungry," she said. "I'll never be hungry enough to eat a child. Now get that away from me."

Stone scowled at her. "It's peanut butter and jelly." He walked into the room and placed the sandwich on the small dresser, then sat beside her on the bed.

Izzy scooted as far away from him as her bindings allowed.

"You have a choice here. You can either eat this sandwich on your own, or I'm going to hold your smart mouth open and force-feed it to you. Either way, you're going to eat."

"I can't eat with my hands tied." Izzy held her hands up for emphasis. "I can't even feel my fingers anymore."

Stone glanced at her hands, which were turning blue. "You shouldn't have been pulling on the cord," he said.

Izzy just stared at him.

"Fine," he said. "I'll untie you, but if you try to get away I'll make sure you can't move at all next time." Stone ran his finger down the side of her thigh.

She jerked her leg away. His touch made her skin crawl. "I need to use the bathroom," Izzy said.

Stone untied her and waited for her to climb off the bed. He walked her into the hall to the bathroom and pushed the door open.

"Go ahead," he said.

"I can't go while you're looking," she said.

"Then you mustn't have to go very bad," Stone said.

Izzy grimaced. She did have to go bad. She'd been holding it for over an hour. No way was she leaving this bathroom without relieving herself.

"Can you at least turn your back?" she asked.

Stone rolled his eyes. "Humans," he said. "You all have so many needless quirks."

"Humor me," she said.

"Fine." Stone turned his back. "But this is another thing you'll need to get over when we reach my realm."

Izzy kept an eye on him while she quickly relieved herself. She did not want him looking at her. Just the thought of him seeing her naked made her physically ill. There was no way she could let him take her to his world. Death was far preferable to whatever Stone had planned.

She had always assumed that *all* monsters operated like Stone. Then she'd met Tristan and her opinion changed. Izzy laughed to herself. Her opinion had more than changed. It had done a one-eighty. She'd gone from fleeing from the monsters to sleeping with them, except...Tristan wasn't a monster. Stone was.

She stared at his back. Izzy had hoped Stone would give her a moment of privacy so she could use her cellphone, but he'd been too smart for that. She washed her hands, then took a quick sip of water to ease her dry throat.

"All done," she said.

"Good," Stone said. "Now eat. I won't ask you again."

He walked her back into the bedroom and took a seat at

the child's desk. Izzy sniffed the sandwich and lifted the bread to examine it.

Stone swore. "It's just peanut butter and jelly. For goddess' sake, just eat it!"

Izzy jumped at his raised voice. She took a tentative bite of the sandwich. It tasted normal, but that didn't mean he hadn't put something in it. *Please don't let it be ground-up little girl.*

Her stomach gurgled.

"Keep eating." Stone kept a close eye on her.

"Why are you doing this?" she asked.

"I told you. You're needed in my realm," he said.

"What's so special about my gift that you have to kidnap me for it?" she asked, taking another bite. Izzy would kill for a glass of milk, but she wasn't about to ask him for anything.

Stone stared at her for so long that she thought for sure he wasn't going to answer. "Nothing," he said.

Nothing? Not the answer she'd been expecting. "Then I don't understand why you went to so much trouble to get me." She set the sandwich down.

"Your gift is necessary, but not needed," Stone said cryptically.

"I don't understand," Izzy said.

"Don't expect you to," he said. "Now eat."

Izzy picked up the sandwich and took another bite. At least her stomach began to settle, though for how long was anyone's guess.

"You said earlier that it wasn't important that I be able to think quickly," she said.

Stone grinned. "That's right."

"Why?" she asked.

"Because you are only needed for breeding."

Izzy dropped the sandwich onto the plate. Her throat worked convulsively as she fought to keep the contents down. The plan was to breed her to monsters like himself.

She shook her head in denial, but Izzy knew from his

pleased expression that Stone told the truth.

"I'm going to be sick." She jumped up off the bed and raced past him. Izzy barely made it to the toilet before she threw up her peanut butter and jelly sandwich.

She heaved and heaved until there was nothing left to expel. Izzy pushed off the toilet seat and grabbed onto the sink to pull herself up.

She glanced in the mirror. The color had bled from her face, leaving her pasty. Izzy splashed water on her face and rinsed her mouth.

Stone stood in the doorway, holding another sandwich. Had he made two? Or had he gone and made another one while she threw up?

Izzy glared at him. "I hope you don't expect me to eat that. Right now I can't keep anything down."

He simply stared at her as if she hadn't spoken.

"Did you hear me?" Izzy sneered.

Stone arched a brow. "Every word. Did you hear me?" He held the plate out to her. "The choice is yours."

Izzy snatched the plate out his hands. "You're an asshole."

Stone had her around the neck before Izzy blinked. The plate dropped onto the bathroom floor a second before he slammed her against the wall.

"I've had about enough of your mouth," he said. "I overlooked the fact that you spread your thighs for that monster. The only reason I didn't rip your womb out was because it's needed, but your tongue isn't." Stone squeezed, cutting off her air.

Izzy clawed at his hand, but he only squeezed harder. She choked, and black dots appeared before her eyes.

"Now you're going to pick that sandwich up and you're going to eat it all, then I'm going to tie you to the bed until we need to leave," he hissed. "Don't worry. It won't be long. Nod if you understand me."

She tried to move her head but couldn't.

His grip on her eased a fraction.

Izzy sucked in much-needed air.

"One word, one whisper, and I will rip your tongue out and eat it," Stone said. "Got it?"

Izzy nodded.

Stone released her.

She fell to her knees.

"Pick it up." Stone pointed to the sandwich.

Izzy's hands shook as she scooped the sandwich up and placed it back on the plate.

"Good girl," he said. "Now get up."

She staggered to her feet. Izzy caught sight of her reflection a moment before he shoved her out the door. Finger marks ringed her neck.

Izzy didn't fight when Stone tied her up. There'd be no escape—at least not alive. He hadn't meant to, but Stone had given her a weapon to use against him. Now all Izzy had to do was get him mad enough to kill her. Given her track record with the monsters, that shouldn't be too hard.

* * * * *

The door opened at three-thirty. Tristan had been debating whether to leave, when he heard the footsteps drawing nearer. Hope soared until he realized there was only one set. The key clicked in the lock, and the door swung open. Everly stepped into the living room.

"Where have you been?" he asked.

Everly yelped and pressed a hand to her throat. "What are you doing in my apartment?" she asked, her charcoal-lined eyes narrowing on him. "How did you get in?"

"The new door wasn't that strong." He glanced at the crack he'd left in it.

She scowled when she saw the damage to the door. "You're going to pay for that. Now what are you doing here?" She glanced around the space. "Where is Izzy?"

"She's the reason I'm here," Tristan said. "Have you heard from her?"

"What's happened?" she asked, ignoring his question.

"Nothing yet," he said, but that wouldn't be the case for long.

Everly pushed the door closed and walked deeper into the room. "Are you alone?"

"Yes." Tristan didn't tell her that the wolves already knew all about her. That would come later. Right now, he didn't want to spook her. "Have you heard from Isabel?"

Everly stared at him for the longest time then sighed. "No," she said. "I haven't spoken to her since I saw you guys in the square." She threw her bag down and took a seat across from him.

Tristan tried to hide his disappointment, but he mustn't have been too successful.

"What's happened to her?" Everly asked. "I thought you were protecting her."

He was supposed to be, but that hadn't worked out well. If he lost her for good, he'd live with the regret for the rest of his life.

"The evil that came to town has her," he said.

Everly didn't say anything. She zoned out for a moment, then her attention snapped back to him. "I can't sense her," she said, her voice thick with emotion.

"Does that mean she's dead?" Tristan's chest tightened to the point of pain. For a moment, he couldn't breathe, as Isabel's face and his brother's blurred together in his mind.

She shook her head. "I don't think so," Everly said. "I think she's on the other side of the river. Water mutes my powers."

Good to know, he thought, but he needed concrete info to find her.

"Tell me about this evil," she said.

Tristan wasn't sure how much he should say to her.

Everly's dark eyes narrowed. "Don't even think about

lying, even by omission. The more I know about it, the more I can help."

"The thing is like my people, but not," he said cryptically. "Everyone and everything has a shadow side. Our shadow side doesn't live in this realm. It exists in another dimension."

"Okay," she said, her brow furrowing as she listened carefully.

"The Darklings—that's what we call them—can cross into this realm. When they do, they bring death and madness in their wake," he said.

Everly's lips pursed. "Is that why I couldn't pinpoint its location?"

"Perhaps," Tristan said. "They have powerful magic behind them. Magic that comes from their dark world."

"Magic? That shouldn't have mattered with me." She kicked off her boots and curled her feet beneath her. "Are they werewolves, or are they sorcerers?"

Tristan sat forward. "They're a bit of both. They use magic, but they shift into a wolf form."

"What does this thing want with Isabel?" she asked.

"Isabel isn't the only one it's after." He gave her a pointed stare.

Everly's eyes widened, and she gulped. "So what does this thing want with me and Isabel?"

Tristan shook his head. "Again, it's not just you two it's after. It's all women like you."

She frowned. "Like us?"

"Sighted-Ones," he said trying to be patient while his beast raged inside him. "The Darklings need women like you."

"Need us for what?" she asked.

She already knew the answer to the question, but she obviously needed to hear it said aloud.

"They want you for breeding purposes," he said. Tristan gripped the side of the chair until he heard the wood groan, then forced his fingers to ease. "They can only mate with Sighted-Ones. Normal women go mad if they're scratched or bitten by them, then they eventually die."

"What happens to a woman if one of these things takes her into their world?" she asked.

"Nothing, other than the obvious, if she's truly Sighted," he said.

"Lovely," she said. "How long has this thing had her?"

Tristan tensed. "He's had her since yesterday."

Everly shot out of her chair. "And you're just coming to me now?"

She had every right to be angry. He was angry, too. Tristan had failed Isabel when she needed him most. He snarled. No, he'd failed her before then.

"The Darkling tried to crush my skull in," he said. "And nearly succeeded. I have no idea why I'm alive, but I assume it's because of Isabel."

Everly put her hands on her hips. "So she saved you, but you couldn't save her."

That about summed it up, though there were extenuating circumstances.

Tristan ran a hand through his hair and scrubbed it over his face. Despite the shift, his head was still sore.

"Have you slept?" she asked, losing some of her fury.

"Not much," he said.

Everly sat back down. "What can I do?"

"I need you to use your gift to try to locate her," he said. "If that fails, I need you to let me know if you hear from her. I doubt the Darkling will simply let her call, but knowing Isabel, she'll wiggle out of his grasp. At least for a short while."

She watched him closely. "You love her, don't you?"

Tristan stiffened in his seat. "Don't be ridiculous."

"You're awful quick to deny it," she said. "But if you don't love her, then why go to so much trouble to find her?"

Because he didn't want Isabel to suffer in the Darkling

world. Because he couldn't imagine never getting to see her again, even if it was from afar. Because she was his, and the Darkling had taken her from him.

"It's my job," Tristan said.

Everly smirked. "Liar. Didn't look like you were doing your job when I saw you guys in Jackson Square," she said.

"I was," he said.

She snorted. "You're not that good of an actor. You care for her."

"You don't know what you're talking about," he said.

"Actually, I do," Everly said. "You forget I had a vision about you guys, and there was a whole lot more going on than just encountering evil."

Tristan's jaw clenched. "Visions can be wrong."

"So you haven't slept with her?" Everly asked.

Heat spread across Tristan's face, and his gaze dropped.

Everly grinned. "That's what I thought. Job, my ass. You like her."

"Will you help me if I say I do?" He'd tell her anything to get her cooperation.

"No." She shook her dark head. "But I will help Isabel."

"Can you try to find her?" he asked.

Everly nodded and closed her eyes. She took several deep breaths, then the muscles in her face relaxed. Minutes passed, and nothing happened.

Tristan tried to be patient, but every minute that went by brought Isabel closer to being taken into the other realm. There was a slim chance that the Darkling had already crossed her over, but it was more likely he'd need time to heal from his injury.

Just the thought that she might be gone forever made his beast howl in agony.

What if this didn't work? What if he was too late?

Everly's eyes popped open. "What I'm seeing doesn't make any sense," she said.

"Tell me everything," he said. No clue was too small.

"I saw flashes of a child. She had fair hair like Isabel and held a stuffed bear," she said. "Like I told you, it doesn't make sense."

A child that looked like Isabel... It wasn't hard for Tristan to imagine such a thing. In fact, it was far too easy.

"Did you see anything else? Anything at all?" he asked.

"Destruction and water, but it could be anywhere in New Orleans. I'm sorry," she said. "If I get anything else, I'll let you know."

"Thanks for trying." Tristan rose. "I need you to do one more thing for me." He grabbed the sheath that held Selene and tucked the lodestone in the side of it.

Everly's eyes widened when she saw the sword, and she jumped off the beanbag. "I won't tell anyone, I swear," she said. "Please don't kill me."

Tristan glanced at the sword in his hand and frowned. "What are you talking about?"

She stopped inching toward the front door. "You're not going to kill me because I know too much?"

He grimaced. "No," Tristan said. "I was going to ask you to hold this until I shift into my other form. Once I do, I need you to tie it around my neck."

"Oh." She sounded oddly disappointed.

Tristan shook his head. Everly was a strange woman.

"Don't you think you'll attract too much attention in your other form?" she asked. "I know this is New Orleans, but even here a wolf running through town with a sword around his neck is bound to raise a few eyebrows."

"No doubt," he said, "but I have no choice. I need my other senses to find the Darkling. If by chance Isabel phones you, please call this number." Tristan pulled a business card out of his wallet and handed it to her.

Everly's eyes widened when she saw the name on the card.

"I take it you know Pierre La Fontaine," he said.

"Know him personally?" She shook her head. "No. But I

do know of him."

"He'll know how to find me," Tristan said. "What you're about to see isn't something the Moonlight Kin share with humans. I'd appreciate it if you'd keep it to yourself."

Everly nodded and took a step back.

Fur rippled over Tristan's arms, and claws extended from his fingertips. He dropped to his knees, and his vision faded before quickly snapping back into the place.

In his beast form, the scents in Everly's house were even stronger, especially the scent of death. He glanced over his shoulder at the Moonlight Kin skull on the bookshelf.

Everly followed his gaze and hurried over to cover it with a cloth. "Don't move," she said. Her fingers shook as she slipped the sheath over his head then put the sword inside it. "Do you need me to open the door?"

Tristan barked.

She flinched but hurried to the door and opened it.

He was about to step through when she blocked his exit. Tristan growled.

Everly thumped him on the head. "Knock it off," she said.

Shocked by her actions, Tristan didn't do anything for a moment. Then his gaze rose, though not very far since they were close to eye level in this form.

"Save my friend," Everly said. "I know you love her, even if *you* don't know you love her."

Fortunately, Tristan couldn't speak in this form. He had vocal capabilities if he performed a partial shift, but not a full one. For once he was grateful for that fact, since he wasn't sure what he'd say.

He barked at her again.

This time Everly stepped aside and let him leave. Tristan raced out the back door, hitting the screen with his shoulder. The world around him came alive, but the one scent he wanted to smell more than any other remained elusive.

Tristan weaved his way through the side streets, avoiding

the more touristy areas, but it would take a while to make his way out of town.

Every mile or so Tristan would glance down to see if the lodestone glowed. At one point the lodestone did, but the magic stopped abruptly. The water from the lakes and rivers dampened the signal just like it had Everly's gift.

Tristan tried to ignore the sun's rapid descent. He raised his head and sniffed the air. *Where are you?* He couldn't lose Isabel. He didn't think he'd survive another loss of that magnitude.

Chapter Sixteen

Stone came for Izzy as the sun dipped below the trees. It wasn't dark yet, but it would be soon. He pulled out a knife and cut through the extension cord binding her hands.

"Time to go," he said.

Izzy clenched her hands to get feeling back into her fingers. She'd need to be able to use her limbs if she stood any chance of escaping. She rolled off the bed.

"Grab your things and anything else you might want from this realm," he said. "We don't have the same things in our world."

"What do you have there?" she asked.

"You'll see." Stone grinned.

Izzy didn't want anything from this house. The place held nothing but death. She grabbed her tote and threw it over her shoulder.

Stone stood in the doorway and waited for her to exit. They reached the front door. There was a gas can sitting on the side table next to the couch. He grabbed it and began to slosh the contents all over the house.

Izzy grabbed his arm. "What are you doing?"

"Getting rid of the evidence, unless you want your

fingerprints found at a crime scene," he said.

"What if they had family?" Izzy asked. "This might be all the family has left to hold onto."

Stone shrugged. "I'm sure you're trying to make a point of some kind, but it doesn't change what I need to do." He went back to pouring the gas around the house.

The sick feeling returned. Izzy clutched her stomach. Somewhere a family missed their daughter and granddaughter. After today, a father would never see his daughter again.

She turned and rushed out the door. Stone was on her before she'd made it across the lawn.

"Where are you going, Isabel?" he asked, blocking her escape.

"Anywhere!" she snapped. "As long as it's away from you." Izzy caught the odor of smoke a second before she saw the flames rise.

"Get in the car," Stone said. "We don't want to be here when the fire department arrives."

Stone drove her in the same direction as the cabin she'd stayed at with Tristan. Izzy saw the exit for Jean Lafitte Park and was surprised when Stone took it.

If Tristan was alive, would he still be in the area? Izzy's mind raced with ways she could contact him.

Frosty, where are you?? she thought. *I need you.*

Stone didn't take the road toward the cabin. Instead, he continued on until they arrived at a swamp tour boat dock. He pulled his car to the end of the road and parked.

"We'll have to walk from here," he said.

The trees leading into the swamp were thick with undergrowth. All kinds of things could be hiding in those weeds. Was it too much to hope that an alligator got Stone?

Izzy glanced at him. He'd probably kill it and eat it. As she lifted her tote, it hit the cellphone in her pocket. She needed to call Everly. Heck, she needed to phone Mindy and say goodbye.

"This way," Stone said, walking toward a fallen tree that concealed a rugged path.

She followed, but Izzy continued to search for a way to escape. She wondered if werewolves were afraid of the water like cats. If so, she would take her chances with the gators.

Even as the thought slipped through her mind, Izzy heard something large splash in the water. She stared at the murky inlet that ran along the path.

"Don't worry," Stone said. "I won't let it get you."

"Being gator bait is preferable to what you have in mind for me," she said.

He laughed. "I won't be one of the ones vying for you," Stone said.

"Good!" she said.

Stone smiled. "You might wish that I was by the time the breeding challenge is over."

Izzy stumbled on a root. "Breeding challenge?"

"Yeah." Stone ran a hand through his short black hair. "When an eligible female arrives in our world, males come from all around to see who can breed her. They each get a shot at the woman until one of them succeeds in impregnating her. The last woman had to endure forty warriors before she was with child." He shrugged. "Nearly killed her. With any luck, it'll take you a hundred."

Izzy's stomach gurgled. She had just enough time to step off the path before she vomited onto the leaves of a plant.

"Not this again," he said as if the whole thing bored him. "You're only delaying the inevitable."

She threw up again then rubbed her mouth with the back of her sleeve.

Stone grabbed a water bottle out of his small tote and handed it to her. "Rinse your mouth. I don't want to have to smell that, too. You already smell *funny*."

She swished water in her mouth then dug into her tote for a mint. She popped it onto her tongue. With any luck, she'd choke on it.

Izzy knew she needed a shower. He didn't have to point it out. "I don't stink," she said affronted.

"Yes, you do," he said. "You smell like that wolf."

She couldn't smell anything, but it made Izzy unduly pleased that Stone thought she smelled like Tristan.

They continued down the trail until they reached a small clearing. At first, Izzy thought the clearing was natural. Once they got closer it was obvious that someone had cleared the area. What wasn't so obvious was how, since none of the trees were cut.

The area reminded Izzy of the crop circle photos she'd seen online. It wasn't as elegant, but there were striking similarities. Did that mean that Darklings were showing up around the world? The people hoping for aliens were going to be very disappointed if that were the case.

Stone pulled out a weird sphere from his bag. He placed it in the center of the clearing and stepped back. "This will take a little while."

"Take your time," she said. "I'm not in a hurry."

The shadows lengthened around them and her heart sank. Tristan wasn't coming. No one was. She was on her own, and she had no one to blame but herself.

"Since we have time, can I call my sister and my friend to say goodbye?" she asked.

"Sure," Stone said. "But if you say anything to warn them, I'll come back to kill Mindy and your friend. Do you understand?"

Izzy frowned. "You know my sister?" The idea terrified her.

"How do you think I found you?" he asked. "I could've killed her anytime, and would have had I known she wasn't a Sighted-One."

She shuddered at how close Mindy had come to dying. Izzy had to do something to protect her. "I'll come with you willingly if you swear to leave my sister alone."

Stone's brow arched in surprise. "Really?"

"Yes," Izzy said. "I want your word."

He laughed. "Sure."

"No, I mean it," Izzy said, advancing on him.

"I swear I won't touch Mindy," he said. Stone didn't bother to mention that it would be difficult to get to her now that she'd mated with one of the wolves.

Izzy studied his face. "Okay."

Stone chuckled at how gullible she was. Izzy pulled out the phone he'd given her and punched in a number. He heard voicemail pick up.

She deflated before his eyes. "Hey, Mindy, it's me. I just wanted to tell you..." She sighed. "I just wanted to say that I love you very much, and I hope you have a long and happy life." Izzy choked on a sob. "I've got to go. Take care of yourself." She disconnected the call.

"I imagine that's disappointing," Stone said. "Your last chance to speak with your sister and she's not home. She's probably with that wolf of hers."

Izzy turned on him. Her eyes narrowed, and her expression became a mask of pure hatred. "I hope so," she snarled. "At least then she'll be safe from the likes of you."

"You'd better make your other phone call while I'm still feeling generous. The energy is building. Soon the portal will open, and this disgusting world will be gone."

Her fingers trembled as she punched in the last number. It rang and rang, then a harried voice came on the line.

"Everly?" Izzy asked.

"Oh my God! Where are you?" Everly asked.

Izzy gave a pained laugh. "You wouldn't believe me if I told you," she said.

"He's there with you, isn't he?" she asked.

Izzy's face paled. "I don't know what you're talking about."

"Tristan came by earlier looking for you," Everly said.

This time Izzy did sob aloud. "He's alive?"

Her palpable relief pissed Stone off. He'd really thought

Izzy was better than that. He should've known that wasn't the case.

"Of course Tristan's alive," she said. "Why wouldn't he be?"

"It's a long story," Izzy said. "All that matters is that he is." Her eyes widened as Stone approached. "Listen, Everly, I just wanted to call to say goodbye. You take care and get out of town."

Stone grabbed her hand before she hung up. "Don't be like that," he said. "Invite her to the party. The more the merrier, I always say."

"No!" Izzy struggled in his grasp. "Run, Everly! Run!"

Stone struck her with the back of his hand, knocking her to the ground. The loud thwack carried over the line. Izzy's grip on the phone gave way. He put the receiver up to his ear.

"You still there?" he asked.

Silence greeted him. He wanted to laugh.

"I can hear you breathing. You might as well answer me, especially if you want your friend to live," he said.

"I'm here," Everly said.

"Good," Stone said. "We're at the tour dock in Lafitte Park. Go past the fallen tree, and you'll see the trail." He glanced at Izzy, who staggered to her feet. "Oh, and come alone, or she's dead."

Izzy screamed for Everly to stay away, but Stone had already hung up.

"You bastard!" She rushed him. Her fists pummeled his chest and grazed his face.

Stone dropped the phone onto the ground and stomped on it.

"No!" Izzy renewed her efforts, but it didn't do her any good.

He countered every blow, waiting for her to wear herself out. It took longer than he expected, but eventually she dropped to the ground.

"I'm going to kill you," she said softly.

"I have no doubt you'd like to," he said. "But we both know you're no match for me. Even your boyfriend wasn't strong enough to take me."

Their gazes met. "He would've been had you not sucker hit him with a pan."

"Believe that if you must, but my people are stronger than the Moonlight Kin. It's why they fear us so," he said. "I really should've killed him when I had the chance."

She hoped that Everly was smart enough to stay home, but even as the thought flitted through Izzy's mind, she knew her friend would come. It wasn't in Everly's nature to run.

Izzy thought of Tristan. He'd been to Everly's house. He was looking for her, but it was unlikely that he'd find her in time. She was just grateful he was alive. It would give Izzy something to hold on to, something to dream about while she walked through hell in the Darkling world.

The air around them thickened.

The leaves swirled *vertically*, defying basic physics. "What's happening?" Izzy asked.

"The doorway is opening," Stone said.

"Then let's go," she said. "We don't need to wait for Everly. She'll delay us needlessly."

Stone chuckled. "Two Sighted-Ones are far better than one. Don't you think?"

He knew. "How?"

"I've been following your trail for a while," he said. "One night I thought I had you, but when I got nearer I realized it wasn't your power I'd been picking up. It was another's. She's a lot more powerful than you. Probably why I hadn't been able to detect her before." He swirled his hands, making odd patterns in the air. "I only caught a glimpse of her, but it was enough to know that I was dealing with two Sighted-Ones. When I return to my world, I will be honored as a hero."

"You're going to be a hero for kidnapping two women?"

Izzy asked. "Your world must have pretty low standards, if that's the title you get for such a despicable act."

"For finding two Sighted-Ones," he corrected. "No one in my world has done such a thing. I will be rewarded for my bravery."

Izzy snorted. "Bravery? You're a coward," she said. "You hide in the shadows. You attack the innocent. You don't fight fair because you know you'll lose."

He hit her again.

This time Izzy didn't fall. "Truth hurts, doesn't it?"

Stone shook his head. "You really aren't bright. If you were, you wouldn't test me this way."

Dark fur rippled over his skin, and his jaw cracked. The bone extended until his human mouth disappeared and a muzzle replaced it. His clothes ripped and fell to the ground. He kept growing and mutating, until a monster stood before her.

Izzy had seen Moonlight Kin in their beast forms. They'd been larger than real wolves, but had maintained the general shape of the animals. Stone didn't. He looked like something out of a bear-themed horror movie.

She scrambled away. "Stay back." Izzy grabbed a stick and swung it at him.

His claws extended, and he sliced the wood in half as if it were a ripe peach. With lightning speed, he struck her, scratching Izzy down her arm. Blood welled on her skin. The wound burned like fire, but she wouldn't give Stone the satisfaction of knowing he'd hurt her.

He slowly shifted back to human form. Sweat covered Stone's naked body, and he was panting from the exertion. He glanced at her arm and grinned, flashing teeth too long for his mouth.

"Now you have to come with me," he said in a garbled voice. "If you stay, that scratch will lead to madness and death. That's what happened to your sister's friend, Celina Gibson."

"Her boyfriend killed her," she said.

"I know," Stone said. "I didn't want to do it, but she got too clingy, and since she wasn't a Sighted-One, I didn't have a lot of use for her." He snorted. "Other than the obvious. Celina was so needy that she let me do whatever I wanted to her."

Izzy glanced down at the wound. The furrows were just deep enough to bleed. "You infected me like you infected Celina?"

Mindy had told her all about Celina's death. It hadn't come as a shock, since Izzy had seen her friend's spirit prior to the phone call. At the time, Izzy hadn't been too surprised, given her friend's dangerous lifestyle, but now she felt horrible for what Celina had gone through. Not only had she been used, but she'd been betrayed.

"In a fashion," he said, then pulled out a clean pair of clothes from his tote.

The sense of evil emanating from him overwhelmed her. "Celina's boyfriend's name was Slade." They couldn't be the same person.

His smug expression said they were. "Slade, Stone, I really don't care what you all call me," he said. "It's unimportant as long as it doesn't interfere with my mission."

Izzy clutched the wound. If she was going to die anyway, then maybe she could take him with her. She turned and ran for the water. The blood would attract the gators. With any luck, they would take Stone out at the same time.

"What are you doing?" he shouted. "Come back here!"

She ran faster. The branches and bushes pulled at her clothes, slowing her down, but Izzy saw water up ahead. This was it. She was almost there. Just a few more feet and the bayou would take her into its watery embrace.

It felt like a truck hit her from behind. Izzy sailed through the air then landed hard, knocking the wind out of her.

"I told you that you couldn't get away," he snarled and yanked her to her feet. "Don't try anything stupid like that again, or I'll knock you out and throw you through the portal."

Izzy tasted blood in her mouth as Stone dragged her back to the clearing. The leaves were swirling faster now, and the darkness at the center of the mass grew. Soon it would be big enough for them to fit through.

Chapter Seventeen

Everly stared in shock at the phone in her hand. Had she just heard Izzy die?

Izzy told her to run, but the guy had sounded serious when he'd threatened her friend's life. What should she do?

She glanced down and spotted the business card Tristan had given her. The thought of phoning them terrified Everly, but the thought of losing Izzy was even more frightening.

Everly picked up the card and punched the number into the phone. It rang twice, then someone picked up.

"La Fontaine residence," the man said. "How may I help you?"

"I'm—I'm..."

"Is this a crank call?" he asked. "If so, you should know that we have caller ID."

Everly swallowed hard. "No!" she said. "My—my name is Everly. I'm a friend of Izzy MacDougal's."

"Hold please," he said.

A strong male voice came on the line a second later. "This is Pierre La Fontaine. Whom am I speaking with?"

"I'm a friend of Izzy's," she said.

"You must be Everly," Pierre said.

She jolted at the mention of her name. How did he know about her? Everly pictured Tristan and swore under her breath.

"Listen, I don't have a lot of time," she said. "I just heard from Izzy. She's in big trouble. If I don't meet her, she's going to die."

"Where did she tell you to go?" he asked.

Everly quickly filled him in.

"You did the right thing by calling," Pierre said. "Sit tight. I'll send some of my men over to guard you."

"What?" Her voice rose before she could stop it. "I don't need a guard. I need to get to my friend before the psycho she's with does something crazy to her."

"He won't harm her," Pierre said.

The deepness of his voice sank into her bones, making her body relax a little. Everly wanted to believe him. He sounded like the voice of authority, but the truth was she didn't know this man, this creature. She wasn't about to take a chance and risk her friend's life, when she knew she could save her.

"I've got to go," she said. "I know what needs to be done. My path is clear."

"Don't hang up!" Pierre shouted, but it was too late.

Everly pushed the disconnect button and grabbed her keys. She didn't know how long it would take him to notify Tristan or to get wolves to her house, so she had to hurry.

"Hang on, Izzy," she murmured, then snatched her gris-gris before running out the door.

* * * * *

Tristan was searching a few miles from the cabin when he heard the wolves howl. He knew what the sound meant. They'd found Isabel. His heart jumped then began to race. Was she alive? He couldn't imagine that the Darkling would kill her—at least not on purpose or without provocation.

His chest squeezed. In the short time he'd known Isabel, Tristan had discovered just how annoying and adorable she could be. Darklings weren't capable of feeling human affection. What if Isabel had spouted off to the Darkling? Fear embraced him. He had to get back to Pierre's house.

Tristan had run a half a mile and was about to turn toward town when he caught Everly's distinctive scent wafting on the air. The only way he could've smelled her was if she was nearby. What was she doing out here? It didn't matter. He had to get back to town. The spicy scent faded.

He took a few more steps then stopped. There was no reason for Everly to be in this area. Tristan sniffed the air. Her scent was faint now. He shook his head and snorted to clear his lungs. When he inhaled again, the scent wasn't just faint. It was moving.

There were only so many directions Everly could be going this far out of town. Tristan kept his nose in the air and followed her scent. Instead of heading toward New Orleans, it led him deeper into the bayou.

Something wasn't right.

The howls came again. This time they were closer, but they were still miles away. Everly's arrival along with the wolves couldn't be a coincidence. Tristan focused on her and prayed to the goddess that Everly didn't drive too fast.

* * * * *

A gaping mouth of darkness stared at Izzy. When Stone had said he came from a world without sunlight, she'd hoped he'd exaggerated. The darkness was so complete it swallowed the light.

Izzy couldn't spend the rest of her life in there. She wouldn't survive. She glanced at Stone/Slade. He grinned now that the portal was open.

He must've sensed her watching because he turned to her. "Are you ready to leave this horrid place?"

"No." Izzy stepped back. At least Everly had been smart enough to stay away. It wasn't much of a consolation, but it was a small victory.

"Come now," Stone said. "Don't be shy. There are a lot of warriors eager to meet you."

Izzy shook her head and ran. She wouldn't get far, but she wasn't about to make it easy on him. Stone caught her and swept her off her feet. Izzy kicked and hit him with all her strength, but he held her easily.

"Let me go!" she cried.

Stone had a bemused expression on his face. "You need to take a deep breath. It's going to hurt."

Her head swam, and her vision dimmed.

"Put her down!" The shout came from behind them.

Stone turned, giving Izzy a clear view of Everly.

"Get out of here!" she shouted. "Run!"

But Everly didn't run. She stood her ground, glaring at Stone. If she noticed the dark opening—and there was no way she could miss it—she didn't acknowledge it. "I said, put her down."

Stone grinned. "I'm so glad you could join us," he said.

"You won't be, when I get done with you," Everly said.

He laughed. "You think your power is stronger than mine?" Stone put Izzy down but didn't release her.

Everly smiled, flashing her vampire fangs, but there was no warmth in her brown eyes. "Not my power," she said. "But the one who's coming for you will be more than your match." She hiked her thumb over her shoulder.

"He won't get here in time," Stone said. "Now be a good little girl and come with me." He grabbed Izzy by the hair and dragged her toward the portal.

She cried out in pain and struggled, but her resistance was useless against his overpowering strength.

"No!" Everly screamed and raced forward.

"Stay back," Izzy shouted, but Everly ignored her and dove for Izzy's legs.

Stone pulled hard to break her grip.

Everly held onto Izzy for dear life.

Izzy felt like a human tug-of-war rope. "Everly, let go! You have to get out of here."

"No," she said. "I can't let him take you."

* * * * *

Tristan saw the ash on the road before he found Everly's car. He touched the hood. Heat rose from the engine. She hadn't been gone long. He scented the area a second before the lodestone flared, indicating dark magic nearby.

He rushed into the woods. Everly and Isabel's scent appeared along with the Darkling's foul odor. Screams and cries rang out. Tristan followed the sound, shifting into human form as he ran.

The leaves parted and Tristan stepped out of the woods, clutching Selene in his hand. He stopped when he caught sight of what was happening. The lodestone pulsed again. Despite its strength, Tristan felt the Darkling steadily siphoning his power. He didn't have much time.

Tristan ran toward the women. He couldn't get a clear shot at the Darkling without the possibility of harming Isabel or Everly. He swung the sword and caught the Darkling in the side. The blade struck true.

The Darkling screamed in agony and staggered back. He dropped Isabel in the process. The move was so unexpected that Everly fell onto her back. She quickly scrambled away on her hands and knees. Isabel didn't move.

It was then that Tristan saw the bruises on her neck and the blood on her arm. The perfect finger placements around Isabel's slender throat made the weapon used easily identifiable. A red haze covered Tristan's vision. It had dared to harm what was his.

Fear filled the Darkling's amber eyes, as he touched the blood and brought it up to his face. He glanced at the sword in Tristan's hand and put even more distance between them.

"That's right," Tristan said. "This isn't a normal sword. It's made for killing your kind."

"I should've finished you when I had the chance," the Darkling said, staying out of reach.

"Yes, you should have," Tristan said. "Go to your friend, Isabel." He never took his eyes off the Darkling.

"Move and I'll gut you," the Darkling said.

"Tristan, stay back," Isabel said. "He's infected me. I'm going to die."

"I won't allow that to happen," Tristan said, glancing at the scratch.

Pain filled Isabel's hazel eyes. "It's too late. Get Everly out of here."

"I will not be leaving without you," Tristan said.

Isabel sniffled. "But I betrayed you."

"That makes us even," Tristan said, then shifted his attention back to the Darkling. "This is between you and I."

The Darkling laughed. "This has nothing to do with you, Kin. Leave now, and I might let you live."

Tristan grinned, flashing sharp, white teeth. "We know that's not going to happen."

"Have it your way." The Darkling held out a hand. Power flowed from his body.

Tristan felt the first wave strike him. The pain nearly knocked him to his knees.

"Come here, beast," the Darkling said, crooking a finger.

"No!" Tristan shouted, but it was already too late. The shift was upon him.

Fur rippled over Tristan's flesh as his beast rose to the surface. The enchanted sword dropped to the ground, useless in his paws. He threw his head back and howled in anguish. Others nearby mirrored the lonesome sound.

The Darkling's head rose, and his eyes scanned the tree line. "Time to go," he snarled and grabbed Isabel, pulling her toward the opening.

Tristan felt his strength drain. Being this close to the Darkling and the opening to the other realm sucked the life right out of him. He wouldn't be conscious for much longer. Tristan leapt, covering the distance between them.

He landed on Isabel, knocking her out of the Darkling's hands. Tristan growled and snapped at him, daring him to try to take her.

Isabel shoved at his fur to try to get away.

Tristan didn't move.

The Darkling took a step forward.

Tristan bared his teeth and growled low in his chest.

The Darkling hesitated then kept coming.

Tristan lowered his head and grabbed Isabel by the throat. He sank his fangs into her flesh where her shoulder met her neck. Blood filled his mouth. It was sweeter than anything he'd ever tasted. He swallowed as much as he could then licked the spot to seal the wound. When Tristan was sure the bleeding had slowed, he released Isabel.

Tears streamed down her cheeks as she clutched her throat and scurried away. Tristan couldn't bear to see the pain of betrayal in her eyes. It hurt too much. But he held no regrets.

The Darkling roared in anger. "What have you done? You can't! She's mine!"

Wrong! Isabel was his. And he'd just proven it. Tristan shook his head to clear it.

The Darkling snarled. "You think biting her is going to stop me?" He ran toward Isabel, who tried to reach Everly's side. The blood flowing from his wound didn't slow him.

No! Tristan shouted inside his mind as he watched in horror. He tried to cut the Darkling off, but he was too weak to catch him.

Tristan staggered forward. He wasn't going to make it.

The Darkling made a grab for Isabel.

"Remember what I told you!" Everly shouted, then shoved Isabel out of the way.

Instead of scooping Isabel up, the Darkling had no choice but to grab Everly or leave empty-handed. The momentum he'd built as he crossed the clearing carried them through the portal opening.

Tristan sprinted toward the portal. If he reached it in time, it would mean his death, but he'd gladly sacrifice his life if it meant saving Isabel's friend for her. After all, she'd saved Isabel for him.

He jumped as the portal snapped shut. The momentum carried him forward into a tree trunk. Tristan hit headfirst. He heard a loud crunch, then the world faded to black.

* * * * *

Izzy stared in horror at Tristan's lifeless form. Everly was gone, and Tristan might be dead. They'd both sacrificed themselves for her. Tears filled her eyes as Izzy struggled to gain her footing. As soon as she was steady enough to move, she rushed to his side.

Blood trickled out Tristan's nose and muzzle.

She dropped to her knees and gently pulled his head onto her lap. When she saw his chest rise, the tears flowed down her cheeks. At least he was alive, but Izzy had no idea how badly he was hurt. Tristan hadn't returned to his human form.

Izzy took off her shirt to put pressure on his bleeding. She kept her eyes on the woods. Would Stone come back for her?

Blood seeped through her shirt. If Tristan didn't wake up soon, she'd drag him to the road. "Please, come back to me," she murmured. "I need you."

Izzy heard a twig snap. Her heart slammed into her ribcage, trying to kick its way out. She glanced around and spotted Tristan's sword. She gently laid his head aside and crawled over to it. Izzy had just wrapped her hand around the handle when wolves poured out of the woods.

She screamed and scurried back to Tristan. "Stay back!" she shouted, swinging the sword wildly around her.

One wolf stepped away from the others. He barked once, and the others grew silent. The air around him shimmered. One moment a black wolf stood in the middle of the clearing, the next Pierre La Fontaine stared at her.

It said a lot about Izzy's state of mind that she didn't even care that he was naked. "Stay back." She kept one hand on Tristan and the other firmly wrapped around the sword.

"Isabel, it's me," Pierre said. "We're not here to harm you."

"I sa—said stay back," she cried.

Pierre held his hands up and motioned for the wolves to move back. Once they were far enough away, he dropped down into a crouch.

"He's in bad shape," he said, indicating to Tristan. "He needs my help."

Izzy glanced at Tristan. He was still breathing, but his breaths were shallow and he was still bleeding badly. "He tried to save me."

Pierre glanced at the wound on the side of her neck. "Did Tristan do that to you?"

Izzy's brow furrowed. "What?"

"Did he bite you?" he asked.

"Yes," she said. "Stone got really mad after Tristan bit me."

"I bet he did," Pierre said. "Where's your friend, Everly?"

Fresh tears filled her eyes until Pierre's image wavered. "He took her," she whispered. "She shoved me out of the way, and he took her instead."

Sadness filled Pierre's amber eyes. "I'm sorry," he said softly, then murmured in French.

Izzy didn't speak the language, but something about the cadence of his voice made her muscles relax. The sword seemed heavier than it had been a moment ago. Her arm trembled and dropped.

"No!" she said, but there was no fighting Pierre's steady voice.

"It's okay." He slowly moved closer as he continued to talk to her.

Izzy's eyes drooped, and the sword fell to the ground.

Pierre moved with lightning speed. He grabbed the weapon, then tossed the sword to someone behind him and still managed to catch her before she fell over.

"It's okay," he said. "You'll be okay."

Izzy had a hard time understanding him. His words were slurring in her mind.

He turned his head to address the others. "Someone get over here and get Tristan. I have his mate."

CHAPTER EIGHTEEN

Izzy awoke in a strange room. The antique furnishings were ornate and exquisitely chosen. She was in a comfy bed with plush linens. A vase full of flowers sat on the bedside table, along with a glass of water.

She tried to recall how she'd gotten there, but came up blank. The door opened, and Tristan stepped inside. Everything came crashing back to Izzy in an instant.

"How are you feeling?" he asked, but didn't meet her gaze. Instead, he leaned against the doorway.

Izzy sat up. "Okay, I guess," she said. "How are you?"

Tristan shrugged. "My head hurts, but I'll live."

"Everly is gone. Isn't she?"

His jaw clenched, and all warmth left his expression. "Yes."

"Can we get her back?" Izzy asked.

Tristan shook his head and winced, then touched the side of his temple. "No."

"Stone told me what he had planned for me on the other side," she said. "It was horrifying. The thought of Everly..." Izzy voice cracked.

"I'm sorry," Tristan said. "I tried to save her. I just wasn't fast enough. I thought if I could get to her, I could toss her back through the opening before it sealed shut."

Izzy frowned. "You told me you couldn't survive in the Darkling world," she said. "Was that true?"

"Yes," he bit out.

"So you would've died had you leapt into their world." The truth punched Izzy in the chest, leaving her winded.

"I might have been able to save her for you," Tristan said, avoiding the truth.

And if he had, it would've cost him his life.

Izzy played with the ends of the comforter. "Everly pushed me out of the way," she said quietly.

"I saw her," he said. "She did it to save you."

She closed her eyes. "Why would she do that? She had to have known what would happen."

"You were her friend," he said.

Her eyes flew open, and she glared at him. "I still am," Izzy snapped.

Tristan nodded. "I think she knew all along what was going to occur. We just didn't listen."

"What happens now?" she asked.

He stared at a spot on the wall. Izzy got the distinct impression that he did it so he wouldn't have to look at her. The thought hurt.

"You'll return to your life with your sister," he said. "And I'll return to mine."

Pain blossomed inside her, but she refused to show it. She wasn't sure why she was surprised. After all, they'd been forced to work together. No sense drawing the situation out. It was already uncomfortable enough.

"I'm..." She cleared her throat. "I'm going to need a ride."

Tristan glanced at her. "It's already been arranged."

"Are you going to take me back?" she asked, knowing the answer before he replied.

"No," Tristan said. "I have... I have things I need to do."

"Of course," she said, unable to keep the bitterness from her voice. "Well, thanks for stopping by. I'm glad you're okay."

Tristan opened his mouth to say something more, then closed it and left the room.

Izzy stayed strong until the door clicked then she let herself fall apart. When she was done wallowing in the pity pool, she threw the covers off and jumped into the shower. Izzy was surprised to find fresh clothes waiting for her when she got out.

They must really want to get rid of her. Or maybe Tristan did.

Well she'd never been one to overstay her welcome. She looked around the room one last time. Nothing of hers was there, so she left.

Pierre La Fontaine waited for her at the bottom of the stairs. Tristan was nowhere in sight. She guessed they'd said their goodbyes earlier. Izzy painted a smile on her face as she approached the Alpha.

"Glad to see you're feeling better," he said.

Izzy rubbed her arms. "Thanks for putting me up. I—uh, guess I'd better be going. Thank you again for—everything."

"Take care of yourself, Ms. MacDougal," he said. Pierre's expression remained pleasant, but he didn't bother to hide the concern in his amber eyes.

Izzy nodded and walked out of the house. A car idled near the curb to take her to the airport. She glanced back one last time at the house, hoping to spot Tristan, but he was nowhere in sight. Her heart broke as she slipped into the car and it drove away.

* * * * *

Tristan pulled the curtains back and watched the black sedan take Isabel away. He had to let her go. It was the right thing to do. She hadn't asked for his bite. Hadn't wanted it.

He wouldn't force himself upon her. He'd already done enough damage.

"Are you going to stand there all night?" Pierre asked, coming up beside him.

"Perhaps," Tristan said.

"She's your mate," Pierre said gently.

Tristan's lip curled. "No," he said. "She isn't. I bit her to protect her."

Pierre had the audacity to laugh in his face. "Is that what you think happened? I was wondering what load of bull you were telling yourself."

He scowled. "I know that's what happened. I was there. You weren't."

Pierre shook his head and walked over to an antique cabinet. He pulled out a bottle of port. "Want a glass?"

Tristan shrugged. "Sure."

Pierre poured two glasses and handed him one. Tristan started to take a sip but stopped short when the Alpha raised his glass.

"Here's to beautiful women," he said. "The ones in our lives and the ones we let get away."

Tristan glared at him.

Pierre clinked his glass then took a sip. "Funny thing about wolves," he said, "they don't do anything they don't want to do."

"She's not my bondmate," Tristan said then tossed the contents of the glass back. The port burned his throat but did little to ease his tension.

"That bite tells a different story," Pierre said, taking another dainty sip. "You really should savor rare things." He glanced at his glass, but Tristan wasn't sure he discussed the port.

Tristan set his glass down on the side table. "The bite didn't happen during sex, so she's not going to become Kin."

Pierre nodded. "Perhaps not," he said. "You're probably

in the clear. You can go back to doing what you do without having to worry about your...Isabel." He finished his port and set his glass down beside Tristan's.

Tristan turned back to the window as Pierre wandered toward the door. The Alpha's footsteps halted. Tristan knew his leaving was too good to be true.

"I do wonder though," Pierre said.

He sighed and turned to face the Alpha once more. "About what?"

"About what did happen during sex," he said.

"That is none of your business," Tristan snarled. He opened his mouth to deliver another scathing response, but Pierre held up his hand to stop him.

"I don't want details," Pierre said in exasperation. "I'm just giving you something to think about."

"Pierre," Tristan ground his name out between clenched teeth.

"Fine," Pierre said. "I'll leave you with one final thought. Isabel may not be your bondmate and she probably won't shift during the next full moon, but if you locked inside of her during sex, then there's a very good chance she's carrying your pup."

Blood drained from Tristan's face, and he grabbed hold of the windowsill to keep from falling over. Was that possible? Had he impregnated Isabel? Just the thought left him light-headed.

Pierre laughed. "You look like you need another drink." He walked over and grabbed the port, then refilled their glasses. "You'll only know for sure if you go after her."

Tristan grabbed the glass and drank the port like it was a shot, then rushed past Pierre. He heard the Alpha laughing as he took the stairs two at a time.

"Thought that might change things," Pierre shouted. "Have a nice flight."

* * * * *

Izzy had been back in Oregon for over three weeks. Tristan had showed up shortly after she arrived, but she had refused to speak with him. Seeing him hurt too much. Everywhere she turned Izzy got a constant reminder of what she'd lost.

Her sister Mindy was so blissfully in love that it was sickening. She was happy for her. Truly happy, but nothing made someone hurting more miserable than hanging around a happy couple.

She continued to mourn Everly but had accepted that there was nothing she could've done to save her. That didn't make her feel any less guilty, but it had brought a modicum of peace.

Mindy had been badgering her for the past two days to come over to the estate where she lived with Nic, her new husband. Izzy tried to digest the fact that her little sister was married. So much had changed in such a short period of time.

And it wasn't just her sister's life. Izzy had changed, too. Now when she saw the monsters, she didn't go the other direction. Not all of them were bad. Most were just trying to get by. Her stomach gurgled. Izzy hadn't been feeling very well lately, but Mindy's cheerful persistence eventually wore her down.

She'd agreed to go to Aidan's place with one stipulation. Tristan wasn't allowed to be there. Her sister readily agreed, which was why Izzy found herself in a car heading toward the estate.

She sat in silence as they drove past the big gates guarding the entrance. Through the trees, Izzy thought she caught glimpses of movement, but she wasn't sure.

The car stopped in front of a magnificent mansion. Mindy turned to her. "What do you think?"

Izzy looked at the house. "It's very pretty."

"Come on." Mindy tugged her hand. "You'll like it more

once you see the inside."

She didn't need to like the house. It wasn't like she'd be living here, but she humored Mindy all the same. Izzy felt eyes upon her as she exited the car.

She didn't see anyone, but they were there. A few times during the week, Izzy swore she'd sensed Tristan in her mind, but that was impossible. They didn't have that kind of connection.

Just the thought of Frosty brought a wave of sadness. Izzy pushed it aside and smiled, but it didn't fool Mindy.

"I'm fine," she said. "I swear."

"I'm not buying it," Mindy said, "but I appreciate the effort."

Okay, she wasn't fine. Far from it. But Izzy would be eventually. It would just take time. *A few years should do it*, she thought.

If only Mindy would wait. Her sister had already talked about setting Izzy up. Just the thought of a strange man touching her made Izzy's skin crawl. She couldn't imagine anyone holding her, but Tristan. She didn't tell her sister because frankly her behavior embarrassed her. Izzy had never been the type of girl to moon over any man.

A handsome man with shoulder-length black hair met them at the door. Next to him stood a willowy strawberry blonde with her arm wrapped around his back.

"Isabel," he said. "It's great to finally meet you. Mindy has told me so much about you. I'm Aidan." He held out his hand.

Izzy shook it. "Nice to meet you, too."

"This is my bondmate, Jenna," he said.

The woman stepped forward and shook her hand. "It's so nice to meet you," she said.

Aidan's nose twitched. He gave Izzy a funny look then glanced at Mindy and Nic.

"Something wrong?" Izzy asked.

"No," Aidan said, recovering quickly. "Please come

inside. We have lunch prepared."

"You didn't need to go to any trouble," Izzy said, feeling uncomfortable by the attention. Though truth be told, she was hungry. More than hungry, ravenous.

"No trouble at all," Jenna said.

After a long leisurely lunch, Mindy gave Izzy a tour around the estate. Unlike Pierre's house, this one was super modern inside and high tech. She tried to picture Pierre going high tech and nearly laughed aloud. He liked his antiques too much to ever do that.

Thoughts about Pierre and New Orleans opened the floodgates on the emotions she'd been trying to suppress. Memories of her and Tristan strolling through Jackson Square filled her mind.

Izzy could almost feel him holding her hand and kissing her. He'd been pretending they were a couple at the time, but the kisses had felt real enough for her to forget for a while.

Her throat thickened. She shouldn't be thinking about Tristan or New Orleans. He wasn't there any longer. Izzy wasn't even sure if he was still in Oregon. Tristan had told her that he lived in the Southwest. Maybe he'd gone home.

Did he think about her and their time in the Big Easy? Did it matter?

Izzy swallowed past the lump in her throat. "Mindy, I'd like to go home now."

Concern filled her sister's brown eyes. "Sure," she said. "Let's just say goodbye to Aidan and Jenna before we leave."

As they drew near Aidan's office, they heard shouting coming from the other side of the door.

"I don't think we should interrupt him," Izzy said, turning to leave.

"I'm not going anywhere until I get to speak with her," a familiar male voice said.

"She doesn't want to see you," Aidan shouted.

Izzy froze. She knew that voice. Knew who it had come

from. *Tristan.* Izzy glanced back at the closed door.

Words were quickly replaced by loud growls.

Izzy moved long before reason raised its ugly head to stop her. She pushed the door open and stepped inside the room. Two sets of glowing eyes turned on her at once.

"Knock it off, Frosty," she snapped.

The growling ceased. Aidan's dark brow shot to his hairline.

"What are you doing here?" Izzy asked, ignoring him and focusing on Tristan.

He inhaled, then his mercury-colored eyes narrowed. "We need to talk," Tristan said.

"There's nothing more to say," she said.

"You may have nothing to say, but I have plenty," he said.

Izzy told herself that she only agreed because she wanted to defuse the situation, but it was a lie. She'd missed him. Missed him so much that it hurt. Being near him made her heart lighter.

Tristan glared at Aidan then walked out the door. He didn't touch Izzy as they stepped off the back patio onto the grass, but he stayed close by her side.

A couple times Izzy caught him scowling at the other wolves they passed as they wandered down a trail in the woods. But she didn't say anything. Izzy simply waited.

She should have heard him out long ago, but she'd been afraid to. Too afraid of what he might say. Izzy couldn't go on like this, though. It was too painful.

When they reached a small clearing, Tristan stopped. He shifted his feet and glanced around, but nothing held his interest for long.

What had him so nervous? she wondered.

"You said you wanted to talk," Izzy said. "So talk."

Tristan rubbed the back of his neck. She saw his gaze dart to the spot where he'd bitten her. It had healed, but the mark didn't look like it was ever going to go away.

Izzy had noticed a similar spot on Mindy's neck. When she'd asked her about it, her sister had been evasive. At the time she'd assumed it was sexual in nature, but now that she'd seen one on Jenna's throat, Izzy wasn't so sure.

He took a deep breath. "I missed you," Tristan said, surprising them both.

She'd missed him, too, but Izzy wasn't about to admit it. "Tristan, what are you really doing here? Does it have something to do with this bite?" She motioned toward her neck.

Tristan's lips thinned. "Yes, and no," he said.

"I think if you try you can be a little more vague," she said.

He laughed, breaking some of the tension between them. "I have missed that mouth of yours."

She gave him a wry glance. "You don't like humans, remember?"

"I remember," he said. "I also recall you don't care for monsters. Has that changed?"

Izzy laughed, but the sound held no warmth. "Yeah, it has." She caught the flare of hope in his eyes. "I didn't know what real monsters were until I met Stone, Slade, or whatever his name is."

Tristan brushed a lock of hair away from her face. "It doesn't matter what his name was, he's dead now."

Izzy blanched. "What do you mean he's dead?"

"The sword I struck him with wasn't a normal weapon," he said. "It was made specifically to kill his kind."

"What does that mean for Everly?" she asked, knowing her friend was now alone in the dark world.

Tristan chose his words carefully. "At least she won't have him to contend with."

Being this close to Isabel and not being able to touch her was sheer torture for Tristan. The proximity was bad enough, but couple that with the aroma coming from her skin and it was enough to make a wolf beg.

He had to tell her the truth about the bite, though it was minor compared to the other news he must share with her.

"You asked what the bite meant," he said.

"Yes," she said.

Tristan pulled her into his arms and kissed her. She pulled back to argue or protest. He wasn't sure which and didn't care. He continued kissing Isabel until she melted against his body. Tristan hardened instantly, wanting her more than he desired his next breath.

Reluctantly, he ended the kiss. Her eyes were glazed when she looked at him. Tristan waited until she focused. "That's what the bite means," he said. "It's what it will always mean, if you'll have me."

He kissed her again before she answered. Tristan was too afraid to hear her response. Couldn't bear the thought of her rejection.

Isabel tore her mouth away. "I can't think when you're kissing me," she said.

"That's the point," he murmured.

She laughed. "You know this probably isn't going to work, right?"

"It'll work," he said. "We will make it work."

Isabel pulled out of his embrace and continued walking until they reached a small clearing.

"You never answered me," Tristan said.

She looked over her shoulder and grinned at him. "I know."

Izzy's hands trembled as she grabbed the bottom of her shirt and pulled it over her head. She felt more than saw Tristan's gaze upon her. It burned her flesh everywhere it touched. She heard him growl behind her.

"What are you doing?" he asked.

"You mean you don't know?" she asked.

Tristan's long legs ate up the distance between them. When he neared, he whipped his shirt off and let it fall to the ground. His godlike beauty left her breathless.

"What now?" he asked, voice harsh.

Izzy wiggled out of her pants then automatically covered her stomach with her hands. "I'm a stress eater. I've put on a little weight since you last saw me."

His eyes flashed with banked emotion. "You're beautiful at any size."

She blushed. "Yeah, well, you won't say that if I continue my cookie dough affair."

Tristan shed his pants and slowly approached her. He gently placed his hand on the small mound she'd been trying to hide, covering it. "It's natural for women in your state to put on weight."

She frowned. "My state?"

"Yes," he said. "You're with child."

"I'm pregnant!" She didn't mean to shout the news. "I can't be pregnant. I'm on birth control, and we only had sex once."

Tristan grinned. "With my kind, once is enough, if everything else falls into place."

Izzy swayed. "This can't be happening!" She glanced down at the small mound and touched it with trembling fingertips. "What am I going to do?"

"Is having my child such a bad thing?" he asked quietly, but there was no mistaking the hurt in his eyes.

Izzy took a deep breath, then took another. She quickly evaluated what she felt. Shock, check. Panic, check. Fear, check. All natural emotions when someone found out they were going to have a baby. The one emotion that she expected to feel was missing. Izzy searched again. Nope, she didn't feel an ounce of regret.

"No," she said, pressing her hand to his chest. "It's not a bad thing."

Tristan shuddered beneath her fingertips.

"What happens now?" she asked.

He flashed a quick grin. "We finish what we started."

* * * * *

Tristan spread their clothes out on the ground then gently laid Isabel upon them. He'd never seen anything quite so beautiful in his life, and she was his.

He dropped to his knees at her feet and lifted her leg to tenderly kiss the inside of her ankle. Isabel sighed.

Tristan continued kissing her, taking care to avoid the areas she wanted him to visit the most. By the time he finished exploring every inch of her, Isabel mewed incoherently.

He grabbed her knees and gently parted her thighs, then settled between them. If he got any harder, Tristan was convinced he'd explode.

"Isabel," he said. "Look at me."

Her lashes fluttered, then their eyes met.

"You asked me about the bite earlier," he said.

She nodded.

"If I do it again when I take you, it'll have a different meaning," he said. Tristan had her full attention now.

"What will change?" she asked.

"For starters, it will bind us together," he said, knowing he was already bound to her with or without the final act. "So I need you to be sure, because there's no going back once it's done."

Isabel bit her lip, and her brow creased. "What's the rest of it?"

"What do you mean?" he asked.

"You said for starters, so there has to be more," she said. "Tell me everything."

Tristan hesitated. There was still time for her to change her mind. Tell him she wasn't ready for this, for him, and there'd be nothing he could do about it. The thought of not being around to raise his child made him ache, but Tristan would honor her wishes—even if it destroyed him to do so.

"If I bite you again, while we're making love, you'll

become like me," he said, then braced himself for her rejection.

"I'll become a wolf?" she asked.

Tristan nodded. Isabel spent her whole life fearing and running from the monsters in the world. The last thing she'd want was to become one of them. This was it. He prepared for the worst.

"Will our child be like you?" she asked softly.

His gaze speared hers. "Yes." Tristan searched for any sign of disgust. There was none. "It'll also be a reflection of you...just as I am."

Her brow furrowed. "What do you mean?" she asked.

Tristan brushed her cheek with his knuckles. "You've brought out my humanity. Made me want to be more human, so that there would be a place for me in your world." He touched her heart. "And in here."

Tears pricked her eyes and she kissed him tenderly. "Then let's do this," Isabel said.

"You need to be sure." Tristan felt his beast rise. It wanted her, wanted their child, and it didn't care if she agreed.

She caressed his cheek. "I am sure. I've had a lot of time to think during the last few weeks. It seems like all I've done is think," she said. "The one thing that kept coming back again and again was you."

"I will give my life for you and our child," he murmured. "I will protect you both with my last breath."

"You already have, Frosty," she said. "You nearly died trying to protect us."

"And I'd gladly do so again." Tristan kissed her hard and entered her with one thrust. The feel of her tight channel surrounding him was like coming home. Isabel was his. And he was hers. Together they were a family.

Emotion welled inside him. Tristan looked away before she glimpsed the tears swimming in his eyes. It had been years since he'd had a family. Years spent wandering the country alone. Now Tristan had someone to come home to. Soon, he'd have two.

He placed his hand upon her abdomen and kissed Isabel lovingly. "Thank you," he said.

"For what?" she asked, placing her hand over his.

"For loving me enough to say yes," he said, then began to move.

Tristan made love to her, taking her body to new heights as he bound them together in the way of his people. He took her blood, savoring it for the gift that it was, then gave Isabel his in exchange. And when she fell apart in his arms and cried out in ecstasy, Tristan followed.

He'd follow her from this life into the next and anywhere else she decided to go. Because this human—*ex-human*—had stolen this wolf's heart.

EPILOGUE

Tristan and Isabel sat in Sticks, waiting for Mindy and Nic to arrive. The dive bar was hopping. Tables had been pushed aside to accommodate the dancers. Even with the added space, they overflowed into the aisles, kicking up sawdust as they moved to the music.

"If they don't get here soon," Isabel said, "I'm out of here." There was edginess to her movements as she scanned the crowd.

Tristan smiled and rubbed her lower back. "Hungry again?"

"Starving," she snapped.

Isabel had eaten two hours ago, but her stomach was already rumbling again. He stroked her rounded belly. She'd deliver in another month—thanks to Weres' short gestation periods. Until then, Tristan would fetch her whatever she wanted, whenever she wanted it.

"They'll be here soon," he said, hoping it was the truth. If not, then he'd leave a message at the bar to meet them at the restaurant.

Isabel looked around the crowded barroom and sighed.

Tristan tensed. "What's wrong? Is the baby okay?"

She touched his arm. "The baby's fine. I was just thinking about Everly. She'd never hang at Sticks, but she would've gotten a kick out of this place," she said.

He squeezed her hand. "I wish we could help her, but there's only been one wolf who has ever crossed into the Darkling world and lived to tell about it."

"Where is he now?" she asked, a hint of hope in her voice.

Hope that he was about to crush. "He's dead," Tristan said, fighting back impotent rage. He wanted to do something to help her, something to make the situation better, but he couldn't.

Isabel didn't bother to hide her disappointment.

"I'm sorry, love," he said.

"Me too," she said, then glanced at something behind him. "Mindy and Nic are here." Isabel pasted a smile on her face and wiggled her way off the barstool. She waddled across the room to hug her sister.

Tristan followed close behind, making sure none of the wolves jostled her. They gave her a wide berth, once they caught sight of him.

"Ready to go to dinner?" Mindy asked.

"I was ready an hour ago," Isabel said.

"Guess that means you don't want to stay for a drink," Mindy said.

"Unless you plan to do a shot, then no," Isabel said.

"Lookout! Pregnant cranky lady coming through," Mindy shouted.

* * * * *

Nic waved to his friend, Lucien.

The bartender smiled and waved back. His jovial mask faded the second the couples left the bar. Lucien overheard Tristan and his bondmate talking about her friend, Everly. She had been taken into the Darklings' world. He shuddered at the thought of a human being trapped there.

Tristan was right. There wasn't much that could be done to save her. But he was wrong about one thing. The wolf that made it out of the Darkling world wasn't dead. He was right here, hiding in plain sight.

Lucien knew firsthand the hell that existed on the other side. He'd barely managed to escape. If he hadn't stolen a portal rune stone, he wouldn't have succeeded.

It had taken months for him to recover his sanity. Months spent trapped between man and beast, raging against the darkness trying to envelop him.

He'd kept his past a secret from everyone, including his best friend, Nic. It had been safer that way—safer for everyone.

Once he'd recovered, Lucien vowed never to return. Not just because the Darklings put a price on his head, but because Lucien knew he wouldn't be so lucky next time.

He pulled the black stone out of his pocket and ran his thumb across the runes etched into the surface. Dark magic snapped at his fingertips, making them tingle. Lucien shoved the rock back into his pocket. Why had he kept it? He should've gotten rid of the stone long ago.

If what they'd said was true about Everly, then she was running out of time and he was the only one who could save her.

If you enjoyed Moonlight Kin 4: Tristan, **LEND IT** to a friend. All my books are lending enabled. If you really loved Izzy and Tristan's story, then please consider leaving a **REVIEW**.

For more information about Jordan's upcoming books, including **Moonlight Kin 5: Lucien**, sign up now for her newsletter: http://eepurl.com/AWu7b

ABOUT THE AUTHOR

Jordan Summers has thirty-one published books to her credit. She's a member of the Science Fiction and Fantasy Writers of America, The Horror Writer's Association, International Thriller Writers, and Novelist Inc.

Connect with her online:
Twitter.com/jordanwriter
www.facebook.com/authorjordansummers
www.JordanSummers.com
Join the Endless Summers Newsletter to find out about upcoming releases and author signings.
Click here to join now!

Other Books by Jordan Summers

Dead World Series
Dead World Prequel: Raphael
Dead World Prequel: Kane
Dead World 1: Red
Dead World 2: Scarlet
Dead World 3: Crimson

Moonlight Kin Series
Moonlight Kin 1: A Wolf's Tale
Moonlight Kin 2: Aidan's Mate
Moonlight Kin 3: Nic
Moonlight Kin 4: Tristan - Coming Soon

Phantom Warriors Series
Phantom Warriors 1: Bacchus
Phantom Warriors 2: Saber-tooth
Phantom Warriors 3: Talon
Phantom Warriors 4: Arctos
Phantom Warriors 5: Linx
Phantom Warriors 6: Riot
Phantom Warriors 7: The Dark King
Phantom Warriors Anthology Volume 1
Phantom Warriors Anthology Volume 2
Phantom Warriors' Box Set
Hawk's Slave

Atlantean's Quest Series
Atlantean's Quest 1: The Arrival
Atlantean's Quest 2: Exodus
Atlantean's Quest 3: Redemption
Atlantean Heat 3.5
Atlantean's Quest 4: The Return
Atlantean's Quest 5: The Dark King
Atlantean's Quest Bundle Volume 1

Atlantean's Quest Bundle Volume 2

Lords of the Night Series
Gothic Passions
Rose's Rapture

Various Standalone Titles
Tears of Amun
Heat of the Night
Paris After Dark
Private Investigations
Hot Shot
Off Limits
Sensational Six Box Set

Transformed in Wonderland

WONDERLAND CHRONICLES
BOOK FOUR

DANI HOOTS

"One of the deep secrets of life is that all that is really worth the doing is what we do for others."

— Lewis Carroll

CHAPTER ONE

What were we to do now?

I held my legs close and sat near the fire, rocking back and forth. Malcolm had quickly located us a cave for the night as we figured out our next plan of action. I bit at my nail—something I didn't normally do, but I was trying everything I could to calm my nerves. None of it was working as nothing could make any of this better.

Glancing around, I wondered if this was the same cave we used when we first hid in the Dark Forest all those years ago. It was damp and dark, and I couldn't help but shiver. It wasn't too cold, but I shook from the fear I had.

The Duchess had control over Wonderland.

I heard steps coming into the cave and found that Malcolm had located some Trisings. As to where he got the jar, I had no idea. I stopped asking him questions long ago. The Dark Forest was a strange place, and I didn't eliminate the fact that he had supplies stored throughout the forest since this was where he used to live.

He set the jar down, and I watched as the fairylike creatures smacked the inside of the glass. I was sort of watching them but at the same time replaying everything that had happened. Kate… she was dead. How was that possible? How could Chase have brought her here and risked her life?

I had given the Duchess what she wanted, and yet I wasn't able to save Kate, and now all of Wonderland was under the Duchess's rule because I went against what Malcolm had said.

What the heck was I going to do?

At least Malcolm and I were able to escape, but as we ran, everything was warping and changing into what the Duchess wanted, which meant it was possible that everyone had already been brainwashed.

So all of our friends were now our enemies.

I didn't know if I could fight any of them after all of the time we had spent together. I considered them to be my best friends, so there was no way I could hurt them even if they were attacking me.

Although I did feel like slapping Chase across the face. But could I really fight him even though he had caused the death of my best friend? I had known him for a couple of years now, and we were close. He and I had so many wonderful memories. How could betray me like that?

More tears formed in my eyes. I couldn't believe what had happened. I would never forgive Chase for what he had done, yet when I thought about all that he went through and the thought of him working for the Duchess, my heart ached. Was it all a lie? Did he not actually care for me and was trying to deliver me to the Duchess? Or did he really want to run away so he didn't have to finish the Duchess's orders? And what would have happened if he had disobeyed her?

Malcolm took a seat next to me and wrapped his arm around me. "We will figure this out. We have each other. You aren't alone in this."

I leaned my head on his shoulder. "Thank you. For saving me, I mean. Even though this is all my fault. If I hadn't gone against your wishes to try to save Kate, Wonderland would still be fine. Kate might still be fine."

"It's not your fault; it's that stupid cat's."

"But I still should have listened to you. I shouldn't have just run off on my own. I just wanted to—" More tears. Would this crying ever stop? I wiped my face and took a deep breath.

Malcolm squeezed me tighter. "I understand. I'm sorry it ended the way it did. We will do what we can."

"Which is what? How will only two of us be able to go up against everyone in Wonderland? Am I wrong to believe that all of our friends are now under the complete control of the Duchess and are searching for us as we speak?"

Malcolm didn't answer as he intertwined his fingers with mine. It was clear he didn't know what we were going to do either. It was different when everyone was under the trance made by Morpheus, as there were seven of us. But now it was just us two, and we were against those who could stop us, like Davis and Melvin. We would have to figure something out.

"We will save Wonderland," Malcolm finally answered. "We always do. Even if the others have been brainwashed—or whatever you want to call it—they might be able to break free. I think as long as we kill the Duchess, it will all be fine."

I nodded even though I didn't know how I felt about using such violence. "Kill the Duchess. You make it sound so easy."

"Well, that's what this land is like—or used to be like. With the Kingdom of Hearts, I used to have to kill all the time. Luckily that ended for quite a long time."

I shook my head. "I'm sorry. I didn't mean…"

He stroked the top of my hand with his thumb. "I know you didn't, but don't worry about having to kill anyone. I will do it."

I didn't know how to respond. It was a bad situation as I didn't like the idea of killing as an answer. The Duchess was, however, supposed to be executed, so her sentence was already determined. But the idea of making Malcolm do the dirty work because of something that was my fault didn't sit well with me. I doubted I could take a life, and as he mentioned, he had killed many in the past.

But I didn't want him to have to relive his past

demons. I wished to help him move on.

Noticing I wasn't going to respond to what he said, he diverted the subject. "Do you think you will be able to sleep? I know this cave isn't that comfortable, but it's all we have until morning. Then we should be able to reach my old home."

"I am tired. I don't think I've slept in over thirty-six hours if I'm honest."

Malcolm shifted and leaned against the cave wall. "Lay your head on my lap, and you can sleep with at least some kind of pillow."

I blushed and wanted to protest as it didn't seem comfortable for him, but I really didn't want to sleep on the ground. I leaned over and rested my head on the side of his leg and closed my eyes. I quickly fell asleep as he stroked my hair gently.

When I awoke, I found Malcolm was still asleep. It was strange—he always was awake before I was. I smiled, as I liked seeing his gentle face. He seemed at peace— something I hadn't seen in quite some time. He usually was stressed and worried about whatever task he had been assigned—or at least that was what it seemed like. After a few moments, he stirred. He blinked a few times and then grinned.

"Good morning."

For an instant I had forgotten everything and was happy—I was happy the two of us were close like this, and I wished it could go on forever. I wished I could wake up like this every day. Then I remembered we were in the Dark Forest, hiding from the entire Wonderland Kingdom. My happiness faded as quickly as it had come.

"Good morning."

Malcolm stretched. "We should probably head to my house in the Dark Forest for the time being. Then we can figure out what to do next."

I raised an eyebrow. "Why didn't we stay in the home last time we were here?"

"Because we weren't going to stay in the Dark Forest. We were moving through it."

That was fair. But now we were stuck here until we figured out a plan. "Well then, it sounds like we should head out there."

He nodded. "Keep your katana near. You never know what is going to attack next."

I put my hand on the hilt. That was true. We had learned that many times before. I didn't want to have to face those beasts again, but I couldn't really complain —it was better than the alternative. Maybe. Hopefully.

We headed out, and I wished that I had some snacks on me. Malcolm was able to pick some plants and berries along the way and assured me that they weren't poisonous, but that was Uncle Iroh said before he poisoned himself. Malcolm had lived there for a long time, though, so I knew he wasn't lying, but I couldn't help but be a bit hesitant. This was the Dark Forest— one would assume that everything was poisonous. The berries were quite tart, but they were something to eat, so I didn't complain.

As we made our way through the forest, I heard the familiar roars and growls of what sounded like large creatures around us. I stayed close to Malcolm, practically stepping on his heels as we moved forward. He never made a comment as I almost pulled him down a couple of times. He didn't seem bothered by the sounds of the creatures around us. Perhaps he knew they wouldn't hurt him. Perhaps they knew to leave Malcolm alone as he used to live there.

I couldn't imagine living in the Dark Forest for what I gathered had been years if not decades before the first Alice came and destroyed the Heart Kingdom. It would seem like you'd be scared for your life every single moment of the day. Perhaps after a while, you'd just get numb to it all. That would explain why Malcolm appeared calm no matter what we faced.

As we moved farther through the forest, Malcolm collected some leaves and stuck them in a bag in his pocket. He did that a few times before I questioned what he was up to.

"What are those for?"

He smiled. "You will see."

I wasn't sure if I should be excited or afraid. He seemed at ease in the Dark Forest, and while I understood he spent a lot of time there, it still freaked me out a bit. Only months before, I had witnessed him kill Morpheus, and yet I had no fear of him. I supposed it was because I knew he wouldn't hurt me but would always keep me safe. Morpheus was a murderer, and Malcolm's old job was to execute those in the Dark Forest. Morpheus knew this, and that was why he made Malcolm chase him out there—so I would witness what he once was. But after seeing what all of Wonderland was capable of, was I really one to judge? There was still a lot I didn't know about this place.

We made it to the table with the teacups, which I had

visited a few times now. This was where Malcolm killed Morpheus—this was where it all went down.

Malcolm stopped and stared at the table for a moment. I was about to say something when he turned and smiled. "Right this way."

He pushed back some of the brush, and there stood a small home. I couldn't believe what I was seeing—there was a house right behind the table that I had never noticed before. Everything was always so overgrown I thought the mound was just a bunch of moss or a dead creature or something.

Malcolm laughed as he saw my dropped chin. "I figured you didn't notice. Yeah, it was here the whole time." He opened the door and whistled like one would to a dog. "Spider. Get out."

I heard a hissing noise, and then the giant spider scurried away. I quickly pulled my katana out and pointed it at the spider.

"That thing is back!"

Malcolm shook his head. "It won't hurt you—not if I am around. But don't go near it on your own."

"So I learned."

I wasn't going to go near it either way. I kept my katana out for good measure and followed Malcolm inside. I gasped, as I couldn't believe my eyes. It appeared unlike anything I thought it would. There were teapots and teacups, cozies hanging on the walls, and the area was lined with bookcases. It almost appeared like an old lady's home.

Maybe this wasn't out of left field, as Malcolm did like his tea, but it wasn't completely what I imagined. I didn't know what I would have expected.

It was rather clean, which made little sense. Perhaps the spider was keeping it clean. That wouldn't make sense in my world, but this was Wonderland—nothing ever made sense.

"Take a seat. I will make some tea with the leaves I picked."

So that was what he was doing. I should have known. I chuckled a little as I took a seat on the floral couch, still on the lookout for spiders. So far I hadn't seen any.

Malcolm made some tea and brought it out on a little tray. The cups were all decorated with flowers like one would see at a British tea shop. I took a sip, and it tasted herbal and rather sweet. It was delicious.

Sitting down across from me, he sighed. "So we will stay here until we figure out what to do next. Does that sound like a plan?"

I nodded. It was really all we could do at that point. At least we had a cozier place to wait.

CHAPTER TWO

It was hard to sleep in the Dark Forest even though I had an actual bed now. I felt like it was a bit worse, actually, as it was a fake sense of security. That, and I worried that the spider would come in while I was sleeping and try to eat me. I didn't want to wake up encased in webbing. It was a worry that I never knew I had until now.

Malcolm and I shared a room at least, as one of the rooms had two small beds. It was the room Melvin and Davis had used when they lived with Malcolm. I could only imagine what Davis was like with all the monsters roaming around. Maybe that was why he was described as drunk in the original story—I know if I had to stay there longer than a few days, I might turn to the bottle as well.

As I imagined what life was like for the three of them, I could hear Malcolm slightly snoring from across the room, which made me feel a little better. If he was at ease, then there was nothing to worry about. Then again, he always seemed to be at ease when scary things were going on. At least right now I could take comfort in knowing he would keep me safe.

I shifted in the bed and stared up at the ceiling. I couldn't get over the fact that this place was still clean. I imagined the spider in an apron with rubber gloves cleaning and tried not to laugh. Perhaps that wasn't what happened. Maybe the home was enchanted, as I wouldn't put it past Malcolm to do something like that. He mentioned having powers that he couldn't use without getting in trouble in Wonderland. I needed to remember to ask him about it now, as it wasn't like they weren't going to arrest him already.

The fact that he escaped with me made me happy. I didn't believe I would have been able to figure out any of this alone. I wondered what would have happened if

I had stayed—whether or not I would have died or if I would have served the Duchess or not. I had a feeling the odds were that I would have disappeared. I was too much of a liability to her. I was the only one who could bring her destruction.

Which was why I knew I had to stop this.

Worst-case scenario, I would eventually disappear. Best-case scenario, I stopped the Duchess, saved Chase, and brought back Kate, but then what? Would I return to my world, or would I have to stay here? Everything was still up in the air, and I didn't know what to expect.

But at least I had Malcolm. At least I wasn't alone.

I took slow, deep breaths and focused on listening to Malcolm snore. After a bit, I found myself drifting off to sleep.

I woke to find Malcolm sitting on the bed. I smiled as I looked up at him. He gently caressed my face.

"Good morning, beautiful."

I didn't know how to respond after everything. It was, in fact, not that great of a morning given where we were, but it made me feel good that he was there, giving me his smile. "Good morning."

"I decided it would be best to wake you before I went

and found something to eat so you didn't wake up alone. But if you wanted, you can join me."

That was a hard choice: go outside and deal with the Dark Forest, or stay here alone and worry about Malcolm's safety and whether that spider would come back. Actually, that was an easy choice. "I think I will go with you."

"I figured. Come, I will teach you about the plants in this area. They are quite spectacular."

I got up but didn't need to change as we slept in our clothes. I straightened them out and ran my hands through my hair a few times, hoping it was somewhat nice and not all over the place like short hair usually was in the morning. People always thought it was easier, but many times it wasn't.

I followed Malcolm outside and found that it still appeared dark out but only due to the foliage. Light barely peeked through now, and I could make out the different trees and the table outside the house.

Malcolm picked a few leaves. "You would be surprised how many of the plants in the forest are actually quite edible. It's the creatures that you have to be worried about. That doesn't go for all the plants, both here and in the forest throughout Wonderland, but it's still pretty easy to identify them here."

He showed me the plant and explained what to look for to identify the plant.

"It sounds easier than it is in my world. There're a lot of plants that look alike, and it's easy to pick the wrong thing. I have always been too scared to ever wild harvest."

"I agree. If you don't know what you're doing, then don't pick plants. But I've been doing this for quite some time, so I definitely know what plant to pick."

I nodded. "Of course."

"And also," he added, "I started a veggie garden a long while ago. Perhaps some stuff is still growing from that."

He picked some of the plants and berries that were growing around the house and pointed out ones that were poisonous. He was right. It was very clear which ones were poisonous from their color and leaf types. The berries that had spots were ones to skip over. Easy enough. I just wished it was that easy in my world.

We moved over to where his vegetable garden used to be, and I couldn't believe my eyes. It looked like a disaster area with random zucchini and tomatoes growing all over.

He grinned. "It's still growing! I wonder if the spider grew them to use as bait."

I peered around again for that creature but didn't see any sign of it. Malcolm picked some vegetables, and we headed back to his home, which was still in viewing distance.

"Feel free to relax while I make something to eat," Malcolm said as we walked inside.

"You're able to cook in the middle of the forest?"

He nodded. "Yes, energy works a bit different here. It is quite nice. You must have been tired yesterday and didn't notice the lamps and lights are, in fact, on right now."

I glanced around. Sure enough, they were.

"Huh."

"So make yourself at home. It won't take long."

I nodded and went over to the couch and took a seat. I still couldn't believe how many cozies and teacups he had hanging around the walls. Where did he even get those? Was he able to go into town when he lived out here? Or did he send others to pick them up? I wanted to ask but felt it would come across weird, so I decided to just ignore the subject.

Malcolm came out with two place settings and

arranged them on the dining table. I moved over to a chair and began eating.

"So…" I poked around with my fork. "What do we do next?"

Malcolm took a deep breath. "I honestly don't know. Maybe wait here for a few years and hope for the best?" I raised an eyebrow at him, and he chuckled. "I joke. But that was what I used to do when something was wrong. It is strange to think I would back down like that. But that was the old me."

I went on. "We are severely outnumbered now. Depending on how the Duchess set up her world, everyone could be on the lookout for us."

"You are right. First I think you need to train a bit more. We need to be at our best before going out. We can't mess up at this point."

Because I already did. I ate some more of my breakfast. "By the way, can you use that power of illusion? I know you said you would be tried for treason if you ever used it in Wonderland and got caught, but what about now?"

He bit his lip. "Well, that is complicated. The rule had nothing to do with the kingdom as much as Wonderland itself. It's sort of like a curse. If I use it, I will automatically die, and I don't think that will change because of the Duchess."

I stared at him. "How did you know it would work in my world?"

Malcolm shrugged. "I didn't in the beginning, but that was before I knew you. I tried it when we went through all the paperwork for the school. Nothing bad happened, so I knew it was fine in your world. Howard was the one who figured it would be fine, and I trusted him. Mainly because he was the one who gave me the curse in the first place."

"Is there a way we can break that curse?"

"Perhaps, but I'd rather not break it. It keeps me in check. Although it would have come in handy right now."

I could understand what he meant. If he had such a strong power, it could corrupt, and by the sounds of it, there was a time in his life where he had too much power. I didn't want him to have to deal with that pain again.

He went on. "So we will train and we will get ready. And what better place to train than here."

I glanced outside as I saw rustling in the bushes. I sighed, knowing he was right. This was the best place to train. It was no wonder he was the strongest fighter in all of Wonderland.

CHAPTER
THREE

I ran through the Dark Forest—branches and stems of hopefully nothing poisonous scratched at my clothes. Luckily I was able to find some of Davis's old clothes that fit me fine. I could just imagine his face as Chase would harass him about being the same size as me.

My heart ached, thinking back to all the fun times we had.

Those memories were what I was fighting for—those memories would get me through this. I wanted to go back to the way things were, and I would stop at nothing to achieve that. And in order to defeat the Duchess, I first had to be able to defeat Malcolm.

Well, not actually defeat him. I had five minutes to start running and find a hiding spot in the forest, without getting killed by all the creatures in here, until Malcolm would come to find me. The goal was to be able to hide well enough that I could surprise Malcolm by striking first. It was some sick mash-up of tag and hide-and-go-seek, but if I could keep myself hidden from him, then we wouldn't have a problem visiting a town and assessing what the Duchess had changed. Apparently this was how all the others trained when they lived out here. I couldn't help but feel sorry for Davis and Melvin, as I bet Malcolm didn't hold back against them. And it sounded like he was a lot scarier back then.

Malcolm promised I wouldn't get completely lost in the Dark Forest, as if I really tried to get him to find me, he would. I was more afraid of getting attacked by a jabberwocky. Again. Yesterday one decided I looked like a pretty good snack and almost chased me out of the woods. Luckily I was able to collect myself and fight it off just as Malcolm appeared. Let's just say I lost that session of hide-and-seek.

But today was different. I could feel it. I would hide well enough where I could surprise attack him, and he would agree to go to town. It's only been a week of training, yes, but I felt today was my day. And I really just wanted to escape this wretched place even if what was waiting for us on the other side was probably nothing good. I wanted to know, and I wasn't sure I could spend another night worrying about that spider. The day before yesterday, it decided to bring some flowers to apologize to me, but it only made my worry grow. But I had to admit, it was adorable.

I was also starting to get familiar with the layout of the Dark Forest, which surprised me. I was never known to be good at directions, but I supposed since I was in constant fear of getting lost, it was possible for me to finally get good at it.

Passing the cave we stayed in on our first night, I glanced around. It was, in fact, possible to climb over the mouth. Would that be somewhere Malcolm would think to look? Deciding to give it a shot, I made it look like I went inside the cave, then backtracked and climbed above it.

The plan was to wait for Malcolm, have him walk

inside the cave, jump down, and surprise him. He would be most impressed with me, and I could hardly stop smiling. I had finally gotten the better of him. Hopefully.

I could hear the howls of creatures that lived in the Dark Forest. Some of them I didn't even know what they were, and I was too afraid to ask. I figured they were all violent and to just always stay on guard.

After a little while of waiting, Malcolm came into the clearing. I still wasn't sure how he was so good at tracking, as one couldn't see the ground in the Dark Forest since it was covered in fog, but he always showed up around five minutes after I stopped, as if he didn't have to put much effort into looking for me.

I watched as he slowly stepped inside the cave. I grinned as I jumped down as silently as I could. Luckily the ground was covered in moss, so footsteps were almost silent. I placed my hand on the hilt and stepped into the cave behind Malcolm.

He was examining around, trying to see if I was hiding behind one of the rocks. I slowly pulled out my sword so that I could attack.

Well, not actually attack. It would be more of a clumsy half swing without actually touching him. He always said to swing like it was real, as he would always be able to block it, but I didn't feel safe doing that.

I was within five feet of him now, smiling. I had actually won. I couldn't believe it. As I went to tap him with the dull edge of my katana, he quickly turned around and drew his own sword and swung. I blocked it in a swift motion, letting out a high-pitched scream.

Malcolm laughed. "You need to be on guard at all times, Alice. I know you don't like fully swinging, but you have to realize there is no room for hesitation when dealing with an enemy who wants you dead."

"I know…"

"But you did very well to block my attack. I think you are ready. We should head to the nearest town tomorrow."

I jumped up. "Yay!"

"But for the record, I did know you were above the cave. I just wanted to see how well you could try to sneak up on me."

I frowned. I really thought I had gotten the better of him. I should have figured. "But I still passed?"

"Yes, I think you will do fine against the others for now. And I doubt they have the same skills as they did before they were affected by the Duchess."

I wasn't sure if that was a complete compliment or not, but I felt better now that we were finally going to figure out what had happened. "Was Bill easier to go up against when he was affected by Morpheus?"

Malcolm nodded. "A bit. He was still smart and good at tracking, but there was something missing. When you aren't able to think for yourself, you aren't able to use all your skills. At least I don't think so. You become more predictable too."

That made perfect sense. I followed Malcolm as we headed back to his home. I decided it was technically a cottage, as I still hadn't come up with a good name for it. It appeared like a cottage on the inside, especially with all the tea cozies. I collapsed on the couch inside as Malcolm went to the kitchen to make some tea. He did that often, and I wasn't sure if it was something I hadn't noticed, or now that we were back to his home, he was reverting to habits he had while living there. Either way, it was some of the best tasting tea I had ever had.

Malcolm brought out a cup of tea, and I took a sip. It tasted floral with a hint of earthy tones. I set it down and peered up at him.

"So, what town will we be checking out?"

"I am not sure. Everything has been rearranged for the new ruler. I don't even know what the districts are, if there are any different districts. I don't think the Duchess is that creative, so they will more than likely be the same, just arranged a little different."

It was crazy how everything could change like that. I didn't want to think about how much of the Wonderland that I had grown to love had changed.

"If each time Wonderland changes, the districts are changed, then how come the Red and White Kingdom and the Heart Kingdom still existed?"

"Because Alice didn't want them to disappear but left them so we could learn from our mistakes. She also made it impossible for anyone else to change them as well."

I supposed that made sense. It was important to remember the past so one didn't repeat it.

"But I do have a feeling none of the districts except the one she is in will be in good shape. She only cares about herself. I don't remember a day she has ever extended a helping hand, at least not without wanting something in return."

That was definitely clear to me. She used Chase as

her puppet and was willing to hurt my friend in the process. It made sense to me that she wouldn't have cared about anything else.

"But there are parts of Wonderland that can't be changed, or at least I don't think. Well, more things outside the actual borders of Wonderland. We will find out tomorrow. For now, get your rest. Tomorrow is going to be a long day."

I nodded and stretched out a bit. These past few days felt long, but I would finally get my chance to save Kate, if that was even possible.

CHAPTER FOUR

I followed Malcolm through the forest, my hand already on my hilt in case we ran into something, whether they be human or monster. The jabberwocky screamed in the distance. I did not want to face another one of those—I was rather sick of them and couldn't believe how many survived in these woods. I supposed it was better than the bandersnatch. Luckily I hadn't run into one of those again. I did hear their roar every once in a while, however, which left me on edge. The jabberwocky was much easier to take down.

I spotted the singing flowers that encircled the forest and felt much more relieved. It meant that we were almost to the rest of Wonderland and would finally understand what had happened. Although I had been training all week, I didn't know if I was truly prepared. Neither of us had any idea what was waiting for us. For all we knew, they could have the entire Dark Forest surrounded and we were walking into a trap.

But it was better than just sitting around.

We would have to face them sooner or later. What surprised me was that none of them dared go into the Dark Forest after us. I presumed it was because they feared Malcolm and that was his home base, so to speak. He knew that place like the back of his hand, and no one could compare to that.

Except Chase.

It seemed like Chase knew the Dark Forest pretty well. He could have tracked us down just like he tracked Malcolm down when he killed Morpheus. I wondered if he still was the old Chase or if he had been brainwashed again. It didn't seem like he needed to be, as he had been working for the Duchess this entire time.

So there was a possibility of him helping us in the

end.

I wasn't going to expect him to—not after everything that had happened. He had his chances, and yet he never tried to come clean or betray the Duchess, other than when he had said he wanted to run away. That wasn't the same, however, as I wasn't even sure he was trying to escape his fate or that he was actually going to take me straight to the Duchess.

We stepped into the field, and the song of the flowers no longer seemed to affect me. I had grown used to the effects of the Dark Forest, which I wasn't sure was a good thing or not. As we marched forward, Malcolm turned to me.

"After here, we won't know the terrain or what is going on. Be on high alert—even more so than when you are in the Dark Forest. And stay close to me. If anything happens to you, there will be no way to reverse this, and the Duchess knows that. I will protect you no matter the cost. Do you understand?"

I nodded, more worried than I had ever been. What would happen if we ran into any of the others? I would have to fight them, but I didn't know if I could do it. Hopefully it wouldn't come to that, as I had a feeling Malcolm wouldn't hesitate to stop them.

Since I had always focused on not listening to the flowers, I never noticed anything else about them. They were quite beautiful with a rainbow of colors decorating the landscape. It was was similar to how the most beautiful flowers had thorns, except in this case it was a song that would put you to sleep and you would eventually die. I tried not to think about how many people might have met their death there. I figured it wouldn't be too many as they knew to stay away from that place. Even the creatures of the Dark Forest knew to stay away.

They also gave off a pleasant aroma. It smelled of candied apples, grapes, and peaches—like those you would find at a carnival. It reminded me of cotton candy and spending time at the Oregon State Fair. Kate and I had a lot of fun at it last year, of which Chase tagged along and lost all his change on one of the rides, as it flipped us upside down and everything fell out of his pocket. The workers wouldn't let us pick up the change either, which was stupid. They probably were just taking advantage of us because we were teens.

The memory of Chase and Kate and how much fun we had made my heart hurt even more. I had so many great memories with both of them. What if I couldn't move on? What if I really couldn't spend another fun day with them?

What if this was the end?

Noticing my distress, Malcolm grabbed my hand. "It will be okay. Even if we run into trouble, I will get us out of it. Don't worry."

I smiled a little. Although I was worried about what we would find and whether or not we would be captured, I was more hurt due to the fact that everything had come crashing down. "Thank you. I am glad I still have you, but I can't help but think of everything we all have been through. If I had just…"

"It's not your fault. It is the Duchess's and Chase's fault. They are the ones who put you in the position to have to choose between Wonderland and your friend."

I nodded a little, but it didn't help the feeling in my stomach—the feeling saying that I was responsible, that I was the cause of all this. I had betrayed everyone's trust. I had destroyed Wonderland.

No, we would find a way to destroy the Duchess, restore Wonderland, and save Kate. And Chase.

We made it through the flower field and stopped to survey the land. Things appeared normal—large flower fields of the Flower District, stretching as far as the eye could see. The Flower District, although one we always visited since the portal dumped us into a random closet, was rather laid-back and quaint. I found it to be quite beautiful, but it wasn't somewhere most people went unless they had to, which was perfect for us as there would be fewer guards. People traded between lands often, so we could just pretend we were traders.

Despite the fact that the visuals were similar to before the Duchess took over, something about the atmosphere did feel off. Although it was sunny out—a perfect day, in fact—it seemed… fake. It felt like the little town in *Big Fish*, where it was perfect and yet something was most definitely wrong.

This was not good.

I glanced over to Malcolm, who had a frown on his face. He must have felt it too. It wasn't just the fact that we had been in the Dark Forest causing this strange sensation.

"Stay on your guard," Malcolm said. "I have a bad feeling about this."

I nodded as we started forward. In the distance, we could make out the town center or at least where the town center used to be. The silhouette was no longer the same, and I wasn't sure what to expect. It appeared as if there were walls that now surrounded the once open and free town. I gulped, not looking forward to seeing how the place had changed.

I scanned the area for any people roaming around or farmers tending their crops, but there was no one. It was almost as if it had all been abandoned, but by the looks of the crops, it was apparent someone was taking care of them. The more I looked, the more I felt a shiver run down my spine. I didn't like this one bit, but at least there were no guards at the ready to fight us.

We approached the town and found that there was only one point of entry on each side of the now large stone walls that surrounded the place. Before we approached, Malcolm stopped us.

"I don't like seeing this security. It reminds me of when the Queen of Hearts was in charge. However, since no one actually likes the Duchess, I'm hoping it is relaxed and they aren't checking people. Just act like you belong, don't look at them, and walk through without hesitating, all right?"

I nodded. "I got it."

Flipping up our hoods, we headed toward the closest entry point. The guards that stood at the gate didn't seem to be checking anyone, just like Malcolm predicted. I didn't look at him but walked past with Malcolm just as he said. The guard never said anything, and we were in the clear. I let out a sigh as I surveyed the area. My mouth dropped, and I covered it with my hand.

This town used to have beautiful flowers that covered the streets and grew up the buildings, but now everything was plain and appeared almost like that of the industrial revolution. Nothing was beautiful anymore but had grown dirty and full of soot. I couldn't believe my eyes.

I stared at the men and women who once were wearing extraordinary gowns but now wore plain clothes that were worn and dirty. It appeared they hadn't been able to bathe properly in days. I didn't understand how this was possible, as it hadn't been that long. Was this truly the power the Duchess had? Did she really want to have her people living like this?

"It's not polite to stare," Malcolm whispered in my ear.

I turned away from them and looked down at what once used to be the most lush grass that was now hard pavement.

"Why would she do this? Why wouldn't someone

ruling want their citizens to be happy?"

"Because it makes it harder for them to gather resources to rebel."

That made sense. Even in my world this was how dictators took advantage of their people. Was this what it was like everywhere? Was this the hardships they had faced with the Queen of Hearts all those years ago? Most of these people weren't alive, but Malcolm had been. Was this what his life used to be like?

Malcolm went on. "Now come, I want to see if we can get an eye on where she is staying."

I followed Malcolm as we ventured through the town. I tried to keep my eyes away from the people as I felt tears streaming down.

CHAPTER FIVE

This madness went on forever.

We made our way through the town. Some parts of the layout seemed familiar, other parts of it did not. We headed forward, however, as we were just trying to get through it so we could head toward the Duchess's mansion. I recognized cafés and some businesses, but ones that had been on the other side of the city were now located where we walked. It was utter madness. Nothing seemed right.

No one seemed to pay us much mind as we ventured through, mingling with traders and such. There were vendors who were selling flowers, which were still beautiful as they had been when we'd passed the fields, but the sellers didn't look too happy to be there. Not many seemed to be purchasing flowers either, which was concerning.

It didn't matter. I would fix this. They wouldn't have to suffer much longer.

I still couldn't believe that only a week had passed. Was this really the same Wonderland? Did they know only that much time had gone by, or did this erase their memories of earlier and they believed they had lived their entire lives like this? How would this affect my world as all the citizens were dreams?

"I still can't believe this is happening," I whispered to Malcolm. "I wish I had known—"

"What the Duchess did is not your fault. She could have easily taken over and been a benevolent leader. As I said earlier, this is what it was like when the Queen of Hearts ruled. My guess is she wants to rule just like her —with fear in everyone's eyes," Malcolm explained.

I shook my head. "I just don't understand. This used to be such a beautiful place. Who would want this?"

"Monsters, that's who. She knew that no one would obey her rule, so she made it so they couldn't do anything to revolt. I've seen it all before. Now let's see what shape the capital is in and if that is where she is ruling all of this. If I had to guess, her mansion is where the capital palace once was."

I nodded and followed him as we left this dreary city behind.

The road from the Flower District to the capital wasn't too long, if it was the same layout. We would have to go through some woods and prairies, but that wasn't difficult. It was mostly flat, and I wouldn't have to climb. I hated elevation changes, more for going down as it always made my knees feel unstable.

There weren't many people on the roads—just a trader here and there. They nodded to us and said hello, but that was it. We kept our heads down when we came across them and waved. They didn't seem to care, so our original notion of everyone being on the lookout for us had been wrong. Perhaps the Duchess didn't have as much power as we had originally thought.

The forest felt like walking through the redwoods in southern Oregon. We had explored these woods many times in the couple of years I had been coming to

Wonderland. They were rather magical and beautiful. I could spend days out here, painting every scenery I found. I was glad they were still in the same shape as they had been before the change. It would have been sad to see such beautiful places disappear.

Glancing at Malcolm, I found him surveying the land as we moved, as if on the lookout. We were wearing hooded capes, but it wouldn't be enough if we found someone looking for us or we ran into Melvin and the others. I gulped, praying that we wouldn't be spotted or have to face them. If we were captured, I didn't know if there would be any way out of this. I had been captured before a couple of times, but this time there wouldn't be anyone to save us. This time it would be the end.

No, I couldn't think like that. I had to stay positive. Just because there were only two of us didn't mean that we wouldn't win. Malcolm would come up with something, and I would go along with it. It was my fault we were in this mess, and I wouldn't argue with Malcolm ever again.

Because my friend still died.

I held back the tears, not wanting to have a complete breakdown in the middle of the path. We would figure out a way to save her—I just knew it.

We made it to the capital, and I couldn't believe my eyes. What was once an intricate and artistic city was now a walled-off manor, similar to the one we'd visited. The more I looked at it, the more I realized it was the same building. Malcolm had been right.

"How…," I began.

"She used your magic spell to move where her mansion was. She must have still wanted it. It is a gorgeous building, to be honest. Just a horrible host."

I nodded. That made sense, as the kingdoms changed. "So the old capital is gone?"

"Seems so. Which is odd…"

"What do you mean?"

Malcolm didn't answer my question but narrowed his eyes at the horizon. He stopped walking, as if searching for something. I stopped as well, not wanting to go any farther into that mess. I saw the familiar nicely cut hedges, the gorgeous roses, water fountains as far as the eye could see. Money didn't seem to be a big deal in this world, but that didn't mean she wasn't guilty living like this and forcing all the citizens into poverty. It just wasn't right.

"What are we going to do now?"

He pursed his lips. "I definitely don't think we should

go any farther. I just wanted to see what we were up against."

That made sense. I turned back to the mansion. I wondered if Chase was in there, still serving the Duchess like he always had been. As for the rest, were they still alive? Were they brainwashed into being her guard, just like what Morpheus did? I had a feeling that was the case as the Duchess would want strong people on her side to protect her from us.

Malcolm glanced around again. "Let's head back. I don't like being out here for any longer than we already have."

I nodded. "Agreed. And I don't think we will want to stay outside the Dark Forest for the night."

"No, we won't. Luckily we are on the side of the Dark Forest that is closer to my cottage. I just figured searching for the Flower District would be the safest thing to do first." He peered over at the mansion. "And I also wanted to see this place with my own eyes."

I agreed—now seeing this place made our situation all the more real. We had to do something before it was too late, but how? Hopefully we could come up with a plan soon. More than likely, it would have to do with killing the Duchess.

As we began to head toward the Dark Forest, Malcolm abruptly stopped and held his hand out. "Stay close to me."

My heart raced as I heard footsteps behind me. I got closer to Malcolm and prayed it was someone just passing by.

"Hey! You two! Stop!"

I knew that voice. It was Bill. I heard Malcolm curse under his breath. I glanced back to find it was just Bill on a horse—there were no signs of the others.

"What are you two doing on the outskirts of the capital?"

Malcolm kept his head down, as not to reveal his face. "We were simply looking for places to work. We didn't realize we were on the road to the capital."

"Oh? And what citizen doesn't know where the capital is?"

"A very turned-around lost one. But since we were mistaken, we are heading back now. Thank you for keeping our country safe." Malcolm grabbed my hand and started forward toward the forest.

"Did you really think I would fall for that, Malcolm and Alice?" He laughed. "Now turn yourselves in before I use force."

"Run! Remember last time!" Malcolm exclaimed as he pushed me forward. I began to run when I realized Malcolm wasn't following. I turned around to find him drawing his sword. No, he wasn't going to do that to me again. If I helped him, we would outnumber Bill. Between the two of us, we could take him down.

But I couldn't clash swords with Bill as I would never want to deal the final blow. I could, however, distract him long enough to let Malcolm knock him out.

I glanced around for anything that I could truly distract someone like Bill with. I bit my lip. What would distract Bill? Then it hit me as he jumped off the horse.

I put my hands around my mouth and shouted. "Oh hey, Kenny! What are you doing over there?"

Bill spun around to see what mess Kenny was getting into but found I was lying. Malcolm picked up on what I had done and used the butt of his sword to knock Bill out. Grabbing his horse, Malcolm led it to where I was waiting.

"I told you to run." He tried to seem mad at me, but I could see the smile trying to appear on his lips.

"Yeah, well, I wasn't going back to the Dark Forest on my own, so I figured I would help."

Malcolm helped me on the horse and mounted as well. With a slight kick, we headed back toward the Dark Forest.

"You could have gotten captured pulling that stunt." He apparently wasn't letting this go.

"But I didn't, and I figured you could use some help. Not to sound like a damsel in distress, but I really don't think I could take down the Duchess by myself. There are too many people after me—people who I recognize are stronger than me. Which is why I will always try to think of easy ways to de-escalate the situation."

"Like yelling 'Hey, Kenny'?"

I nodded. "Yup. Admit it, it was clever and kind of funny if not for the fact we almost got arrested."

"It was, but he's going to have one heck of a headache when he wakes up, not to mention be mad about his horse."

"Speaking of which, what are we going to do about the horse once we get to the Dark Forest?"

"We will let it go. The military horses we have are quite smart and always head back to the capital once set free. Sometimes even when you don't want them to, leaving you stranded and having to walk all the way back."

I smiled as I could imagine a horse doing that. We set forward and prayed that we wouldn't run into any of the others.

CHAPTER SIX

We jumped off the horse, and Malcolm whistled at him. He abruptly turned and sauntered off, as if that was the cue to go home, or perhaps he didn't want to be near the Dark Forest any longer than he had to. I didn't blame him.

Malcolm turned to me. "Well, ready to go back home?"

He used the word *home* ironically, as he knew I didn't want to be back in the Dark Forest. I rolled my eyes as we stepped through the singing flowers.

It was nice having time with Malcolm after we had

spent quite a few months ignoring each other. It was also nice to see him in good spirits, given that fact that Wonderland was now controlled by a ruthless madwoman. It meant he had hope, and if he had hope, then so did I.

I didn't like the fact I felt so helpless right now, not to mention anxiety randomly overtaking me at any moment. What was I supposed to do when it felt like there was nothing I could do. I had the entire world shatter before me, and it was my fault.

Grabbing my hand, Malcolm squeezed it. How he always knew when I was distraught, I wasn't sure, but it was comforting to know that he was there for me when I needed him most. I just had to make sure to be there for him and the others.

I would save them all if it was the last thing I did.

We reached the denser part of the Dark Forest, past the singing flowers, and I was welcomed back by the roars of the jabberwocky. I sighed as we moved forward, which made Malcolm laugh a little. I was getting used to the sounds, but they still made the hair on the back of my neck raise a bit. I couldn't wait to get out of there again.

"So what are we going to do next?" I asked as we

crouched under some thick branches.

Malcolm let out a sigh. "I'm working on it. I am playing all the possibilities in my head and going through everything I know about Wonderland and determining what our safest plan of action can be."

I nodded. "Safest, huh? Is there really a safe plan?"

"I hope so."

That made me chuckle in the way one laughs when there was nothing else they could do. I didn't know Wonderland like Malcolm did, so I doubted I could come up with the best solution; however, sometimes a newcomer could bring different eyes to the table and solve a problem in a way no one else thought of.

So I began to let my mind wander about what I did know about Wonderland. I knew that there were different eras and that the old kingdoms were still standing, although no one went there anymore. I knew that Chase would look there first for us, so it wouldn't be a good hiding spot long term. I knew since the mansion was where the king and queen once lived, that it was likely they had been erased from this era. I knew if Chase's memories were altered, that he would be the only person we could convince to help us. However, no one in the Flower District seemed to care that we were walking around. Even if they didn't see us under our hoods, one would think that the guards would check everyone coming in and out of the town.

Which meant she had less control over everyone than we realized.

"Do you think the Duchess focused more on those with roles than the dreams in this world? Since they would be the most powerful to take her down. Then she just made living hard for everyone else so they couldn't use resources to fight her."

Malcolm glanced at me. "That makes sense. It seemed odd that none of the guards stopped us. Perhaps we can trust certain people after all then. However, I don't want to lower my guard, as we can't have any screwups."

That was fair. But it was something we could potentially use. I smiled, satisfied that I deduced something. Now I just needed to figure out how to use it to solve my problem.

It occurred to me that we didn't really know anyone outside our circle. "Why don't you guys befriend people outside your circle? I mean, besides because you were in my world a lot. But it doesn't seem like you interact much."

Malcolm shrugged as he moved some hanging moss out of the way to walk under. "It's not that we don't want to interact with them, but more… that they don't stick around."

"Ah. I guess I never thought of that."

"We are much older than all of them, and we will continue living after they are gone. It's hard to make connections. So typically those with roles stick together."

"But that would make broken friendships even that much harder, I bet."

He nodded. "Yes it does. You hold grudges and learn whether or not someone is worthy of trusting again. Take Chase for example. It had been decades since he said he broke ties with the Duchess, but I never believed because I knew he was a liar. And I was right."

I realized I shouldn't have brought it up. I let out a breath. Their fight never seemed to end. However, now I understood what type of betrayals would cause such strife between two people. It made sense that he wouldn't trust him, as I doubted I could ever trust Chase again.

We made it back to the cottage, and I double-checked

the couch for the spider before collapsing on it. My body started shaking as I realized what had happened—we had almost been captured by Bill, and the past week of training would have been for nothing.

"Are we going to be able to do this?" I peered over at Malcolm as he hung up his cloak. He looked at me with sad eyes for a moment, then turned to the kitchen.

"I'm going to make us some tea."

I closed my eyes and rubbed my face as he went into the kitchen. It was clear Bill had been brainwashed, but at least his love for Kenny hadn't changed and I was able to use that to our advantage. But it all was still concerning.

How were we going to get past them in order to take down the Duchess?

I thought back to how the citizens didn't seem to be brainwashed like Bill was. Did that mean Zachariah and Penny remembered who we were? They and their daughter were the only people I had really gotten to know here in Wonderland. Would they turn us in if they recognized us? Or would they help?

The problem was they had no skill in fighting, and I wouldn't want anything bad to happen to them if they helped us. So it was out of the question to talk to them.

Besides, Chase knew of their existence and was probably keeping an eye on their home.

"Here you go." Malcolm stepped into the room. I opened my eyes to find him holding two cups of tea with a smile. I sat up as he handed one to me.

"Thank you." I blew on it some and took a sip. It was a mix of berry, black, and green tea with a hint of rose. It was one of my favorite blends he had. It was sweet yet hearty. I could drink it every day and not get sick of it.

He took a seat across from me. "Now, to answer your question, I don't think just the two of us will be able to take down the Duchess by ourselves. Not after seeing what we saw."

I frowned. I didn't think he would be so upfront about his thoughts. He wasn't one to say something was impossible unless it really was. What did that mean for us?

"What are we going to do then? I don't particularly want to live here for an eternity, not to mention they will eventually come out here for us."

"That is true. I give it about a month before they try, but they will have a good plan by then. I doubt we would win, even on my own turf."

Well, at least I wouldn't have to be out there for that long. I gulped, waiting for him to go on.

"But I think there is a way for us to win. The problem is, we will have to find Dodo."

Like the one in the caucus race. I knew that there were other characters in the novel, but I never asked about them in case it brought up bad memories, like Howard.

"And what is wrong with that?" I asked. "I mean, if you think it is possible. And why wouldn't he have been affected by the change?"

"Well, Dodo gave up on being involved with Wonderland affairs and now lives outside the boundaries. So, therefore, he isn't affected by anything that is happening within Wonderland."

"Well, that's good news for us. Why don't we go now?"

He let out a sigh and set down his tea. It was never a good sign when he set down his tea. "The problem is that Dodo… He always asks a price for whatever he helps with. We have to be willing to give up whatever he asks."

That didn't seem like a big deal, given the circumstances. "I'll do anything. Wonderland will be destroyed at this rate, not to mention the Duchess wants me killed anyway."

"There's another thing."

How could there be more? It seemed like nothing could get more complicated than it already was, but Wonderland always seemed to like to surprise me. "What is it?"

"He… he might be able to bring back Kate."

I couldn't believe what I was hearing. This entire time, he knew of a way to bring back my best friend? Why hadn't he said anything earlier?"I'll do whatever he asks."

"He could ask for your life in exchange. Or my life, or maybe even Wonderland. You can never tell with him."

But could he really be any worse than the Duchess? I shook my head. "There is only one way to find out. Let's go find him."

CHAPTER SEVEN

"So why don't we just head toward where the Dodo is? I mean, if he isn't within the boundaries of Wonderland, then he shouldn't have been moved in the change, right?" I asked as I watched Malcolm pace back and forth. We had made a decision the night before that we would visit the Dodo, but after that, Malcolm seemed to be deep in thought, as if there was more to this than he was letting on.

Malcolm stopped pacing and took a sip of his tea.

Today it was an Earl Grey-tasting tea. Setting the cup down, he glanced over at me. "Although he hasn't changed locations, I'm not completely sure which direction to head."

I furrowed my eyebrows. Malcolm was supposedly the greatest tracker in all of Wonderland. How would he not know how to find someone? "Wouldn't north, south, and all that be the same?"

He shook his head. "When we went out yesterday, the sun rose and set in different spots compared to normal. The Duchess did a real number in regard to knowing which was north and south. I was able to orient myself so I could find the Dark Forest fine, but to find the Dodo, we will need a map. He isn't someone I visited regularly, not to mention he could have moved. But with a map, I might be able to deduce where he is and which way to head."

I leaned farther back into the couch and clutched a pillow against my chest. Why was everything always harder than it needed to be in this place? Why couldn't we just be able to find someone easily?

"Not only that, but since Bill found us, I'm afraid they are going to heighten security, not to mention someone might figure out we will go to the edges for help. I doubt anyone would side with her, since they all know how corrupt she is, and they have more power on the outside so she won't dare cross them. But she might have rearranged the edges so he and a few others will be hard to find for us."

"What others? Is there anyone else we can find? Maybe we can gather them all and they can help us."

Malcolm shrugged. "We can, but I know they won't help at all. Dodo is the only one with power and knowledge of Wonderland that we can use. It's crazy, but he is said to be older than time itself."

It wasn't the strangest thing I had heard, but it was definitely up there. "You're right. That is crazy."

Malcolm let out a chuckle to my comment and rubbed his forehead with his hand. "He was also Howard's mentor and taught him everything he knew. Since he knew Howard, I'm hoping he will help us."

I sipped my tea, thinking back about Howard. I hadn't known him that long, but from what I could tell, he seemed like a pretty nice guy. He was Malcolm's mentor and was wiser than anyone else I'd known. Having witnessed his death, I clutched the pillow even more, trying to rid myself of those images. I could only imagine how Malcolm felt as he was standing closer to him.

But if he'd taught Howard, then he had to be wise and willing to help us. Then again, Count Dooku taught Qui-Gon Jinn.

"Have you ever meet Dodo?"

Malcolm hesitated. "Well, sort of. It was while I was the executioner. He might have been on a list. But he survived. One of the few that did. He was saved by Alice, actually."

So he was supposed to kill him but didn't only because of Alice. That was a great start. "Ah."

He smiled. "But I'm hoping since you are with me, he will listen. And because I worked with Howard. And because it's been a few centuries... I'm hopeful. Although some people do hold grudges against others in Wonderland, most people get over things after a while. If everyone were to hold grudges, then no one would like me, if I were honest."

Sort of like how no one liked Chase. Then again, all their suspicions were correct. I let out a sigh. "Well, hopefully he's forgiven you. Or he listens because I am there."

"Exactly. And although you aren't the same Alice, the old Alice did save him, so he owes her. He's never one to forget a debt."

"Which means he might not ask for something in return because of that debt, doesn't it?"

He shrugged. "It depends what he thinks is of equal value. But yes, you do have a point. But there is still a chance he will ask for something in return, especially if we are asking more than one thing of him. Hopefully it isn't something too horrible. Unless it's the Duchess's head. I could work with that."

I didn't know how to answer that. After everything that had happened in Wonderland, I still didn't believe violence was the answer unless truly necessary. But right now it felt necessary to have to kill her. I just wished the king and queen could have succeeded in ending her life before Chase messed it all up. Before Kate was teleported there and vanished.

I pushed back the thought of my best friend. "So what should we do now?"

Malcolm let out a long breath. "Well, we need to go back into town to get a map. However, when a change happens, everyone automatically knows where things are, within reason. They at least have a concept of where all the lands are."

"So if we ask, there is a possibility that they will

realize we weren't part of the change and that we are wanted."

"Exactly. Not to mention maps aren't in great demand. People do need them to plan routes and such, just in case someone gets lost. But other than that, there aren't many sold."

"So asking around where to get a map and then buying the map will both seem suspicious?"

He nodded. "Yup. So we will need a plan on what to say to not seem odd."

I bit my lip, thinking of excuses that seemed reasonable. We couldn't just say we were lost nor that we were on a journey as it seemed that many didn't journey. We couldn't pretend to be traders as we didn't have any goods on us.

Then it hit me.

"What if we say we are looking for work in the districts due to how poor everything is and we need a map that lays out the districts so we can mark them off?" I asked.

Malcolm took a sip of tea. "That's not a bad idea. It would definitely be a good idea and wouldn't be out of the ordinary. Although, no matter the excuse, it could be possible that everyone who asks about maps is checked out and interrogated."

That was a big possibility. "So should we just sneak in and steal one?"

"That would probably just get us arrested. I think your first plan would be all right and hope that they haven't sent out word that we were spotted yet. The guards in the Flower District didn't seem to care that we walked in, so we should try there again."

I nodded. "That makes sense. Even if they had been given the orders, perhaps since they have been treated so poorly, they will just ignore them and not care we waltz in all over again."

"Precisely. But we should still come up with a backup plan in case they attack."

I sighed. "Are you saying I will have to go hide in the forest again?"

Malcolm chuckled. "No, but perhaps we do some sprints later today just to warm up in case something does happen. And we should come up with a meetup area."

"But in order to make a meetup area, we will need a map."

Malcolm gave me a look, and I smiled. "But seriously, we aren't one hundred percent sure with the layout, and so a meetup area might not be as easy as that. I'm getting better at directions, but that doesn't mean I would be able to find something."

"Well, what if the meetup area was here?"

I wrinkled my nose. "But then I would have to go through the Dark Forest on my own."

"You are getting better at knowing the layout of this area. No guard would follow you in here."

He had a point there. Even most of the others wouldn't follow us in there, which is why they hadn't come searching yet. "But what if it was Bill or Melvin or something?"

"Well…" He took a sip of tea. "Let's just hope that it isn't."

I put my finger to my chin. "What if we made the meetup spot be somewhere we pick along the way outside the Dark Forest but close enough so that if we need to get anyone off our tail, we could? We can mark it with some nondescript paint or something; and then we will know which spot it is and hopefully I will remember where it is."

Malcolm nodded. "That could work. Just hopefully you remember."

I gave him an innocent smile. "I'm getting better, I

swear!"

A smile appeared on the edge of his lips. "So you say. But hopefully it won't come to that. We should be able to stick together the entire time."

"Right. But a backup plan is always nice to have. Is there anything else we need to think of?"

Malcolm shook his head. "Nothing we need to do until we get the map. We might need some gear to camp with, but that will make our journeying to find work story appear even more real."

"Right then." I took a sip of the tea. "Shall we train?"

CHAPTER EIGHT

Malcolm made me wear a cloak again. It didn't really make us blend in. In fact, we stood out more as it was kind of warm and no one else was wearing a jacket. It was obvious we were trying to be inconspicuous.

Everyone always tried wearing a hood and cloak to hide who they really were, but I always thought that made them stand out even more. However, a lot of people knew our faces, or at least a good chunk of them did, so we couldn't exactly move around without something to shadow our faces. Either way, it was like we were walking around with a target painted on ourselves. Or maybe like a neon blinking sign that said Here They Are.

As we approached the town, I let out a slight sigh. Seeing the once beautiful Flower District now surrounded by walls and the beautiful plants now ruined made my heart ache. This place, once the circus had been destroyed, was always open and full of magic. Now it felt like something out of industrial Europe or even the Middle Ages, except more advanced. But the feeling of exclusion and defense was there, which was not something I was used to in Wonderland. The original story, yes, but not the Wonderland I had gotten to know and love.

I turned to Malcolm. "Too bad you can't use that illusion magic. It would really come in handy right about now."

Malcolm let out a small laugh. "Wouldn't that have been convenient? But that is not the case, and I will more than likely never get to use it again."

I felt a little bad for bringing it up, but I didn't like the quiet as we made our way to the town. It made me even more nervous. After what happened just a couple